MRS. JEFFRIES
and the
Merry Gentlemen

MRS. JEFFRIES
and the
Merry Gentlemen

Emily Brightwell

BERKLEY PRIME CRIME, NEW YORK

THE BERKLEY PUBLISHING GROUP
Published by the Penguin Group
Penguin Group (USA) LLC
375 Hudson Street, New York, New York 10014, USA

USA • Canada • UK • Ireland • Australia • New Zealand • India • South Africa • China

penguin.com

A Penguin Random House Company

This book is an original publication of The Berkley Publishing Group.

Berkley Prime Crime Books are published by The Berkley Publishing Group.
BERKLEY® PRIME CRIME and the PRIME CRIME logo are trademarks
of Penguin Group (USA) LLC.

Library of Congress Cataloging-in-Publication Data

Brightwell, Emily.
Mrs. Jeffries and the Merry Gentlemen / Emily Brightwell.—First edition.
pages cm
ISBN 978-0-425-26808-7 (hardback)
1. Jeffries, Mrs. (Fictitious character)—Fiction. 2. Witherspoon, Gerald (Fictitious
character)—Fiction. 3. Stockbrokers—Crimes against—Fiction. 4. Women household
employees—Fiction. 5. Police—Great Britain—Fiction. I. Title.
PS3552.R46443M634 2013
813'.54—dc23
2013026904

FIRST EDITION: November 2013

PRINTED IN THE UNITED STATES OF AMERICA

10 9 8 7 6 5 4 3 2 1

Cover illustration by Jeff Walker.

*This book is dedicated to
my literary agent and friend, Donald Maass.
With thanks and gratitude for many years of hard work,
excellent advice, and incredible integrity.*

MRS. JEFFRIES
and the
Merry Gentlemen

CHAPTER 1

"I'll get the door, Mrs. Clarridge, you go on with the others." Orlando Edison smiled at his housekeeper as he crossed the black and white tiled floor of the foyer. "You don't want to be late."

Emma Clarridge stopped by the staircase and continued pulling on her gloves. "It's carolers, sir. I saw them from the window, and I'll be happy to pass out the coins if you don't want to be bothered. It'll only take a moment."

"No, no, go on, the others are waiting for you. It's going to take time to get to the theater and I don't want you being late." His spirits lifted as he saw that she was wearing her best hat, the blue one with the striped ribbon and the veiling on the crown. She and the others were obviously excited about their outing and, to his way of thinking, considering what he was going to announce the following day when he got back from court, it was the least he could do. "Besides, I enjoy seeing the carolers and hearing them sing."

"We'll be off, then, sir. I'll lock up the servants' door as we leave." She nodded respectfully, turned, and hurried down the corridor to the back staircase.

From outside, he could hear the murmur of voices and the shuffle of feet as the carolers took their places. He opened the heavy front door. A mixed band of men and women swathed against the damp evening in overcoats, scarves, hats, and gloves clustered together in front of his doorstep.

In the middle of the group, a man wearing a black great-coat and a stovepipe hat suddenly raised his hand and waved it in a flourish and they began to sing.

God rest ye merry gentlemen, let nothing you dismay. Remember Christ our savior was born on Christmas day, to save us all from Satan's power when we were gone astray. O tidings of comfort and joy, comfort and joy . . .

The song struck him as ironic, of course, and that made him smile. The real Merry Gentlemen were most certainly going to be dismayed tomorrow. Nonetheless, he was going to miss this; not that there was going to be a shortage of carol singing where he was going, but it would be a long while before he'd stand in his doorway with the damp, acrid smell of London in his nostrils. It wasn't a particularly pleasant odor, but it was the smell of home.

In Bethlehem, in Israel, the blessed babe was born, and laid within a manger upon this blessed morn . . .

From the road, he heard the distinctive jingle of a horse's harness pulling a hansom cab as it trotted past and he found himself hoping it wouldn't be too long before he heard that sound again. He knew they had cabs there, but he suspected they didn't sound like the ones in London.

The which His mother Mary did nothing take in scorn. O tidings of comfort and joy, comfort and joy. O tidings of comfort and joy . . .

Orlando hated self-pity, but as the melody filled the chill night air, he couldn't stifle the wave of misery that threatened to engulf him. It wasn't fair! He shouldn't have to be the one to go. He'd done nothing wrong—well, not that wrong—but he was the one who was going to suffer. She was furious with him, she thought him the worst kind of cad, a blackguard who ran off like a thief in the night. But by tomorrow, she'd know the truth. She'd know that it had to be done, that he'd had no choice if he was to honor his obligations.

Now to the Lord sing praises, all you within this place. And with true love and brotherhood each other now embrace. This holy tide of Christmas all other doth deface. O tidings of comfort and joy, comfort and joy. O tidings of comfort and joy . . .

Orlando forced his attention back to the carolers as they sang the final verse. As the last note ended, he clapped in appreciation, reached into his coat pocket, and grabbed a handful of florins. "Thank you, ladies and gentlemen, that was lovely." He stepped out onto the stoop and passed out the coins. "You ought to go along to Sunningdale Gardens, it's just across Holland Park. There's a real Merry Gentleman that lives there. I'm sure he'd love to hear you sing."

"We'd like to, sir." The leader nodded gratefully as he

took the money. "But we're going in the other direction, to St. John's Church. The weather's turning, so we'll be getting along." He ushered his group down the walkway as they waved and shouted their thanks and good-byes. "Thanks for your generosity, sir," he called over his shoulder as they reached the street.

Orlando watched them go and fought off a feeling of overwhelming loneliness. "Get hold of yourself, man," he muttered under his breath as he turned and went into the house. "You've no other choice, not if you want to make things right."

He'd started to close the door when he heard footsteps behind him. Thinking one of the servants had forgotten something, he whirled around, his hand still on the door handle, and said, "You're going to be late . . ." His voice trailed off and his eyes widened in surprise. "What on earth are you doing here?" It was then that he noticed what his visitor was holding. "What are you doing with that . . ."

His unexpected guest said nothing, but lunged forward with the weapon raised and ready. It came crashing down against Edison's skull. The blow stunned him and he fell to his knees. His assailant struck him again and Orlando's last thought before his soul left this earth was that he wished he'd not given his servants the night off.

"That was a wonderful meal, Fiona. Please convey my compliments to your cook," Mrs. Jeffries said as she followed her hostess, Fiona Sutcliffe, into the drawing room of her elegant Mayfair home.

"I'll be sure to do so." Fiona accepted the compliment with a regal nod. She was a tall, attractive woman of late middle age with a smooth, relatively unlined face, brown hair done in an elaborate but flattering coiffure, and a grace of carriage the envy of women years her junior. As always, she was fashionably attired in a dress of green and gray stripes with lace at the collar and cuffs.

Mrs. Jeffries, a short, slightly plump woman with graying auburn hair, a ready smile, and sharp brown eyes that missed nothing, suspected that her sister-in-law had deliberately worn a less formal outfit than was her habit either out of deference to Mrs. Jeffries' own limited wardrobe or because she thought a less formal gown might actually help both of them relax. In either case, Mrs. Jeffries appreciated the gesture.

"We'll have coffee as soon as John joins us." Fiona gestured at the sofa. "Do sit down and make yourself comfortable. I'm so glad you came tonight. I was afraid you wouldn't. It's Christmas and I wanted to see you."

Mrs. Jeffries stifled a flash of guilt as she sat down. Until recently, her sister-in-law's comment would have been absolutely correct; family or not, she'd have ignored any invitations from her. Fiona Jeffries Sutcliffe had "married up," as the saying went, and for a number of years Mrs. Jeffries had bitterly resented her for the way she'd treated her own brother and Mrs. Jeffries' late husband, David. But life had a way of changing one, and after Fiona had come to her needing help, they'd found their way to a better relationship, one that was slowly allowing them to become friends as well as in-laws. Truth be told, despite the closeness she'd developed with everyone at Upper Edmonton Gardens, where she served as housekeeper to Inspector Gerald Witherspoon of the Metropolitan Police Force, sometimes she felt a bit lonely. "Of course I'd come, Fiona. First of all, I wanted to see you and John; secondly, you have a wonderful cook; and thirdly, we both agreed to put the past behind us." She glanced around the room as she spoke.

An evergreen wreath decorated with a red velvet bow and made even brighter with strips of gold and silver ribbon woven among the branches hung over the double doors leading to the hall. Boughs of ivy and pine were strung along the marble fireplace, and on the mantelpiece itself a carved Italian crèche complete with delicately painted Mary, baby Jesus, Joseph, shepherds, and angels held pride of place in the center. Tall silver candelabras holding red candles stood at each end of the mantelpiece. Three holly wreaths with polished crimson and golden berries hung along the wall opposite the fireplace and two huge potted poinsettia flowers blooming in brilliant splendor flanked the cream and pink drapes on each side of the windows. "You've outdone yourself, Fiona. These decorations are lovely."

"It's kind of you to say so. I wanted to do something special this year as we're having guests for Christmas. Usually it's just John and me, but this year, we've invited Henry Anson and his wife, Amy."

Surprised, Mrs. Jeffries blinked and tried to think of what to say.

"Don't look so alarmed, Hepzibah." Fiona laughed. "I'm quite alright with the situation. Believe it or not, it's taken a huge burden of guilt off my shoulders."

"But you have nothing to feel guilty about," Mrs. Jeffries protested, though she understood exactly what was meant by the remark. "It's not your fault you and John never had children. David and I weren't blessed, either. Many couples aren't."

"We've been blessed in other ways." Fiona shrugged philosophically. "Logically I know that being unable to carry a child is not something any woman can control, but that doesn't mean you don't feel it's somehow your fault. But once I got over the shock of learning about Henry, I have to tell you, it made me feel much better. John now has someone who'll inherit his legacy and it's not as if John was unfaithful to me. He didn't even know me when——" She broke off as the door opened and John Sutcliffe stepped into the room. He was a tall handsome man with a full head of gray hair and the posture of an admiral.

"Have you taken care of your business, John?" Fiona asked. "I do think it could have waited. Hepzibah and I want our coffee."

"Forgive me, ladies, but it was rather urgent. I had to send a note to my broker."

"Oh, for goodness' sake, the exchange is closed right now." Fiona sighed heavily. "It could have waited till tomorrow."

"Indeed it could." He grinned at his wife. "But I'm getting to the age where it's important to take care of business while one still recalls precisely the business one needs to take care of." He sat down next to his wife as the door opened and the butler stepped inside pushing a silver coffee service atop a trolley. "And with all the rumors circulating about the City, I want to make sure I get rid of those Boer shares."

"Excellent, the coffee's here," Fiona said.

Mrs. Jeffries watched the interplay between man and wife curiously. She'd seen no evidence of senility from John during dinner and wondered what he meant by the reference to his age. John and Fiona were only a few years older than herself. Curiosity warred with manners and, as was usual in her world, curiosity won. "Surely you're not frightened of going senile," she said to him as the butler poured their coffee.

"Of course not." It was Fiona who answered. "He simply

wanted to make sure his broker received the notice first thing in the morning. He's been fretting over those mining shares for months now."

"You're exaggerating, my dear," John said. "The fretting only started when I found out the Granger and two other mines have gone bankrupt. It's beginning to look as if the Boers hoodwinked a number of English investors about the amount of gold in their mines. Add to that all the other unsavory rumors about directors being bribed to sit on boards and surveys being falsified, I think it's wisest to simply sell the lot of them."

"We don't have to worry about missing the last omnibus home," Phyllis Tomlinson, housemaid to Inspector Gerald Witherspoon, said to her companion. "I've got money for a hansom cab. Come on, hurry, the curtain will be going up soon and we've got to find our seats. We're in the upper gallery." She turned and pushed her way through the packed throng in front of the Gaiety Theater toward the doors.

Susan Jordan hurried to catch up with her. "You're so lucky." She raised her voice so Phyllis could hear her over the din of the crowd. "I only get one half day off a week and your guv's given you that and tonight as well."

"It's a special Christmas treat," Phyllis called over her shoulder. "The inspector is having dinner out so he decided we should have an evening out as well. The only one who stayed in is Mrs. Goodge. She doesn't like to go out at night." She handed her ticket to a uniformed usher.

"Entrance to the upper galleries are on the left and right, all the way to the top of the stairs," he told them.

As the two young women crossed the lobby, they gawked at the women in elegant gowns and the men in evening dress heading for the expensive box seats and stalls. Susan stumbled and Phyllis grabbed her arm to keep her from smashing into the well-dressed matron in front of them. They were out of breath by the time they reached the upper gallery and found their seats.

"You're going to love this," Phyllis enthused as she turned to her friend. "It's ever such a wonderful story."

"*The Shop Girl.*" Susan nodded absently as her gaze darted back and forth, from the beautifully clad women in the lower stalls to the lavish appointments of the theater itself. "You've seen it before. Again, lucky you. This is only the second time in my life that I've ever been to the theater." She turned and her hazel eyes narrowed speculatively. "Are there any positions going?"

Phyllis' smile faded as she saw from the expression on Susan's broad face that she was dead serious. "Positions. You mean a job? No, it's a small household and I only got hired because the maid before me got married and left."

Susan's thin lips pursed in a frown. "But it's a huge house, I've seen it from the outside. Surely they need more than one housemaid."

Phyllis was at a loss. Making friends, indeed, human connections of any kind, was hard for her so she didn't want to make Susan angry, but she didn't want to encourage her, either. It wouldn't work. She felt bad for her as Susan's current employer was harsh and she knew the poor girl worked her fingers to the bone. But on the other hand, having someone like her at the inspector's household would be disastrous.

Susan couldn't keep a secret. Her tongue ran away with her all the time.

And there was a huge secret at the Witherspoon household.

Namely, that Inspector Gerald Witherspoon, the policeman who'd solved more murders than anyone in the history of the Metropolitan Police Force, had substantial help on his cases. His staff. Under the leadership of Mrs. Jeffries, the housekeeper, Witherspoon's servants used their extensive resources to track down clues, watch suspects, and find out just about everything to do with his cases. Mrs. Jeffries would then pass the information along to Constable Barnes or cleverly feed the bits and pieces directly back to the inspector.

When she'd first gone to work there, Phyllis hesitated to get involved; she'd feared losing her job if Witherspoon got wind of what they were doing. But then she'd taken the plunge and found that she not only enjoyed working for the cause of justice, but she was actually quite good at it.

"Well, don't just sit there like a statue," Susan demanded. "Tell me what you think. Shouldn't he have more help?"

"But there's not that much to do."

"But even so, it's a big place, you can't do all the work yourself. You've said yourself your inspector's rich and don't have to work. Can't you put in a good word for me?"

"Of course I will," she lied. "But don't get your hopes up. I'd not like you to be disappointed. It's a big house but there's only him there. Most of the upper rooms are closed off and, what's more, the footman and the coachman do a lot of work around the place. But I'll ask Mrs. Jeffries."

"Good, don't forget. I'm counting on you. Goodness, will you look at that dress." Susan leaned over the railing and pointed at a girl on the lower balcony taking off her cloak. "What a horrid color, it looks like mustard. Mind you, Miss Pringle—that's the mistress's friend—wears that color all the time and it doesn't suit her. Even the mistress says she ought to be more careful in her clothes . . ." Her voice trailed off as the house lights dimmed. "Oh, good, it's starting."

The butler knocked once on the drawing room door and stepped inside. "Excuse me, madam, sir, but there's a Constable Barnes insisting he must see the inspector."

"Show him in," Lady Ruth Cannonberry replied. She put her coffee cup down on the table and glanced at her companion, Inspector Gerald Witherspoon. "Oh dear, this certainly doesn't bode well. Constable Barnes would never interrupt your evening without a good reason."

"I imagine this means that something dreadful has happened." Witherspoon pushed his spectacles up his nose and smiled wanly at his hostess. He was a man of medium height with thinning brown hair, a pale bony face, and deep-set, kindly eyes. "This is most unfortunate, I hoped to spend a lot of time with my darling goddaughter this year. She's getting to the age where she can really enjoy the holiday."

Ruth tried not to smile. His godchild, Amanda Belle, had turned one in October and, precocious though she was, she wouldn't have a clue what Christmas was about. But she didn't want to spoil anything for him so she merely nodded.

The butler returned, followed by Constable Barnes. Barnes was an older copper with a head full of thick gray hair under his policeman's helmet and, despite his aching knees, a ramrod-straight back. He gave them a rueful smile. "Sorry to disturb you, Lady Cannonberry, Inspector, but I'm afraid it's bad news. We've a murder and the chief inspector wants you to head the investigation."

"Chief inspector?" Witherspoon repeated.

"Would you like a cup of tea or some coffee?" Ruth gestured at the silver coffee service.

"I'm not sure we've time." Barnes looked at the inspector as he spoke.

"You've put in a full shift today so we've time for a cup of tea," Witherspoon said. "The body isn't going anywhere."

"Have you eaten?" Ruth asked. He gave a negative shake of his head. "Everton, please bring two roast beef sandwiches with the tea," she instructed the butler.

"Right away, madam," he said as he left.

"Do sit down, Constable, and rest your feet."

"How did you happen to be at the station this late?" Witherspoon glanced at the clock on the mantelpiece. "It's almost half past seven."

Barnes nodded gratefully and sank into an armchair. "I left a package there to do a bit of shopping for the missus and when I went back to fetch it before going home, the chief had sent word that we've a murder on Holland Road."

"Holland Road, that's less than a quarter mile from here," Witherspoon muttered.

"Apparently, the chief was one of the first at the scene and he sent Constable Young to the station to send someone to call you in just as I went to get my package. The duty sergeant caught sight of me and he sent me along to fetch you, sir. As you'd mentioned you were having a meal here, I came straight away."

"Chief Inspector Barrows was at the scene," Witherspoon clarified. "That's odd. I don't think he's taken a murder case in years."

Barnes allowed himself a wry smile. "The word at the station was that he found the body. Luckily, old habits die hard and he had his police whistle with him. When he realized the fellow was dead and not just drunk from too much Christmas cheer, he blew it and raised the alarm. Sorry to ruin your evening."

"Don't be concerned, Constable," Witherspoon said. "It most certainly isn't your fault that people haven't stopped murdering one another."

"True, sir, but we always seem to get us a nasty one right at Christmas."

"Let's hope for the best," Ruth said. "Perhaps this will be a nice, simple case you can solve right away."

Witherspoon knew they should get to the murder scene as fast as possible but if the chief inspector was already there, then a short delay was permissible. If they had a murder to investigate, they might be up all night and Barnes needed to keep up his strength.

"I'll inform your household that you've been called out," Ruth offered. She started to get up but he waved her back to her seat.

"There's no rush. Everyone, save for Mrs. Goodge, is out for the evening, and she's probably asleep by now. You can send one of your servants over. I don't want you walking across the garden alone. It's already dark outside."

Ruth nodded meekly, but she had every intention of going herself. "Of course, Gerald."

"Do we know who is dead?" Witherspoon asked Barnes.

Barnes nodded. "The duty sergeant said it was a man named Orlando Edison."

The butler returned with a tray loaded with food. He set it down on the table next to Barnes, nodded respectfully, and withdrew.

"Don't stand on ceremony, Constable, go ahead and eat," Ruth ordered.

Barnes nodded his thanks and reached for a sandwich. He was used to eating on the run and tonight was no exception. Within minutes, there was nothing but crumbs left on the sandwich plate. He drained his tea and put the cup down. "Thank you, Lady Cannonberry, that was won-derful."

The two policemen took their leave. Ruth waited till the front door closed behind them and then raced for the back stairs. Everton stepped out of the butler's pantry as she descended the stairs. He was holding her cloak and a lantern. "I took the liberty of getting these ready for you, madam. Shall I accompany you across the garden?"

"Thank you, but that's not necessary." She slipped the cloak on, grabbed the light, and crossed the garden to Inspector Witherspoon's house.

"I'm sorry to bring you out when you're off duty, Wither-spoon," Chief Inspector Barrows muttered. "But frankly, when I realized who the victim was I knew we needed to get this sorted out quickly. Gracious, that's a very bold scarf you've got there. Even in this dim light I can see the colors."

Witherspoon stroked the red and green stripes of the soft wool lovingly. Ruth had knitted it for him and he was very pleased to wear it. "It's a gift, sir, just given to me by my hostess and as I didn't have my other scarf with me, I wanted to wear it. It is most colorful. How did you happen to get involved, sir? I understand you found the body?"

Barrows made a face as he pointed to the house next door. "I was there visiting my friends. We were having an aperitif before dinner with when one of their maids rushed in and said there was something wrong here. She said the door was wide open and she'd seen someone lying here." He pointed to the body. "Naturally, I suspected it was someone who'd had too much to drink but, as a policeman, I thought it my duty to have a look. When I got close, I saw the blood, gave him a quick examination, and then blew the whistle.

The fixed-point constable from the corner came so I sent him along to the station to send for you."

"Why me, sir?" Witherspoon avoided looking at the corpse. He was very squeamish about bodies and the quick glance he'd taken when he first arrived convinced him this one was going to be very bad indeed. "Isn't Inspector Blodgett on duty tonight?" He knew there was some talk around the force that he "hogged" all the cases and he didn't want bad blood between himself and other officers.

"He is." Barrows fixed him with a steely glare. "But I want you to take this one. Inspector Blodgett is an excellent officer, but he's not had much experience with murder and, frankly, when I realized who this fellow was"—he jerked his chin toward the dead man lying across the doorway—"I knew the Home Office would want it sorted out as quickly as possible. Don't worry about Inspector Blodgett, I'll make sure he knows I insisted you take this one."

"Thank you, sir. What time did you find the victim?"

"Six ten. I checked the time as soon as I realized the death wasn't an accident," Barrows said.

"The victim is a Mr. Orlando Edison, is that correct?"

"That's right and he was due to testify in that Granger Mine bankruptcy fiasco tomorrow. Unfortunately, he'll not be talking to anyone, seeing as how his head's been bashed in with that shovel." He pointed to a small, two-foot-long implement that was lying next to the body on the top step. "The killer very kindly left us the murder weapon."

"What on earth is it?" Witherspoon edged closer, his eyes squinting in the pale glow of the brass door lamps.

Barnes took a hand lantern from one of the other officers and held it up, casting additional light on the murder weapon and the corpse.

"I'm not really sure, my best guess is that it is some sort of odd knickknack." Barrows shrugged. "It appears to be a miniature version of a mining shovel. It's been bronzed so we know it wasn't used as a proper gardening implement." Barrows rubbed his hands together. "Now that you're here, I'll go back to my friends. As you can imagine, they are a tad upset. You can take my statement tomorrow when you come to the Yard to report." He turned on his heel and started down the short walk.

"Has the police surgeon been notified?" Witherspoon called.

"Yes, he'll be here shortly." Barrows turned. "The house-maid who raised the alarm told me that none of Edison's household would be back until late. Apparently he bought theater tickets for all his servants and sent them off for an evening out." With that, he pulled his coat tighter and set off.

"They'll be in for a rude shock when they get here," Barnes muttered. Still holding the lantern, he slid past the inspector, knelt down by the body, and shone the light on the victim's face. Gently, he grasped the chin and slowly turned the head to one side. "I'm no expert, sir," he said, letting the head move back to the original position, "but it looks like he's been hit more than once. There's not much left of the back of his skull."

Witherspoon swallowed the bile that rose in his throat. "I'm sure the police surgeon will be able to tell us more." He forced himself to move, stepping around to the other side of the corpse.

"Careful where you step, sir." Barnes grimaced. "There's bits of him all over the door stoop."

Witherspoon froze, looked down, and realized he'd

almost stepped on a dark, wet chunk of something. He decided to stay still. "Thank you for the warning. Can you shine the lamp up and down the corpse? I want to make certain there aren't any other signs of violence."

Barnes shifted position so that he could move the lamp freely. Witherspoon studied the body as the light drifted up and down the dead man's frame. But all he saw was a prone body in a nicely tailored gray suit coupled with a white shirt and a green cravat. A large gold ring was on the finger of the left hand. "It doesn't look as if there are any other wounds," he finally said. "Nor was robbery the motive. He's still got his ring and a robber would most definitely have taken it."

"I agree, sir. But let's see if he's got any other cash or valuables on his person." He opened the jacket far enough to stick his hand into the inner pocket. "There's something here, sir." He pulled out a bundle of paper, flattened out the stack, and held it up toward the light so they could see. "Five-pound notes, sir, and no robber would leave this much cash. Besides, a professional thief wouldn't leave the body lying here with the door wide open."

"This killer wanted the victim found quickly," Witherspoon said.

Barnes continued checking the pockets. "He's got coins, sir, a lot of them," he said. "Looks like florins." He groaned slightly as he got to his feet.

"Are you alright, Constable?" Witherspoon looked at him sharply. Barnes would never shirk his duty but he wasn't a young man and what had to be done tonight could be done by one of the other officers.

"It's just my knees creakin' a bit, sir." Barnes smiled gratefully. "I'm fine. I'll have one of the constables take the cash and coins next door to the chief inspector. He can put it in the safe at Scotland Yard." He took a moment and counted out the bills. "By my count, there are fifty pounds and a dozen florins."

"Excellent notion, Constable. That's a lot of money; I'd rather it was at the Yard than the station."

Barnes motioned for one of the three constables standing guard at the end of the walkway to come. A sizeable crowd had now gathered and the constable realized they would need more men. "Then I'll get the lads started on the house-to-house. Someone might have seen something."

The inspector looked down at his feet and then moved cautiously, watching where he stepped until he could reach the shovel. Picking it up, he examined it closely. "It's very heavy and the back is covered in blood and other bits. It feels like cast iron."

"Yes, sir?" the young constable said.

Barnes handed him the bills and coins. "Take this next door to Chief Inspector Barrows and ask him to take custody of it. Then come back with the evidence box for the murder weapon and take it to the station. Mind you, don't muck up the sticky end. We'll need that for the court case. When you get to the station, have the duty sergeant send along three additional constables. But before that, have Constable Sanderson there"—he pointed to the tallest constable holding back the crowd—"take charge of the house-to-house and interviewing witnesses."

"Right, sir." He took the money and raced off.

Witherspoon put the shovel down beside the body, turned his head, and studied the foyer through the open doorway. "It appears as if Mr. Edison had just stepped out for a moment. There's plenty of light coming from the interior of the house and I can see that one of the gas lamps in the hallway is lit. As soon as the police surgeon gets here, we'll search the place."

"Third time is the charm," Ruth muttered as she balled her hand into a fist and banged on the back door of Upper Edmonton Gardens. Putting her ear to the wood, she listened for the telltale shuffle of Mrs. Goodge's feet, but she heard nothing. Frowning, she silently debated her next course of action: Mrs. Goodge was the only one home tonight, so should she go back to her own house and wait until the others came back from their various outings or should she try knocking again? She'd knocked as hard as she dared and it was getting cold out here.

From behind her, she heard footsteps and someone whistling. She whirled around just as Wiggins, the footman, stepped off the path and onto the small kitchen terrace.

He came to an abrupt halt. "Cor blimey, who's there?"

"It's me, Ruth Cannonberry," she replied.

"Oh, you gave me a start." He shook his head and stepped toward her. "What are you doin' 'ere? Is the inspector alright? 'E's not taken ill, 'as 'e?"

"He's fine, Wiggins." She sighed in relief. "But he's been called out on a murder and I've been standing here for five minutes trying to get Mrs. Goodge to answer the door."

"Murder, huh." Wiggins pulled a ring of keys out of his pocket. "I'll get us in. Mrs. Jeffries left me with her keys before she went out. She knew I'd be the first one back. I was just 'avin' a drink with one of my mates at the pub. Mrs. Goodge 'as probably dozed off."

He got the door open and led her down the hallway and into the large, warm kitchen. Mrs. Goodge, her head resting on her chest, had indeed fallen asleep. She woke with a start. "What is it? Who's here?"

Fred, the household's dog, a black, brown, and white mongrel, who had been curled up asleep on his rug next to the stove, got to his feet, his tail wagging. Wiggins patted him on the head as he stepped into the cook's frame of vision. "It's me, Mrs. Goodge. I've got Lady Cannonberry with me. The inspector's been called out on a murder."

"A murder?" She blinked to clear the sleep out of her eyes. She was a portly, gray-haired woman with wire-rimmed spectacles and several chins. "Gracious, they always happen at such inconvenient moments. What should we do? Everyone's out tonight. Phyllis has gone to the theater and Mrs. Jeffries is at the Sutcliffes' for dinner. We can't even get Betsy or Smythe because they're at a Christmas party tonight."

"I don't think we'll be able to have a meeting." Ruth slipped into the chair next to the cook. "All I wanted to do was let everyone know that the inspector has been called out to a murder. But"—she glanced at Wiggins—"even though I don't have the exact address, the scene is quite close. The victim lives on Holland Road, so if you wanted to nip over there and see what you can learn, that would be useful."

Wiggins refastened the buttons of the jacket he'd started to take off and slapped his cap back on his dark brown hair. He got up. "Do we know who was killed?"

"A man named Orlando Edison. But be careful, I think Chief Inspector Barrows is in the area. Constable Barnes mentioned he'd found the body."

"I'll be careful." Wiggins grinned broadly. "Don't worry, I'm good at keepin' out of sight. All the constables round here know my face. But if I do get spotted, anyone sees me, I'll just say I was coming back from the pub, saw the crowd, and wondered what the fuss was all about."

"Crowd?" Ruth repeated.

"There's always a crowd at a murder 'ouse." He gave Fred one last pat and started toward the back door.

"Take your scarf," the cook ordered. "You don't know how long you're goin' to be outside and the temperature's dropping fast." She looked at Ruth. "I knitted that for him."

He doubled back to the coat tree, grabbed the long, light blue woolen garment, and wrapped it around his neck. "I like to save it for best," he explained with a grin.

The cook snorted. "You like to wear it where a pretty girl will notice that it matches your eyes. Mind you be careful out there."

"Will do, Mrs. Goodge. I'll be back as quick as I can." He headed for the back door with Fred at his heels. "Sorry, boy, I'll take you out when I get back," he promised. "I can't take you walkies now, we've got a case."

"He knows me, so if you'll trust me, I'll take him out," Ruth offered. "But he'll need to be on a lead. I'm afraid he won't come when I call."

Wiggins smiled gratefully. "Ta, he does like his evening walk." Fred danced up and down as the footman grabbed the lead off the coat tree and clipped it to his collar. "You be a good dog, now," he ordered as he handed the end of the lead to Ruth.

She got up and the three of them headed for the back door. "We'll be back in fifteen minutes," she called over her shoulder.

"What do you think of this, Constable?" Witherspoon handed Barnes a copy of the *Times*, which had been neatly folded on page eight. "See, under the Shipping Intelligence, two vessels have been circled."

Barnes angled the paper so that it caught the lamplight. His eyesight wasn't what it used to be. "There's one circled for December twenty-second and another for December twenty-third. Both ships are leaving from Liverpool and sailing to New York. Perhaps he was planning a trip, sir." He handed the paper back to Witherspoon.

"But he's testifying in that Granger matter at the bankruptcy court." He frowned.

"Perhaps he thought he'd be finished by then, sir." Barnes pulled open another desk drawer. They were searching Orlando Edison's study. The constable was going through the desk while the inspector examined the cabinets and bookshelves.

"And just because he's circled those ships, it doesn't necessarily follow that he was planning on leaving the country," Witherspoon said.

From outside, they heard the sound of an angry female voice.

"What do you mean I can't go inside? I'm Mr. Edison's housekeeper. What on earth is going on here?"

Barnes headed for the door. "Shall I bring her in, sir?"

"Please do."

The constable stepped out into the hall and saw a thin, middle-aged woman standing in the open front door. She was glaring at the policeman who was doggedly darting from one side of the doorway to the other to stop her from coming inside.

"If you'll just wait a moment, ma'am, I'll get the inspector," the young constable said as he lunged to his left when she tried to elbow her way past him. "Careful where you step, ma'am, there's still bits of him about the place." He glanced nervously down at the door stoop. The body was gone, but they hadn't had a chance to gather any other parts that might have flown off the poor fellow's skull.

Barnes winced as he heard the constable's warning. "Let the lady come in," he ordered.

He moved aside and she lunged past him and raced toward Barnes. "I'm the housekeeper. What's going on here? Why are there policemen at all the doors?"

Barnes smiled kindly. Despite her bravado, he could see the fear in her eyes. She knew something awful had happened.

"What's your name, ma'am?"

"Emma Clarridge, and I demand to know what's happened."

Barnes said nothing but merely led her into the study where Witherspoon stood waiting. He advanced with his hand out as he introduced himself. "I'm Inspector Gerald Witherspoon. Please forgive our being here, but I'm afraid I've bad news."

"I'm Emma Clarridge, Mr. Edison's housekeeper." She paled and her eyes glazed with tears as they shook hands. "Something terrible has happened, hasn't it?"

"Yes, ma'am," he replied. "Your employer, Mr. Orlando Edison, was murdered this evening. One of your neighbors saw him lying in the doorway and raised the alarm."

Tears poured down her cheeks and she stumbled backward toward an overstuffed leather chair. "Oh, dear Lord, murder. But—but—but he was alive and well when we left. He sent us to the theater—it was to be our Christmas present."

Witherspoon grabbed her arm to steady her and gently eased her into the chair. "Please sit down, Mrs. Clarridge, I can see this has been a great shock to you."

She shook her head, her expression confused. "But he can't be dead, he can't be. Oh, my gracious, the others, the cook and the housemaids, they're waiting at the servants' entrance. I've got to . . ."

The inspector interrupted. "The constable will see to them." He glanced at Barnes, who was already on the move.

"I know this is difficult, Mrs. Clarridge, but can you tell me when you last saw Mr. Edison?"

"Six o'clock." She took a deep breath, closed her eyes, and swiped at her wet cheeks. "There were carolers coming and even though we were leaving, I went to answer the door but he waved me back. He said he'd take care of it, that he enjoyed hearing them sing."

"How did you know the carolers were coming if you didn't answer the door?" Witherspoon asked.

"I saw them from the drawing room window. I'd gone in to close the curtains and I saw them coming across the road. They were heading straight for the house." She sniffed as a fresh batch of tears pooled in her eyes. "We've had carolers before, sir, and Mr. Edison was uncommonly generous. He always gave each of them a florin. I think word had gotten about, if you know what I mean."

"Yes, I think I do," he replied. That explained why the victim had over a dozen of those particular coins on his person.

"Had Mr. Edison actually opened the door while you were here?" Witherspoon asked. He wasn't sure what, if anything, the carolers had to do with the murder, but he felt it wise to get as many details as possible.

She thought for a moment. "No, we were in a hurry to leave. The others were shouting at me to come along so we could get the next omnibus."

"Did you hear him open the door?"

"There was too much of a racket for that. As I said, we were in a hurry and not minding how much noise we made."

"You left by the servants' entrance at the side of the house?" he clarified. Barrows had found the body at six ten and if they'd left at six, then the killer would have had to have done the murder in that ten-minute period of time.

She smiled through her tears. "Mr. Edison was a very generous and liberal employer but it would hardly be fitting for the staff to use the front door."

"What about the downstairs front door?" he asked.

"That's the tradesmen's entrance and it's kept locked. It's only opened when deliveries are made."

"Did you lock the servants' door when you left?"

"Yes." She rummaged in her coat pocket, pulled up her hand, and held up a key. "It was locked tight as a bank vault and I had the key with me."

"Would Mr. Edison have locked the front door after listening to the carolers?"

"Most definitely. Once the sun was down, we kept the house locked. If he went out in the evening he took the key to the front door with him. That's what he was going to do tonight. He was going out to dinner."

"Do you know what time he was to leave?" Witherspoon asked.

"No, he didn't tell me, he just said he had plans for supper and we weren't to worry about him." She shook her head. "I'm sorry, I can't understand this. Mr. Edison was a good man. Who would want to kill him? Who would do such a wicked thing?"

"I don't know, Mrs. Clarridge," Witherspoon said softly. "But I assure you, we'll find that person and bring them to justice."

CHAPTER 2

Now that he was here, Wiggins knew exactly what to do. Finding the murder house was dead easy. Despite the cold, half the neighborhood huddled together in small groups on both sides of the street, pointing and gawking at the constable standing guard on the doorstep. The victim had lived in the last house at the end of the road. Wiggins had passed it many times over the years and knew it to be a posh, four-story light brown brick home with a brightly painted green door and windows with white-painted trim. A concrete walkway led the short distance from the street to a low, wide set of steps going to the front door while a second path branched off to a lower staircase going down to what was probably the kitchen.

He stomped his feet to get the circulation moving in his toes and rubbed his hands together to keep warm while he surveyed the crowd, looking for a likely source. This was his neighborhood and as his gaze flicked from face to face, he realized he recognized half these people by sight and it was a good bet they knew him, too. Good, that could work to his advantage.

He moved through the groups huddled along the pavement until he spotted a skinny young lad wearing an oversized jacket and a green knitted cap with dangling earflaps. It was Georgie Marks, the delivery boy from Wynn's, their grocer's shop. "Hey, Georgie," he said as he sidled up to him, "what's all the fuss about 'ere?"

Georgie pointed to the house. "You should know, your guv's in there already."

"I've not seen my guv since early this mornin'. I've not even been home yet, I was out with my mate Tommy at the pub."

"There's been murder done." Georgie's eyes brightened with excitement. "The poor feller was lyin' right out on his doorstep. I know—I saw it myself. He had his head bashed in. I got a real good look before they carted the body over to the wagon."

"Cor blimey, a murder! That's awful. Who was he, then, the one who was done in?" Wiggins asked.

"Mr. Orlando Edison. He buys his groceries from our shop."

"He does his own shoppin'?"

Georgie looked at him as if he was stupid. "Don't be daft! 'Course not. His housekeeper does that. But he stops in every month to settle the account. Mrs. Wynn is goin' to be upset at him dyin' like this. He was a right good customer. Paid promptly and was always as polite as could be."

"Did ya ever meet him yourself?" Wiggins scanned the crowd to see if there were any additional sources he could tap.

"'Course I did," Georgie boasted. "He were in the kitchen just last week when I was doin' the delivery. He give me a few bob, said it was a Christmas tip. Most rich men don't do that, they don't give you nuthin' and look at ya like you're supposed to be grateful to be servin' them. But 'e weren't like that—'e was a nice bloke. Just yesterday I overheard Kitty Long, she's one of the maids, tellin' Mrs. Wynn that Mr. Edison was givin' the 'ousehold a special treat tonight."

Wiggins gave the lad his full attention. "What kind of treat?"

Georgie's eyes narrowed. "You tryin' to 'elp your guv by askin' questions?"

He smiled ruefully. "Nah, I'm just bein' nosy. Come on, then, tell me what's what."

Georgie leaned closer. "Well, I don't know if it's worth passin' on, but Kitty told Mrs. Wynn that he was payin' for all them to go out to the theater tonight. They was goin' to the Gaiety and Mr. Edison was givin' them pocket money to pay for hansom cabs home and a bit extra so they could buy them sweets they sell."

"He sounds an even nicer man than our guv," Wiggins muttered.

"That's what I thought, too, and everyone round here knows how good your guv is to his household. I said as much to Mrs. Wynn, I said, 'That Mr. Edison sounds even better to them that works for him than Inspector Wither-spoon,' but Mrs. Wynn, she just snorted and said there was more to it than him bein' a decent master. She claimed he was only good to his people so they'd keep their mouths closed about his shenanigans. Mind you, she says that sort of thing about everyone."

Wiggins nodded as his mind worked furiously. Despite the way she smiled as she bustled about her shop, Mrs. Wynn was as two-faced and catty as anyone he'd ever seen or heard. The woman never had anything nice to say about anyone or anything. Mrs. Goodge called her a crepe draper and some of their neighbors had actually stopped shopping at Wynn's. But he'd once heard Mrs. Jeffries say that even though Mrs. Wynn's tongue was unpleasant, it was often truthful. "Did Mrs. Wynn say what she meant by that remark?"

"Huh?" Georgie pulled a crumpled handkerchief from his pocket and blew his runny nose. "What do ya mean?"

"Cor blimey, Georgie, it's as clear as that drippin' snout of yours. What was she talkin' about? Come on, lad, you're a sharp one, you know what I'm askin'. Was she just bein' mean or did she have a reason for what she said?"

Delighted by the backhanded compliment, Georgie grinned broadly. "For once she wasn't just bein' her usual nasty self. She did have a reason for what she said. Mrs. Crumley was in the shop when Kitty was natterin' on about what a wonderful master Edison was, and Mrs. Wynn is always lookin' to best her when it comes to bein' in the know. So the minute Kitty left the shop, Mrs. Wynn turned to Mrs. Crumley and said Mr. Edison wasn't a saint, that she'd seen him in Holland Park a few days back with a young woman and the woman was cryin' like a baby."

"Did she tell Mrs. Crumley what the two of 'em was talkin' about?" Wiggins pressed.

"I don't know what she said then—I 'ad to get on with the morning deliveries." Georgie wadded the hanky up and stuffed it back in his coat pocket. "Still, I don't care what Mrs. Wynn thought of him, he was a nice fellow and treated the people who worked for him like they wasn't just dirt under his feet. Kitty said he was always good to them. Why do people like him have to get murdered? Seems to me that if God was doin' his job properly, he'd only let the horrid ones get their heads bashed in."

Wiggins understood what poor Georgie was trying to say and, in his own way, he'd often had the same thought. Why did seemingly good people get murdered when there were so many wicked ones about? He and Mrs. Goodge often discussed that topic; but right now, he needed information. "Wonder what the killer used to bash 'im."

"I heard it was a club of some sort," Georgie said.

"It was a shovel," a female voice said from behind them.

They both turned. A young woman who Wiggins recognized as the maid from the last house on the corner of Upper Edmonton Gardens stood there. She was a tall, dark-haired girl swathed in a heavy cloak and scarf that had slipped off her head and pooled around her neck.

"It was a miner's shovel," she continued.

"How do ya know that?" Georgie demanded. "And what would Mr. Edison have been doin' with a miner's shovel, diggin' for gold? I've been standin' here as long as you 'ave and I didn't hear that."

"Then you're not listening closely. One of the coppers carryin' out the stretcher said as much to the other coppers. Mind you, I can't imagine why there'd be a miner's shovel in a big, fancy house like this." She pointed toward the front door. "But maybe the copper got it wrong and it was just a plain old gardenin' shovel."

A pot of fresh-brewed tea was on the table when Mrs. Jeffries came into the kitchen. Surprised, she stopped in the doorway. "I thought I heard voices but I assumed it would be Phyllis and Wiggins. What on earth are you doing here?" She untied the black ribbons from underneath her chin as she headed to the coat tree. "I thought you were having dinner with the inspector."

"We did have dinner," Ruth replied. "But during coffee, Constable Barnes came and got Gerald. There's been a murder; that's why I'm here. We're waiting for Wiggins now."

"The lad came home just as Ruth arrived, so he scarpered off to see what he could find out at the murder scene." Mrs. Goodge poured a cup of tea and put it at the housekeeper's spot.

"It's close by, then?" She took off her bonnet and hung it on the peg and then unbuttoned the fastening of her cloak.

"Less than a quarter of a mile, on Holland Road," Ruth said. "The only other bit of information I heard was the victim's name is Orlando Edison and Chief Inspector Barrows found the body."

"Chief Inspector Barrows found the body?" Mrs. Jeffries put her cloak up. "Gracious, that's a bit unusual. He's normally behind a desk at Scotland Yard."

"We'll know more when Wiggins gets back," Mrs. Goodge said.

"Orlando Edison . . ." Mrs. Jeffries came to the table and sat down. "That name sounds so familiar. But for the life of me, I can't place it now. Perhaps we ought to notify Smythe and Betsy . . . no, that can wait until tomorrow morning. Besides, they're out this evening."

"Wouldn't you just know that our inspector would get a case on the one night everyone's gone," the cook complained. "Luckily for us, he was having dinner with Ruth; otherwise, we'd not be able to find out anything until tomorrow. And it's lucky Wiggins came home at a decent hour so we might find out a few bits and pieces from the neighbors." It was the household's custom to get "on the case" as quickly as possible.

"I hope he's being careful," Ruth murmured. "Most of the constables know him by sight."

"As do many of the neighbors." Mrs. Goodge frowned. "But he's a clever lad and he'll know what to do."

"Mrs. Clarridge, you shouldn't have gone to so much trouble." Witherspoon put the stack of business correspondence he'd looked through back in the wooden tray on the corner of Edison's desk.

She carried a tray holding a pot of tea, two mugs, a jug of milk, and a bowl of sugar. Their earlier interview had been interrupted. When the maids learned their employer had been murdered, they'd set up an unholy racket that had the housekeeper leaping up and racing for the kitchen.

Witherspoon had used the break to finish searching Edison's study while Barnes had tactfully withdrawn to let the housekeeper minister to the sobbing girls. He'd come up and commandeered the dining room to use for his interviews. He was in there now with the cook, a stoic older woman not given to displays of emotion or hysteria.

"It was no trouble, Inspector, and making tea gave the girls something to do. I'm sorry they lost control and made such a fuss, but they're both very young." She set the tray down on the small table between the brown leather love seat and matching chair sitting catty-corner to Edison's desk. She gestured for the inspector to sit.

"I hope you don't mind, Inspector, but I took tea to the constables outside. It's very cold tonight." She sat down on the love seat and handed him a mug of tea. "I've added milk and sugar but if you need more, it's here."

"Thank you, ma'am, that's very thoughtful of you." He smiled gratefully as he took the cup. "I'm sure this will be fine." Her eyes were red from weeping, but she had herself well under control.

"I'm sure you've a lot of questions for me." She straight-ened her spine and folded her hands in her lap.

"When you left the house, did you notice anyone suspi-cious hanging about on the street?"

"I wasn't really paying attention, Inspector, but I don't recall seeing anyone in particular. There were people out and about, of course. It's a busy street and there's shops just around the corner."

"Did Mr. Edison have any enemies?" He hated asking that question. Of course the man had enemies; he'd had his skull bashed in and that wasn't the act of a friend. Nonethe-less, it was an inquiry he had to make.

She said nothing for a moment. "I wouldn't say he had enemies, per se," she finally said. "But there were people who were upset with him."

"You mean because of the Granger Mine bankruptcy?" Witherspoon remembered what Barrows had said earlier.

"I'm sure there's some that would blame him, but it wasn't his fault. Mr. Edison is—was—a businessman. All investments carry risk and most people know that."

"Had anyone threatened him about this matter, this bankruptcy?" He took a sip of tea.

"Not that I know about," she said. "But that's hardly the sort of subject he'd discuss with me."

"Did Mr. Edison do anything out of the ordinary today?"

"Out of the ordinary?" she repeated. "I'm not sure what you mean. Unless he was meeting with a potential investor or going to the stock exchange, he was often at home during the day." She waved her hand around the room, gesturing at the file boxes on the lower bookshelves and then at the desk with the wooden correspondence trays overflowing with papers, the crystal ink pot and cloisonné pen, and the green ceramic jar that housed a dozen pencils. "This was his workplace and today was like any other. He didn't have any appointments so after breakfast he came in here and went through his correspondence, wrote his replies, and then called Kitty to take them to the postbox on the corner."

"That was his usual habit?" Witherspoon asked. Experience had taught him that familiarity with the victim's routine was often very helpful.

"That's right." She nodded as she spoke. "After luncheon, he'd often go to the exchange, but not always. Today he stayed home. He said he had some personal correspondence to see to and that he'd need Kitty to take a letter to the postbox."

"Did he have any visitors?"

"Mr. Ralston came by. Mr. Ralston is one of the directors of the Granger Mine, and this was the first time he's been here since the bankruptcy was made public."

"Was Mr. Edison surprised or upset by the visit?"

"Oh no, they were quite cordial to one another. But then, Mr. Edison never let business sour him on people."

Downstairs, Barnes had finished speaking to Mrs. Green, the cook, and was now with the maid, Kitty Long. She was a chubby, blonde-haired young lass with blue eyes red rimmed from crying and nice, even features. "Are you feeling better, miss?"

"Yes, sir, thank you, but it was such a shock." She dabbed at her cheeks with a tear-stained handkerchief. "Mr. Edison is—I mean was—such a good master. Why would anyone want to kill him? I don't understand. How can this be happening? Where will I go? I only just got this job a few months ago."

"Now, now, I'm sure you'll be fine. I imagine you can stay on here until everything is sorted out, but if we're to catch the person who did this, you must get hold of yourself and keep calm."

She sucked in a lungful of air and exhaled heavily. "You're right, I mustn't be so selfish. Mrs. Clarridge has already said she'll make sure we all get a good reference and she has a friend who runs a domestic employment agency. But I don't know what I can tell you. We were all gone when he was killed. Mr. Edison had bought us tickets to the theater."

"This was a Christmas treat, was it?" Barnes opened his little brown notebook and picked up his pencil.

"It was a surprise." She grinned. "He told us yesterday morning: He came right down to the servants' hall just as we finished breakfast and announced he'd bought us tickets to *The Shop Girl* at the Gaiety. Everyone was so excited and then he said he was giving us pocket money to buy sweets and come home in hansom cabs. Can you imagine, sir, hansom cabs!"

"He sounds a very generous employer." Barnes nodded encouragingly as he flipped open his notebook.

"He was, sir." Her eyes flooded with tears but she blinked them back. "Mrs. Clarridge offered to stay back in case he needed something, but he wouldn't have it. He said he could fend for himself and that he was meeting a friend for supper at Barnaby's Restaurant and we were to go and enjoy ourselves. So as soon as we had our evening meal, we tidied up and then left."

"What time did you go?"

"Six o'clock," she replied. "We caught the omnibus on the corner and then changed to the Strand omnibus on Haymarket Street. That got us to the Gaiety a half hour before the curtain went up."

"When you left the house, did you notice anyone hanging around, anyone suspicious looking?" He always hated asking this. Most murderers, especially ones that had planned their crime, went to great lengths to fade into the background. But it was a question that needed to be asked.

Her brows drew together as she thought back to the start of the evening. "I didn't notice anyone. But this is a busy street"—she pointed toward the front of the house—"and there were lots of people out shopping, carolers, and tradespeople making deliveries. That's why we left so early for the theater, because there was so much traffic."

"Did you leave by the front door?"

"No, the servants' door."

"The one on the lower ground floor at the front of the house?"

"That's the tradesmen's door, sir; it's only used for deliveries. It's a bit bigger than the other doors. It's always kept locked."

"Does Mrs. Clarridge keep the key?"

"She doesn't, sir. It's one of them big, old-fashioned locks, so the key hangs on a nail by the door." She grinned. "I don't think she wants to come dashin' down all the stairs in this house every time we get a delivery. She's got bad knees."

"And was it locked today?"

"It was, sir. I locked it myself after the laundry was delivered early this morning and that was the only time the door was opened."

"To your knowledge has Mr. Edison been worried about anyone lately? Has anyone threatened him or upset him?"

She drew back, her eyes widening in surprise. "I'm only a maid, sir. I'd not know anything like that."

"I didn't mean anything untoward," he assured her quickly, realizing she made an assumption he'd not meant.

"Of course he'd not say anything to his servants about such a matter, but you seem like an intelligent and observant young woman. I was hoping you might have noticed something or perhaps overheard something that might prove useful."

Pleased by his words, she smiled. "Well, I wasn't eavesdroppin' or anything, but two days ago when I was dusting the drawing room, I overhead him arguing with Mr. Downing. Mr. Charles Downing. He's one of Mr. Edison's business associates."

Barnes wrote down the name, then looked up and gave her a conspiratorial smile. "Do you know what the argument was about?"

She glanced over her shoulder at the closed dining room door. "I didn't hear much of it. Mrs. Clarridge come in and sent me upstairs to get her more brass polish and by the time I got down, the study door was open and both Mr. Edison and Mr. Downing were gone. But before that, Mr. Downing was shouting that Mr. Edison had better be careful, that people wouldn't take kindly to losing their money. Mr. Edison yelled right back at him that any kind of investin' was risky and that just because things went bad, it wasn't his fault. Mr. Downing screamed that it was his fault. That's when Mrs. Clarridge come in and sent me upstairs. I don't think she really needed the brass polish, she only wanted to stop me from overhearin' the argument." She glanced at the closed door again. "I think she just wanted me out of the way so she could have a good listen, if you know what I mean."

A quarter of a mile away, Mrs. Jeffries yawned as she and Fred stepped into the back hall. She reached down and unhooked his lead, and together they trudged up the corridor to the kitchen. Ruth had wanted to stay and wait for Wiggins, but Mrs. Jeffries had pointed out that even if the footman had learned something of significance, there was nothing that could be done until morning. So with Fred acting as their guard, she'd seen Ruth safely home.

Mrs. Goodge was still sitting at the table when they came into the kitchen. The dog immediately flopped onto his rug and curled into a sleepy ball.

"Is Phyllis back yet?" Mrs. Jeffries hung her cloak on the coat tree.

"Not yet, but she said she might be late. Her friend is a bit of a nervous Nelly and Phyllis was going to have the cab drop her off first."

"You're going to wait up," Mrs. Jeffries said as she slipped into her seat. It was a comment rather than a question.

"Of course." Mrs. Goodge grinned. "I dozed off earlier this evening and once I've had a catnap, it's ages before I can get back to sleep. One of the few advantages of getting old is that you don't need as much sleep as the younger ones. Besides, I want to hear what our Wiggins has found out."

"So do I. I feel rather badly for the inspector, though—I know he was anticipating the holidays with Amanda Belle."

"Luty and I were, too. But it's only the eighteenth, so if the crime isn't complicated it might get solved quickly. Then all of us godparents will be able to enjoy the season with our baby."

"But it will be complicated." Mrs. Jeffries helped herself to a cup of tea. "That's precisely why the chief inspector interrupted Inspector Witherspoon's evening. Once he identified the victim, he knew it wasn't going to be an easy case and he wanted his most experienced officer to take charge."

"It doesn't seem fair, does it? Our inspector wasn't even

on duty tonight." She glanced at the clock and pursed her lips in a frown. "I do hope Wiggins is alright. It's miserable out there and I'd not like him to catch frostbite."

"He's young, he'll be fine. Where did he go this evening? I heard him mention something about going out tonight, but frankly, when he started talking about football I stopped listening."

She laughed. "He went to the pub with his friend Tommy. They were going to make plans about a game this Saturday—" She broke off as they heard the back door open and Fred, who'd been sleeping in front of the cooker, reared up and then trotted toward the back door.

"Hello, old boy, do you need to go walkies again?" Wiggins' voice was clear as a bell. "Or did you do all your business when Ruth took ya?"

"He's fine. I took him out again when I walked Ruth home," Mrs. Jeffries called out quickly. "So you can come straight in and sit down."

"Good. It's freezin' outside and you know Fred, 'e likes to sniff every leaf and bush in the garden." He patted the dog on the head and then slipped into the chair next to the cook. Fred flopped back down on his rug.

"Here, drink this." Mrs. Goodge pushed the mug of tea she'd poured toward him. "It'll warm you right up. Now, did you hear anything useful?"

He nodded his thanks and took a quick sip of the hot brew. "I don't know if it's useful, but I did find out a thing or two." He told them about his encounter with Georgie and how everyone, save Mrs. Wynn, thought Orlando Edison was a wonderful master.

"So he was well liked by his servants," the cook murmured. "Then it's a safe bet none of them had anything to do with his death. Good positions with decent masters are rarer than gold nuggets from the Thames."

"Mrs. Wynn didn't think much of 'im," Wiggins reminded her.

The cook snorted. "She doesn't think much of anyone except herself. Mrs. Wynn is the sort of person who'd criticize the Second Coming."

"But she doesn't out-and-out lie," Mrs. Jeffries mused. "So we should do our best to find out who the weeping woman might be and, more importantly, what had Edison done that made her cry?"

"If that will be all, Inspector, I really must see to the household." Mrs. Clarridge rose to her feet. "The girls are still very upset and I've got to write notes to the local vicar and Mr. Edison's solicitor."

"Did he have any family?"

She shook her head. "Not that I'm aware of, Inspector, and if there is, his solicitor would know." She pointed to a slip of paper on the desk. "That's his name and address. I'm sure you'll want to speak with him yourself."

"Thank you, Mrs. Clarridge, you've been very helpful." He got up and grabbed the paper off the desk. He'd covered the victim's last day and whatever other questions he might have could wait until another time.

She started to leave, took two steps, and came to an abrupt halt as Constable Griffiths' voice thundered through the closed doors. "Just a moment, sir. You can't go in there. There's been a crime committed here."

"Crime, what crime?" The voice was male and accent American. "What are you talking about? What in the name of all that's holy is going on here?"

Witherspoon, giving in to what Mrs. Jeffries called his "inner voice," shot past the startled housekeeper and into the hall. Constable Griffiths stood like a sentinel, blocking the front door with his arms. On the doorstep, a man wearing a black top hat bobbed and weaved from side to side trying to see inside.

"Let the gentleman in, please," he ordered the constable.

"Yes, sir." Griffiths moved aside and the man stepped inside.

Witherspoon studied him as he crossed the small space. He was a rather youngish-looking fellow. He swept off his hat as he moved, revealing a face with pleasant features, dark brown hair, and light gray eyes.

"I'm Yancy Kimball," he announced. "Where's Orlando? Why is this place thick with police?"

"You're a friend of Mr. Edison's?" Witherspoon asked. Mrs. Jeffries had always told him to trust the voice, that part of himself that saw and understood on a level that was different from the rational part of his brain. So, despite the man's aggressive manner, the inspector wasn't alarmed. The fellow looked more anxious than threatening. "If so, I'm afraid I've some very bad news."

Kimball's eyes widened and his face visibly paled. "Oh, God, what has happened? Is he alright? Has he been hurt?"

"Please, do come sit down, Mr. Kimball, and I'll explain everything." Witherspoon turned and went back into the drawing room.

Kimball followed after him, unbuttoning his coat as he walked. He was now as white as a sheet as he slipped onto the seat at the end of the sofa. "Tell me, sir, why are the police here? Where's Orlando? We were supposed to meet at Barnaby's Restaurant for supper, but he never arrived. That's not like him."

"I'm afraid Mr. Edison is dead." Witherspoon watched Kimball carefully. "He was murdered earlier this evening."

For a moment, Kimball simply gaped at him. His mouth gaped open and his eyes flooded with tears. "Murdered? Orlando? No, that can't be right. He can't be dead. I saw him yesterday as I was coming out of Thomas Cook's. That's when we made our plans to have supper together tonight."

"You're planning a trip, sir?" It was always wise to know what plans witnesses made, Witherspoon thought.

"I'm leaving for New York after the new year. I was booking my passage." He closed his eyes and sighed heavily. "I can't believe this is happening. I can't believe he's dead."

"How long have you and Mr. Edison been friends?" Witherspoon asked.

"All of our lives," Kimball murmured. "Orlando is—or was—my cousin."

The inspector frowned. "But you've an American accent and Mr. Edison was English."

He drew back and stared at Witherspoon. "I left England when I was twelve and went to New York when my mother got a job as a housekeeper to an American. But what does that have to do with my cousin's death? It happened years ago."

"When did you return to England?"

"I've been back many times."

"So you and your cousin have kept in close touch?" the inspector pressed.

"Our mothers did. They were sisters and wrote one another often." He drummed his fingers on the arm of the chair. "Inspector, I don't know what my personal history has to do with Orlando's murder."

"Perhaps nothing," he agreed. "But it's important to

establish relationships during a homicide inquiry. Are there any other family members we should notify?"

Kimball shook his head. "No, just me. Both our mums passed within a year of each other and Orlando and I lost touch."

"How old were you when you lost your mum?" Witherspoon had no idea why he was pursuing this line of inquiry, but somehow, he felt it might be important.

"Sixteen. By that time, both Orlando and I were making our way in the world, me in New York and him in England. A few years back, I had business here and I looked him up. I was pleased to see he was doing so well for himself but, then again, he always did have a good head for money."

It occurred to Witherspoon that Kimball might well be the dead man's heir. He glanced around the elegantly furnished drawing room. The room reeked of wealth and he'd learned that money was often the motive for murder. "What is your occupation, Mr. Kimball?"

Kimball cocked his head to one side. "Occupation, well, I guess you could say I'm a professional gambler."

Downstairs, Barnes gave the second maid, Mary Gunnerson, an encouraging smile. She was a slender young girl with a longish face, very pale skin, brown hair, and such a terrified expression you'd think the poor lass was facing a firing squad. "Don't be nervous, Mary, just tell me again what you heard yesterday afternoon."

Mary chewed her lower lip. "I don't know that I ought to repeat it, sir. Mrs. Clarridge doesn't like us to gossip."

"This isn't gossip, Mary," he explained patiently. "This is a murder investigation and what you overheard could be very important. I want to make sure I understood exactly what you were saying." He was making her repeat herself because when she'd rushed through it so quickly the first time, he wasn't sure he'd understood the lass.

"Well, sir, as I told you before, Mrs. Green had sent me upstairs yesterday to ask Mrs. Clarridge for the keys to the spice cupboard. She'd run out of nutmeg, sir, and needed it for the puddin', but just as I reached the top of the back stairs, I heard Mr. Edison. He was yellin' something fierce and I don't mind tellin' ya, it scared me to death. Mr. Edison never raises his voice. I didn't know what to do so I just stood there."

"Where exactly was Mr. Edison when you heard this?" Barnes was very tired. He'd worked a full day shift before tonight and he was feeling his age in every bone in his body, but he knew this might be important so he forced himself to listen closely.

She pointed up. "In his sitting room. It's toward the back of the house—that's why I could hear him so clearly when I come up the staircase. Anyways, he was yellin' that they were happy to make money off him when things went right so it was only fittin' that if things went south—that's the words he used, sir—then they had to take the loss."

"Do you know who Mr. Edison was arguing with?"

"I'm not sure. I think it might have been Mr. Ralston or it could have been Mr. Bagshot. But Mr. Edison often opened the door himself, so I don't know."

Barnes nodded. In his interview with Kitty Long the only thing she'd mentioned was Downing's argument with Edison two days ago. She'd not mentioned anyone named Bagshot or Ralston coming to the house yesterday. But then again, he'd not asked that specific question. He sighed inwardly; sometimes getting complete information out of people was a bit like pulling hen's teeth. "What happened then? Did you hear anything else?"

"No, sir. Mrs. Clarridge came down the hall and hustled me back to the kitchen. She said it wasn't fittin' for us to be eavesdroppin' on Mr. Edison's personal troubles."

Barnes looked up from his notebook. "Do you know either Mr. Bagshot's or Mr. Ralston's Christian name?"

"No, sir, I don't, but I expect Mrs. Clarridge does."

Phyllis hummed to herself as she unlocked the front door and stepped inside. Mrs. Jeffries hadn't wanted her to come across the garden at this time of night, so she'd given her a key to the front door. She closed her eyes, thinking back to the wonderful story she'd seen. Perhaps, one day, she'd have a house like this, too; perhaps, one day, she'd find she was the long-lost daughter of a rich man. She untied the strings of her bonnet as she walked down the hall to the back steps, grabbed the newel post, twirled dramatically, and started to go up to her room, when she noticed the light coming up from the kitchen. She couldn't imagine anyone would be up; surely she was the last one home. She hurried down the stairs.

"It's about time you got home." Mrs. Goodge frowned at the maid as she entered the kitchen. "We were startin' to worry."

Flustered, she yanked off her bonnet. "No one had to wait up for me. Mrs. Jeffries gave me a key to the front door."

"We're not waitin' up just for you," Wiggins said. "But now that you're 'ere, we can get on with things."

"What things? What's wrong?"

"Nothing is wrong, so to speak," Mrs. Jeffries said calmly. "But we were getting concerned."

"I'm sorry, I didn't mean to worry anyone. It's just that

we couldn't find a hansom right away. We had to walk half a mile up the Strand before we got one." This was an out-and-out lie. She didn't like deceiving them and she wasn't very good at lying, but she couldn't tell them the truth, they'd never understand. She and Susan had ignored half a dozen empty cabs so they could have more time together to talk about the play. They'd not wanted the evening to end. She slipped off her overcoat and hung it on the peg. "But I'm here now." She took her seat at the table.

"We've got a murder," Mrs. Jeffries said.

"And the inspector is at the murder house now but he might come home at any moment," Mrs. Goodge said.

"So we'd better make this quick," Wiggins added.

Mrs. Jeffries, Wiggins, and the cook gave her the pertinent details of what they knew thus far.

"I do hope this one will be easy to solve," Phyllis muttered when they'd finished speaking. "Our inspector was so looking forward to having time with Amanda over the holidays." She didn't add that she'd been hoping for some free time herself. She wanted to go back to the theater, to be taken once again out of her normal routine and shown a different world. For the first time in her life, she could afford to buy tickets. In this household, she didn't have to pay for sugar or tea out of her wages and she'd managed to save practically all of what she'd earned. But she knew her duty. If they had a case, she'd do her part.

In the sudden quiet that descended upon the room, the clock struck the hour, startling Mrs. Goodge. "Oh dear. I'd love to wait up for the inspector but I'm suddenly tired. I'm going to bed."

Phyllis got up. "I'll clear off the tea things."

"I'll lock up the back," Wiggins said.

"No, both of you go on up to your beds," Mrs. Jeffries ordered. "I'll take care of the teapot and the back door. I couldn't sleep anyway."

"You goin' to wait up for the inspector?" Mrs. Goodge asked around a yawn.

"I'm going to try," she replied.

It was another two hours before the inspector came home but Mrs. Jeffries stayed awake. She'd heard the hansom cab pull up and that gave her enough time to meet him at the front door.

He raised his eyebrows when he saw her. "Good gracious, you didn't need to wait up for me. It's dreadfully late. You must be tired."

"No more tired than I'm sure you are, sir." She reached for the bowler he was in the process of taking off his head. "But I've a roast beef sandwich and a glass of sherry waiting in the study, sir. I thought you might be a bit peckish."

"You are an angel of mercy." He smiled gratefully, shed his overcoat, and a few moments later followed her down the hall and into his comfortable study.

As was her custom, she'd poured herself a glass as well. "Now, sir, we hear from Lady Cannonberry's household that you've been saddled with another murder. I take it that's where you've been this evening."

He took a sip of his drink and nodded. "The murder house is close by. Poor fellow got bashed on the head. Chief Inspector Barrows found the body and sent for me. It was quite dreadful, really." He took a quick bite from the sandwich, chewed vigorously, and swallowed. "The victim's name is Orlando Edison and, from what I could gather from his servants, he made his living promoting foreign mining stocks. Unfortunately, even though the man was murdered on his front door stoop, we've no witnesses as yet."

"It's early days, sir," she murmured.

"Indeed it is," he agreed. "Mind you, he doesn't seem the sort of man to actually get murdered; though, of course he must have been because it happened."

"Whatever do you mean, sir?"

"He seemed very well liked by his servants—as a matter of fact, he'd given all of them the night off and paid for them to go to the theater this evening."

"So he was home alone?"

"Oh yes, I expect the killer must have counted on that being the case, but my earlier point was his servants seemed to genuinely care about him. He had no quarrels with his neighbors and the only family he has is a cousin who came to see what was wrong when Edison didn't show up for supper." He told her the rest of the details about the evening, beginning with finding the body and continuing on through his interview with Yancy Kimball.

She listened carefully, occasionally nodding or murmuring a comment. "It's odd that the housekeeper didn't mention either of the arguments the victim had prior to his death."

He frowned thoughtfully. "She seemed to have herself under control, yet, despite her demeanor, I sensed that she was more upset about Mr. Edison's murder than she wanted to let on."

"You mean you think she simply forgot both incidents?" She stared at him over the rim of her glass.

"Not really, no, but sometimes a terrible shock makes one forget very important details."

"When you speak with her again, it will be interesting to see if she volunteers this information. As you said, sir, arguing with two different people right before being murdered is a most important detail and we know from the housemaids' statements that Mrs. Clarridge was aware of both incidents."

"True, but I don't think she deliberately kept anything from me, I think the poor woman was just overwhelmed."

"Do you think his cousin, this Mr. Yancy Kimball, is his heir?" she asked.

"It's very possible but I won't know until I can speak with his solicitor and I hope to do that tomorrow."

"You'll be going back to the Edison house?"

"Of course. We've more questions to ask, but by the time we took everyone's statement tonight Constable Barnes and I were both so tired we felt it best to come back when we've had a bit of rest. We left a constable on duty by the front door and came home." He sighed heavily. "But it doesn't seem fair. We always seem to get stuck with a dreadful murder every year at this time. You'd think that even killers would have some respect for the holidays!"

CHAPTER 3

"We weren't at our best last night and I know we missed something." Constable Barnes put his empty mug down and got to his feet. "But we're going to make up for it today. Everyone in Edison's household is going to be interviewed again."

"Don't be so hard on yourselves." Mrs. Jeffries smiled kindly. "You both put in a full day's work before you even got the case. I think you learned quite a bit."

"And thanks to young Wiggins I now know Edison had some sort of emotional ruckus with a young lady in Holland Park." He frowned. "That was good work on his part but now I've got to figure out a likely source before I can pass that particular tidbit along to the inspector."

"You'll come up with something. You always do." Mrs. Goodge wiped her hands on a clean tea cloth and reached under her worktable for a bag of flour. "If push comes to shove, you can always just say one of your informants passed it along to you."

Barnes shot her a grateful grin. As was his custom when working a murder, he'd stopped in the kitchen to have a word with Mrs. Jeffries and Mrs. Goodge before going upstairs to fetch the inspector. During one of the inspector's earlier cases, the constable had realized the household was actively involved in gathering information and seeking out clues. Barnes understood the value of "amateurs" and took full advantage of the situation. Many of London's good citizens would sooner die than give a policeman the time of day, but those same people would then turn around and talk a blue streak to anyone who'd put a pint of beer or even a cup of tea in front of them. Mrs. Jeffries and the others could also skirt the edges of the law with a bit more ease than either himself or the inspector. In return for the information they passed to him, he freely shared with them, and this morning he'd given them additional details he'd picked up from the victim's household.

"I'd best get upstairs, then. The inspector's probably finished his breakfast and we've a lot of ground to cover today." He headed for the staircase, pausing just long enough to give them a cheerful wave. "I'll see you ladies tomorrow morning."

"Nell's bells, the traffic gets worse every day," Luty announced as she swept into the kitchen. Her butler and constant companion, Hatchet, trailed behind her. "I was scared ya was goin' to start without me."

Luty Belle Crookshank was a small, elderly American with a love of bright clothes and shiny jewelry. She unbuttoned her crimson cloak and let it slide off her thin shoulders and into Hatchet's waiting hands. Her dress was the same color as the cloak but trimmed with white lace at the collar and the cuffs. Gold earrings dangled from her lobes and a matching pendant hung around her neck. A star-shaped gold broach was pinned at her throat.

"I told you they wouldn't start without us." Hatchet took their outer garments to the coat tree and hung each on a peg. He was a tall, white-haired man with a ready smile and a quick wit. As usual, he was dressed in a perfectly tailored black suit, a white shirt, and, in honor of the season, a maroon tie. "Honestly, madam, there was no need to keep shouting at poor McGregor to go faster. I believe half of London must have heard you."

"Fiddlesticks. McGregor loves to make that carriage fly! He was grinnin' like a fool." She stopped and surveyed the faces around the table, her eyes narrowing as her gaze stopped on a lovely blonde. "Alright, Betsy, where's my baby?"

Luty Belle, along with Mrs. Goodge and the inspector, was godparent to Smythe and Betsy's one-year-old daughter, Amanda Belle. They'd met and fallen in love while working for the Inspector as a coachman and housemaid. After marrying, they'd moved into their own flat.

Betsy grinned. "She was up half the night so she's taking a quick nap in Mrs. Goodge's room. I'm sure she'll be up before we get out and about. She's not sleeping as much as she used to."

"Neither are we." Smythe yawned. He was a heavily muscled man with thick black hair going gray at the temples and hard, sharp features. His face was saved from being harsh by the kind light in his brown eyes and his ready smile.

"Stop your fretting, Luty." The cook smiled broadly. "You'll get equal time to play with our little one." There was a good-natured, but real, rivalry between the two women over time with the baby. Neither woman had ever had children and they both doted on the child. "Now sit down so we can get this meeting started. We've lots to discuss." She picked up the big brown teapot and began to pour.

Mrs. Jeffries slipped into her chair. There was an air of excitement around the table, but then, there always was at the beginning of an investigation. She glanced at the faces of the others.

Ruth had arrived first, coming in the back door at almost the same moment the inspector and Barnes had gone out the front. She'd begun helping on the inspector's cases some time back and now was a special friend of both Witherspoon and the household. The widow of a peer, she was the daughter of a country vicar who took the teachings of Jesus seriously. She worked tirelessly to love her neighbor as herself. To her way of thinking, that meant treating everyone, even servants, as her equal, so in the privacy of their meetings, she insisted the inspector's household call her by her Christian name rather than her title. Publicly, she understood that none of them could refer to her as anything but Lady Cannonberry.

Ruth turned her head and caught the housekeeper looking at her. "Is something wrong?"

"No, no, I was just thinking that perhaps you ought to start," Mrs. Jeffries suggested quickly. "It's important that all of us know the details as they happened."

"Certainly." Ruth nodded her thanks as the cook handed her a mug of tea. "Gerald and I had finished dinner when we were interrupted by Constable Barnes," she began. She repeated the sequence of events carefully, making sure she left nothing out of the recital. "And then Wiggins left to go to the murder house," she concluded.

"So we had the victim's name right from the beginning," Hatchet murmured.

"And we knew where he lived, more or less," Wiggins added. "I'll go next." He told them everything he'd heard, starting with the shovel being the murder weapon and finishing with the tidbits Georgie Marks had gotten from Mrs. Wynn.

"Mrs. Wynn." Betsy snorted in derision. "For goodness' sake, you can't trust anything that old witch says. That woman is a terrible gossip—she doesn't have anything good to say about anyone."

"Don't get so het up, lass." Smythe patted his wife's hand. "I know you don't like her."

"Nobody likes her." She jerked her hand away, her blue eyes flashing angrily at her husband. "And if you'll recall, she said some nasty things about me when we got married."

Smythe winced at the memory. Mrs. Wynn had hinted to everyone who set foot in her shop that the only reason Betsy and he had married was because they'd *had* to because Betsy was in the family way. That hadn't been the case at all; they'd been engaged for ages before they wed. But that hadn't stopped the old lady's tongue and when the rumor had gotten back to Betsy she'd stormed into the shop, given the woman a piece of her mind, and vowed to buy her groceries elsewhere. "Sorry, love, I wasn't tryin' to defend the woman."

"Well, it sounded that way to me."

Mrs. Jeffries knew she had to intervene. "Mrs. Wynn does sometimes start ridiculous rumors based on speculation," she interjected quickly. "And she was both unfair and unkind to you. But she's the sort of woman that is always going to think and say the worst about younger, prettier women like you."

Somewhat placated, Betsy reached over and squeezed her husband's hand. "Sorry, I didn't mean to fly off the handle like that, but it's still a sore spot with me."

"And it is with me, too. Add to that we're both tired from our little one's nightly shenanigans." He yawned again. "But let's get on with the meeting. I could use getting out and about."

"I'm all done," Wiggins said.

"Good, then I'll go next." Mrs. Jeffries repeated the information she'd heard from the inspector and when she finished, she turned to Mrs. Goodge. "Tell everyone what we found out from the constable this morning."

"It wasn't that much, but he did mention that so far, the house-to-house hadn't turned up any witnesses and that there were several groups of carolers out last night," she replied. "They're going to try and track down the singers that came to Edison's door. But that might take some doing."

"Why are they doing that?" Ruth asked. "Is the constable thinking one of them might have seen someone lurking about the area?"

"That's what he's hoping," the cook replied.

"We've now got the name of the victim and his address as well as the names of several individuals that had quarreled with him on the days leading up to his murder," Mrs. Jeffries said. "So we're well on our way on this case."

"Orlando Edison, Orlando Edison," Luty muttered. "I know I've heard that name before."

"Ralston, Downing, and Bagshot," Smythe said. "Too bad we didn't get their first names. That would 'ave 'elped a bit."

"Even without them, as Mrs. Jeffries says, we've still got a fair bit to go on," Betsy said.

"Of course we do," Hatchet agreed. "We also know the

name of the one person who might benefit the most from Edison's death: his cousin, Yancy Kimball." He looked at Mrs. Jeffries. "Do we know where Kimball's staying?"

"The Larchmont Hotel on Pringle Street in Paddington," Mrs. Goodge said quickly. "Sorry, I should have told you before."

"But just because this Mr. Kimball is the victim's cousin, it doesn't mean he gets the estate," Phyllis said. "Maybe Edison left a will givin' it to someone else. When I worked for the Lassiter family, the master had a rich old bachelor cousin who died. Mr. Lassiter expected to inherit the lot, but the cousin had left both his house and all his money to the Royal Society for the Prevention of Cruelty to Animals. He liked cats more than his kin."

"It's certainly possible that the victim left a will," Mrs. Jeffries said. "But according to the inspector, he was only thirty years old. That's relatively young and as he had no wife or children, he might not have thought it necessary to have one. In which case, the law generally specifies that the nearest relative inherits the lot."

"So one of our first tasks will be to find out who inherits." Ruth tapped her finger against the handle of her cup. "That shouldn't be too difficult."

"And then we need to find out who wanted him dead . . ." Phyllis' voice trailed off. "Sorry, that's silly, that's what we always do."

"It's not silly," Mrs. Jeffries said quickly. Phyllis had very little faith in her own worth or intelligence. The housekeeper suspected that the maid had spent most of her life surrounded by people telling her she was dull and stupid. That most certainly wasn't the case; the girl was as bright as a button and had a talent for detecting, and Mrs. Jeffries was determined to help her develop these and all her other positive qualities. "Oftentimes we get caught up in the details of a case so intently that we ignore the basics. It was good of you to remind us and equally important that it become our first priority."

Embarrassed, but pleased by the praise, Phyllis grinned and ducked her head.

"Findin' out who wanted 'im dead isn't goin' to be our only problem," Smythe said bluntly.

Betsy looked at her husband. "What do you mean?"

"I mean, this is our neighborhood; the murder was committed less than a quarter mile away, so when we're out and about talkin' to shopkeepers, neighbors, and hansom cab drivers and sussin' out bits and pieces at the local pub, everyone will know what we're doin'."

"But this isn't the first time there's been a murder in this district," Hatchet pointed out. "We ought to be able to manage if we're careful."

"Of course we'll be able to manage," Mrs. Jeffries repeated. "But Smythe's correct, we'll need to watch our tongues when we're asking questions. The locals all know we're employed by the inspector."

"But we've asked questions round 'ere before," Wiggins protested. He didn't want them making this case any more complicated than it was. He knew his duty and working for the cause of justice was important to him, but cor blimey, this was shaping up to be a right miserable Christmas season. He'd wanted a bit of time to himself, especially this Saturday. He had to go all the way across London. Millwall Athletic Football Club was playing Clapton at the Old Spotted Dog. So even if he could steal a couple of hours off for the game, by the time he took the train to either Upton Park or Forest Gate, he'd need half the day. Plus he'd promised to meet Tommy at the pub across from the ground so they could go to the game together. He really wanted to see this match; he'd missed the Millwall–Clapton one in November and that had been a corker. "Seems to me as long as we just act like we're doin' a bit of gossipin' and not really askin' questions, we'll be alright. Besides, it's only the victim that we know for certain lived round 'ere. Could be that once we know who all our suspects are, they might be from other neighborhoods."

"That's certainly true." Mrs. Goodge glanced at the carriage clock on the pine sideboard. "It's gettin' on and I've got to do more baking for my sources—"

Mrs. Jeffries interrupted. "How are you fixed for provisions?"

The cook did all her investigating right from the kitchen. She had an army of tradespeople, delivery boys, gasworks men, and street vendors that popped in and out of her little empire on a daily basis. With buttery scones, cherry tarts, seedcake, and currant buns she plied her sources with mouthwatering treats and endless cups of tea. She extracted every morsel of gossip that was to be had about the victim, the suspects, and anyone else whose name popped up in the course of an investigation. Mrs. Goodge had worked in some of the finest homes in all England. If her street sources failed her, a lifetime spent in service had given her a vast network of former colleagues that she could call upon for information. She'd come to the Witherspoon household after getting sacked from her previous position for being "too old." When she'd first arrived, she'd been a hidebound old snob who considered working for a mere policeman a step down in the world. But once she'd been pulled into the inspector's investigations, once she'd seen that the rich and powerful were capable of the most heinous crimes while some of the poorest and the least were capable of self-sacrifice and honor, she'd changed. Now she took her commitment to justice very seriously and she was as proud of her accomplishments in contributing to justice as she was of her cooking.

"I've got plenty in for the baking"—she glanced in the direction of the dry larder—"but I could use some vegetables. I need some carrots and turnips for tonight's stew."

"I'll get them for you," Phyllis volunteered. "It'll give me an excuse to speak to Mrs. Preston at the greengrocer's. She might know something about our Mr. Edison."

"And I'll take Amanda in her pram and talk to some of the shopkeepers over on the Kensington High Street," Betsy offered. "We might as well cover the whole area."

"Mind you wrap my lambkins up warmly," Mrs. Goodge said. "It's cold out there."

Everyone looked at Luty, who always jumped in whenever the baby was mentioned. But she was staring off in the distance, her brows furrowed in deep concentration.

Hatchet reached over and tapped her hand. "You're uncharacteristically silent, madam. Is everything alright?"

Luty started. "Yup, I'm fine, I'm just tryin' to remember where I've heard them names before. Now Orlando Edison, he was easy. He's that stock promoter that's always pushin' mining shares, especially the ones in South Africa."

"South Africa?" Ruth repeated. "You mean places like Cape Town?"

"No, not there, the other place, the one that's got all the gold—Johannesburg. Gossip was that he made a bundle during the Witwatersrand Rush in '87 and '88 but then he figured out that it was lots easier makin' others do the actual prospectin' and took to promotin' mines rather than swingin' a pickax. But it's them other names . . ."

"What other names?" Hatchet asked irritably.

Luty's eyes widened. "Ralston, Bagshot, and Downing, yes, yes, that's it. Now I remember where I've heard of 'em. They're the Merry Gentlemen."

"Mrs. Clarridge, Mr. Edison had two arguments on the two successive days prior to his murder and you heard both of them. Yet when I asked you if anything out of the ordinary had happened recently, the only thing you thought to mention was Mr. Ralston's visit yesterday afternoon." Witherspoon stood in front of the unlighted fireplace and watched the housekeeper's face. She was sitting on the sofa in the drawing room and the inspector wanted to ascertain if she'd deliberately misled him the previous night. He wasn't very good at reading expressions but it was a skill he was trying his best to master.

"What are you implying, Inspector?" she demanded. "That I was purposely trying to deceive you?"

"Not at all, ma'am," he said quickly. Perhaps he'd practice his face-reading skills at another time. "But sometimes, people are hesitant to make comments about the deceased. Especially if they admired and respected that person, they don't want to mention anything that might diminish them in the eyes of others. I sense that Mr. Edison was the best of employers and very well liked by his staff."

Her face softened and her eyes filled with tears. "He was a wonderful man, Inspector, and this is the best post I've ever had. But I wasn't keeping anything a secret, I simply was so rattled I forgot all about the other incidents. It was late and when we came home to find the house filled with police, well, between trying to calm the others and make sense of what happened in my own mind, I'm amazed I could even remember my own name. But rest assured, the moment you'd gone I realized I ought to have told you about both incidents and that they might have been important."

Witherspoon believed her. "Could you tell me now? Let's start with the one from two days prior to Mr. Edison's murder. Who exactly was arguing with the victim?"

"It was Mr. Downing. He arrived unexpectedly and insisted on speaking to Mr. Edison."

"What's Mr. Downing's full name?"

"He's Mr. Charles Downing," she replied. "And he lives on Argyll Road in Kensington."

"And the other one?"

"Mr. Martin Bagshot was the one who quarreled with Mr. Edison the day before yesterday. Like Mr. Downing, he lives quite close by, on Sunningdale Gardens in Kensington."

Witherspoon nodded encouragingly. "Excellent. And can you tell me what relationships Mr. Downing and Mr. Bagshot had with Mr. Edison?"

"They did business together. Both men were investors in the Granger Mine and both of them are on the board of directors." She broke off as the sound of loud voices came from the foyer.

Witherspoon turned just as the drawing room door crashed open and three men, followed by a constable, charged into the room.

"Ye gods, it's true, then?" The portly man leading the pack directed his question to Mrs. Clarridge. "He's really dead?"

"Get back into the hall," the constable shouted as he scurried in front of them and tried to herd them back toward the foyer. "Sorry, sir," he said to Witherspoon. "I tried to keep them out."

"Not to worry, Constable. Let the gentlemen come

inside. It's alright." The constable glared at the intruders, nodded respectfully to the inspector, and left, closing the door behind him.

Mrs. Clarridge stared stonily at the trio of newcomers as she rose to her feet. "You're correct, sir. To the household's great sadness, our master, Mr. Edison, has passed away," she announced. Then she pointed toward one of the men, who was middle-aged, with curly light brown hair, noticeable jowls, and a huge handlebar mustache. "That's Mr. Downing," she said to Witherspoon. "You can ask him yourself why he was arguing with Mr. Edison."

"Now see here, I don't know what you're talking about," Downing blustered.

"Presumably, you're the policeman in charge here." A much younger man, who'd been standing behind the other two, stepped past them and looked at Witherspoon. He had dark hair, ears that stuck out, and blue eyes. "So I take it it's true, Orlando was murdered?"

Before the inspector could reply, Mrs. Clarridge touched his sleeve. "I must go downstairs, sir. Cook and I are going over the menu for the funeral reception. I'll be in the kitchen when you're ready for me again."

"Thank you, Mrs. Clarridge, I'll come speak with you further when I'm finished with these gentlemen."

As soon as she'd gone, Witherspoon said, "I'm Inspector Gerald Witherspoon. I assume you're all friends of the victim."

"Victim?" The man who'd led the pack into the room spoke now. He had thinning blond hair streaked with gray, a very ruddy complexion, and a potbelly that his well-tailored blue suit couldn't quite hide. "Good gracious, then it's true, he was murdered."

"That's right. Now, why don't you all introduce yourselves and tell me how you found out about Mr. Edison's death?"

The youngest man extended his hand to the inspector. "Forgive us, sir. We've forgotten our manners. I'm Paul Ralston, a business associate of Mr. Edison's. This"—he nodded toward the tubby blond fellow—"is Martin Bagshot and, as Mrs. Clarridge pointed out, the other gentleman is Charles Downing."

"We're all business associates," Bagshot said quickly. "This is unbelievable, I'm not sure I can take it in." He moved to the sofa and flopped down. "Murder? That simply doesn't happen to people like us."

"I assure you it does, sir," Witherspoon said as he moved toward the door. He stuck his head into the foyer. "Can you please go and get Constable Barnes and Constable Griffiths," he called to the policeman at the door. Barnes and Griffiths were both downstairs reinterviewing the servants.

He turned back to the drawing room. "How is it that all three of you arrived here together?"

It was Downing who answered. "We had an early morning meeting together, Inspector, at my home. We heard talk that he'd died and came round to see if it was true."

"How did you learn of his death?"

"From my housekeeper," Downing said. "She'd heard about it from someone in the neighborhood. I live very close by, just around the corner. She mentioned it to my wife, who mentioned it to me."

Witherspoon wished Barnes and Griffiths would get here soon. He wasn't sure questioning them all together in the same room was wise. Yet now that he'd started, it was difficult to stop. He tried to think of a somewhat innocuous one. "Was Mr. Edison supposed to be at your meeting this morning?"

"Absolutely not." Bagshot's heavy brows drew together.

Oh dear, Witherspoon thought, perhaps this line of inquiry wasn't prudent, either. "And why is that? You said Mr. Edison was a business associate, and apparently he was closely enough involved in your affairs that you rushed over here to confirm whether or not he was dead."

"Edison wasn't there because we were trying to decide if we ought to take action against him." Ralston smiled faintly. "Legal action, Inspector. We think we might have had grounds to show he'd deliberately misled and defrauded us."

Phyllis hummed faintly as she rounded the corner onto the high street. She daydreamed as she made her way up past the butcher's, not bothering to notice that the place was empty and she'd have had a good chance to talk to the girl behind the counter. Her mind was full of the story she'd seen again at the theater, the tale of Bessie Brent, a working girl like herself who had been discovered to be the long-lost daughter of a miner and she herself an heiress. Well, she wasn't exactly like the heroine in the play—Bessie worked in a London shop while Phyllis was only a housemaid—but it was close enough to her own life, except that she didn't have a young man in her life like Bessie did.

A scruffy lad raced past her, bumping her arm just as she came to the baker's shop. "Sorry, miss," the boy yelled over his shoulder. Sighing, her reverie interrupted, she glanced in the window and saw Hilda Ferguson, housekeeper to one of their neighbors from Upper Edmonton Gardens, talking to the clerk. Mrs. Ferguson wouldn't let her get a word in edgewise, so she moved on, crossing the road to the butcher's shop. But there were three people in line waiting to be served. She moved on toward the greengrocer's. It was empty but that was probably because it was more of an open stall than a proper shop and it was freezing. But beggars couldn't be choosers and she had promised Mrs. Goodge she'd pick up the vegetables.

Stepping inside, she smiled at Dulcie, the clerk on the far side of the bins. "Good morning," she said cheerfully. "Is your mum not working today?"

"She's got the sniffles so she's stayin' home this morning. It's cold today." Dulcie Preston, a thin, red-haired girl wearing a heavy jacket under her apron and gloves with the fingers cut out, blew on her hands. "Too cold for Mum to be here—she had pneumonia last year and Da didn't want her takin' ill again. I heard your inspector got that Edison murder from round the corner. I saw Georgie Marks this mornin' and he was there last night and he said poor Mr. Edison had his head bashed to bits."

"That's what we heard, too," Phyllis said. "Did you know him?"

"I didn't know him, but I've seen him before. He was a nice-looking man, handsome, if you know what I mean. But his household has always bought from us. His housekeeper, Mrs. Clarridge, would come in once a week with their fruit and veg order."

"How exciting," Phyllis exclaimed. "Did she ever say anything about him?"

Dulcie shook her head. "She isn't much of a talker. Mum says she's the kind that thinks herself a bit above the likes of us. One time Mum commented that the master of the house must have done a lot of entertainin' because he was a single gentleman who always ordered so much, but all that Mrs. Clarridge would say was that she didn't comment on her employer's circumstances with tradespeople. What'll you have today?"

"Two pounds of turnips, please, and a pound of carrots." She let her mind wander while she waited for Dulcie to fill her order. She kept thinking about the theater, about the wonderful play she'd seen, and wishing she could go back and see it again.

She was jerked out of her reverie by angry shouts. "Are you bloomin' blind? Watch where you're goin'!" a red-faced cabbie screamed as he pulled his hansom sharply to the right to avoid smashing into a laundry wagon that had cut in front of him.

"Here you are," Dulcie said. "Give us your basket, then, and I'll put the veg in."

Phyllis, who'd been staring at the laundry wagon, shoved her shopping basket onto the narrow counter. "You said that Mr. Edison's housekeeper dropped his order off every week?" she said.

"That's right." Dulcie dumped two bundles wrapped in newspaper into the basket and brushed off her hands. "She'd bring the order on Fridays and Da would deliver it that afternoon. I don't know what's goin' to happen now. Da liked going there—he never had to wait long before they opened the tradesmen's door. Not like some places where you have to hang about for ages while they fetch up the housekeeper to go over the order."

"Mrs. Clarridge didn't look at the order when it came in?" Phyllis thought that was odd. Mrs. Jeffries didn't go through household deliveries, either, but she was the exception rather than the rule. In every other household where she'd ever worked, either the lady of the house examined everything coming in or the housekeeper did.

Dulcie shook her head. "Nah, one of the maids would unlock the door, Da would take the order into the wet larder, and then the girl would lock up behind him. Straight in and out, that's what he liked. Will there be anything else?"

Wiggins stood outside the pub on Throgmorton Street and watched as people went inside. This was the financial heart of England and before he went inside he wanted to make sure the place wasn't going to fill up with toffs in shiny black top hats who wouldn't give him the time of day.

Coming here had been his second choice. He'd first tried to find a servant from Edison's household to chat up, but after waiting for what seemed ages without seeing so much as a housemaid stick her nose out for a bit of air, he'd decided to try his luck elsewhere. But once he'd made that decision, he wasn't sure where to go next. The only other address they had was Yancy Kimball's hotel in Paddington, or he could try to find out something about the men Edison had been quarreling with before he was killed, the ones Luty had called the Merry Gentlemen. They were professional investors and financiers and this was their territory, Throgmorton Street. It was close enough to the Bank of England and the stock exchange so that the money lads didn't have to walk too far to get a nice pint at lunchtime.

Two men, both of them wearing ordinary business suits, went past him and into the pub. He glanced down at his own brown jacket, white shirt, and tie, and decided he looked respectable enough to give it a go. He took a deep breath, opened the door, and stepped inside.

It was just after opening time and already the pub was filled with jobbers hanging on to their bowlers, accountants in navy suits and regimental ties, and ordinary clerks. Wiggins elbowed his way through the crowd to the bar. He wedged himself into a space next to two lads who looked to be about his age.

"What'll you have?" the barman asked.

"Pint of bitter, please." He pulled some coins out of his pocket and had them at the ready when the barman put his beer in front of him. "Ta."

Wiggins eased to one side to scan the room, looking for someone on their own who might be in the mood for a chat. It was a cut above a working-class pub, with booths along one wall and small tables packed densely in the remaining floor space.

"Southampton St. Mary got lucky."

Wiggins turned his head sharply.

A dark-haired young man with deep-set brown eyes and pale, pockmarked skin tapped his fingers on the counter to make his point. "Two of those goals shouldn't have even counted. Seems to me the real score should have been a ruddy draw. Swindon Town played better."

"Are you daft?" His companion, a young lad with wispy blond hair, snorted contemptuously. "All of those goals were good. Swindon's got a lousy team. Luton Town beat 'em by two goals last month."

"And Millwall has thrashed them both," Wiggins interjected. "They beat Luton last month and Southampton the week before."

The two stopped their conversation and eyed him curiously. Wiggins knew he should have kept his opinion to himself, but he'd not been able to stop himself. Except for his friend Tommy, he'd no one to talk football with. "Sorry, I didn't mean to interrupt, it's just that—"

"You a Millwall supporter?" the first one asked.

He nodded.

"Then you must be looking forward to this Saturday." The dark-haired lad grinned broadly. "I hear Clapton is out for revenge considerin' the way you thrashed them last month."

"My mate's a Clapton supporter and even he says they're a sorry bunch," the blond added. "They play like a pack of schoolgirls."

Wiggins couldn't believe his luck. He jumped into the conversation with relish. When their glasses were empty, he ordered a round for the three of them and it was only as the two lads left to go back to work that he realized he'd not asked one single question about Orlando Edison or the Merry Gentlemen.

Jon Barlow, deliveryman for Hubbard's, the inspector's local wine merchant, put his cup down. "Are you talkin' about that fellow that got himself bashed over the head?" he said to Mrs. Goodge. "Is that who you're askin' about?"

Mrs. Goodge forced herself to smile and ignore the brown-paper-wrapped package that had been brought to the door by special messenger only moments before Barlow had arrived with a crate of wine for the holidays. She was dying to know who had sent her a present but she knew her duty: She had to see if Barlow knew anything. "Yes, that's who I'm asking about."

Barlow scratched his chin. He was a short, wiry man with thinning black hair that stood up in tufts around his ears. "Yeah, he gives us his business. The guv liked him 'cause he always ordered the best whiskey and wine and, even better, he paid his bill right and proper every month."

"Did you ever meet him?" Again, her gaze strayed to the package.

"Last week, I was deliverin' to the house when he come into the kitchen to tell the cook he'd not be home that night for dinner. Sad him gettin' coshed the way he did. The scullery maid there said he was always good to the servants." He paused and stuffed another piece of shortbread into his mouth.

"Indeed it is awful when good people get murdered," she murmured as her attention wandered to the bundle at the end of the table. Who would send her a present and what could it be? It couldn't be from anyone here at the house; they always waited till after Christmas breakfast to exchange presents. "But that's the way of it, isn't it."

"The good die young and bad live to be a hundred." Barlow took a sip of tea. "That's what my old gran used to say. Would you mind if I had another biscuit?"

"Go ahead, help yourself," she murmured. Barlow loved the sound of his own voice so she only half listened to him. Perhaps the present was from one of her previous employers. No, why would they suddenly start sending gifts now— none of them had ever done it before.

"Mind you, my gran could also spout a lot of nonsense." He reached for another biscuit and gobbled it up. "But it is a shame about Mr. Edison. You can always tell what kind of person someone is by the way they treat their people, can't you."

"Uh-huh," Mrs. Goodge muttered absently. She could barely understand the man. He was talking with his mouth full.

Barlow noticed the cook wasn't paying any attention to him, so he grabbed one last piece of shortbread, shoved it into his mouth, and chewed frantically. "Mind you"—he swallowed with a loud gulp—"not everyone liked Mr. Edison. Mrs. Morton—she runs the Nag's Head Pub at Shepherd's Bush and when I made her delivery this morning, she brought up the murder. She told me that she'd seen Edison getting his ears boxed last week. He was out in the mews

behind the pub with a woman and, the way she was swing-
ing her fists, she surely weren't no lady."

But Mrs. Goodge had stopped listening. She was thinking so hard about who could be sending her a present and
what it could be that she completely missed what he was
saying.

"Mr. Ralston, where were you yesterday at six o'clock?"
Witherspoon and Paul Ralston were now alone in the drawing room. Constable Barnes had taken Downing off to the
study and Bagshot had gone with Constable Griffiths to
the small sitting room at the end of the hall.

Ralston, who was sitting at the end of the sofa, looked
surprised by the question. "Surely you don't think I had
anything to do with Orlando's murder?"

"It's a routine inquiry, sir." Witherspoon gave him a
reassuring smile.

"I was shopping." He shrugged. "I was looking for Christmas gifts."

"You went shopping directly after leaving here?"

Ralston relaxed against the cushions and smiled. "So
Mrs. Clarridge mentioned I'd stopped in to see Orlando. I
thought she might have, but in answer to your question, I
went home first and had tea with my fiancée, Anne Waterson. When she left, I went out."

"Did you go to any particular shops?"

"The Burlington Arcade. They have some fine jewelers'
shops there. I stayed for about an hour until the shops started
closing and, as I couldn't find a hansom, I walked home."

"Did you go into any specific shops, someplace where the
clerk might remember you?"

Ralston thought for a moment. "I went into Minsky's,
but it was very crowded so I doubt any of the shop assistants

will remember me. Actually, Inspector, I was just having a look at the jewelry. I finally decided that I'm going to take my fiancée shopping and let her pick out what she wants."

"You made a statement a few moments ago about legal action against the deceased," Witherspoon said. "Would you explain what you meant, please?"

Ralston looked down at the floor and then back up. "One hates to speak ill of the dead, Inspector, but I might as well tell you the entire sordid story. You're bound to find out anyway and it's best you hear it from me."

"Yes, do go ahead."

"Two years ago, the three of us and another man by the name of Ezra Amberly were approached by Edison to serve as directors to a company he was forming to buy a gold mine on the Transvaal in southern Africa, specifically in the Witwatersrand."

"Mr. Amberly is on the board of directors as well?"

"He is, but he's not been active for weeks now. He's ill and confined to bed. But my point, Inspector, is that Edison approached us with what we thought would be a great opportunity."

"I understand that, sir. I'm aware of the fact that a substantial amount of gold has been found in that part of the world."

"Huge fortunes have been made," Ralston continued. "So the four of us thought this could be a great opportunity."

"And England has almost been dragged into a war with the Boers over the area as well," the inspector said.

"There's always conflict when the stakes are so high. Are you an investor, Inspector?"

Witherspoon hesitated. He didn't like to reveal personal details to suspects, but on the other hand, he might get more information by being candid about his own investments.

"Yes, and I freely admit I have shares in two mines there and that they've done very well."

Ralston smiled thinly. "You've very lucky, then. Not all investors have been as fortunate. A number of these mines have turned out to have very little, if any, gold. Unfortunately, my colleagues and I have recently found out that the mine we invested in and serve as directors of, the Granger Mine, is worthless."

Witherspoon wasn't sure he understood. "Was Mr. Edison an investor as well?"

"We thought he was." Ralston got to his feet and began pacing in front of the fireplace. "He certainly led us to believe he'd put his own money into the venture. But it turned out he was merely a 'promoter,' I believe the expression is, for what turned out to be a completely worthless piece of land. The Granger Mine is now in bankruptcy court and every single one of us has lost every penny we put into it."

"I'm not sure I understand. Didn't you know Mr. Edison either personally or by reputation before you invested in a company he recommended?"

"Of course we knew him." Ralston waved around the opulent room. "Look at the way he lives—we thought he was one of us. He was at the exchange a fair bit and he had a good record of success. He'd recommended a number of other enterprises that made a great deal of money for their investors."

"But no one is successful all the time." Witherspoon smiled faintly. "Any good broker will tell you that all investments carry risk." His own broker, Roger Linley, a stodgy and conservative fellow, had recommended he buy shares in a tea plantation only days before the entire crop and the plantation itself was destroyed by a typhoon. Losing money hadn't made him happy, but he certainly hadn't blamed Mr. Linley nor did he think he would have had grounds for a lawsuit against the man. "Even if he was just promoting the mine, I don't understand on what grounds you could take legal action against Mr. Edison."

"We're not sure we had grounds—that's what this morning's meeting was about."

Ralston flopped back onto the sofa and crossed his arms over his chest. "We heard a rumor that Edison might have had prior knowledge that the Granger Mine was worthless. Which would mean, of course, that getting the four of us to invest and to use our reputations to attract other investors was nothing short of fraud."

"Reputations?" Witherspoon repeated.

Ralston cocked his head to one side. "I thought you said you were an investor, sir. Surely you've heard of us. We're the Merry Gentlemen."

CHAPTER 4

"Luty, you should have let me know you wanted to see me. I'd have been delighted to come to you." Angus Fielding came from around his desk and hurried across his office.

"Don't fuss, Angus." Luty chuckled. "I was in the neighborhood and hopin' you could spare me a few minutes of your time."

"Now, now, Luty, I always have time for you. You will have refreshments?" She nodded and Fielding glanced at his secretary, a fine-looking young fellow who'd escorted her into the room and was now at the door on his way out. "Just a moment, Phillips—please bring us a pot of tea. The Assam will do nicely," he instructed.

"Yes, sir."

"Do come and sit down." Fielding grabbed her hand. "It's been ages since I've seen you."

Luty let herself be led to one of the overstuffed leather

chairs in front of his desk. Middle-aged, balding, and one of the worst snobs she'd ever met, Angus Fielding was one of her many bankers. She sank down in her chair and waited while he went back behind the desk. "I know how busy you are," she began, only to be interrupted.

"Nonsense, I always have time for you." He leaned forward. "I say, you don't happen to have any more of that delightful drink I had at your house a few years ago, do you? You remember, it had a most unusual flavor as well as an odd name. I believe it was called 'pale lightning' or 'sunshine.'"

She smiled in spite of herself. Fielding was indeed an elitist, but not about money, social class, or position. He claimed to have the most discriminating palate in England and, by all accounts, it might be true. He drank like a fish but didn't waste his time or cash on anything as ordinary as a pint of bitter or good Scots whiskey. Only the odd, the unusual, and the rare would do for him. He claimed to have a wine in his cellar from every country that grew a grape as well as a collection of exotic brews from all over the world. Rumor had it that he'd spent a fortune obtaining beverages like aquavit, sake, retsina, and even one from Korea called soju for his personal cellar. Luty sometimes thought he was nothing more than an alcoholic with plenty of money.

"You mean white lightning or moonshine." She laughed and shook her head. "No, sorry, I don't have any. The friend that brings it to me hasn't been to England in a while. But the next time he comes, I'll be sure to let you know and we'll have us a high old time again."

She'd once gotten him drunk on the Appalachian home brew when she was after information. But today she didn't need to be so sneaky. She had a perfectly legitimate reason for seeking him out.

He hid his disappointment well, but Luty could see it in his eyes. "Well, keep me in mind if you do get more. I found it absolutely delicious."

Delicious wasn't what she'd have called it, but she nodded in agreement. "You'll be the first in line for it. I was hoping you could tell me a little about the Merry Gentlemen. My stockbroker has been listening to that bunch some and seems to want me investin' in some of the shares they recommend. Now, Angus, you know how much I value your opinion, so I told my broker I wasn't goin' to let him invest in anything until I spoke to you."

Flattered, he sat up straighter. "That was very wise of you, Luty, very wise indeed."

His office door opened and Phillips stepped in, carrying a tray with the tea. He set it on the desk. "Shall I pour, sir?"

"Thank you, no, we can manage," Fielding said. As soon as the secretary had gone, he walked around, perched himself on the edge of the desk next to the tea tray, and began to pour. "As I was saying, Luty, it was wise of you to come see me." He handed her a delicate porcelain cup filled with the fragrant brew. "In my opinion, the so-called Merry Gentlemen aren't any more knowledgeable than half of the other financial men in the City. They simply got lucky a few years ago and they've been riding that particular train ever since."

"What do ya mean?" She took a sip. It was delicious tea.

He put his cup down on the corner of the desk, stood up, and then sat down in the chair next to hers. "Surely you remember how they got their reputation and formed their little group? Martin Bagshot and Ezra Amberly were both

traders on the floor of the exchange, as was Charles Downing. Paul Ralston, the fourth member, was nothing more
than a jobber without floor privileges. Supposedly, Bagshot,
Amberly, and Downing were all in dire straits financially
when Ralston gave them a tip about buying diamonds and
other minerals in the Transvaal."

"But why would they listen to him if he was just a jobber?" Luty asked.

He leaned closer. "This isn't common knowledge, but do
you remember those riots, the ones by the stock exchange
on Throgmorton Street?"

She remembered them well. "They weren't really riots,"
she argued. "It was just a bunch of jobbers and brokers trad-
ing after hours and blockin' the traffic."

"It was a bit more than that," he claimed. "Arrests were
made and that's how the Merry Gentlemen were formed."

Nell's bells, she'd forgotten that it took him forever to
get to the point. "What do ya mean? I thought they formed
their group after they'd pooled their resources and bought
some stocks that had done real well."

"They did do that, but not until later. The Merry Gentlemen were actually formed in jail."

"Jail?"

He grinned proudly. "Indeed. If you'll remember, a
number of respectable people in the financial community
were caught up in the confusion and arrested. Downing and
Bagshot were two of them and they happened to be in the
same cell as Ralston. By the time their friend Ezra Amberly
showed up to facilitate Bagshot's and Downing's release,
Ralston had impressed them with his knowledge of the
market. They were all in such cheerful moods as they left
the police station that one of the reporters who had covered

the riots asked why they were such 'merry gentlemen.' Apparently, one of them retorted they were merry because they intended to make a lot of money."

"And that's what they've done," she finished.

"That's what they'd like us to think they've done." Fielding sniffed disapprovingly. "Even though the rest of the City might hang on their every word and seek out their advice on investing, I'm of the opinion that, to some extent, they owe their past success to luck—and rumor has it, their luck had run out."

Barnes didn't like Charles Downing; the fellow was puffed up with his own importance, dismissive of anyone he didn't consider his equal, and, from his attitude, behaved as if he didn't have to answer questions from a lowly policeman. But the constable had a lot of experience with men like this and knew precisely how to handle him. When they'd entered Edison's study, Downing had looked quite stunned when Barnes had commandeered the leather chair behind the massive mahogany desk, leaving Downing the choice to either pull over the straight-backed chair from beside the door or stand up like a naughty schoolboy in the headmaster's study. The man had glared at him, opened his mouth as if to protest, and then, wisely, dragged the chair over and sat down. "Let me ask you again, sir, what were you and Mr. Edison arguing about two days before he was murdered?"

"I don't know what you're talking about. I stopped in to see Orlando that morning, but only to invite him to dinner," Downing insisted.

Barnes fixed him with a cold stare and said nothing for a moment, letting the room fill with silence. Downing looked away first, making a show of taking his watch out of his waistcoat and noting the time. Finally, Barnes said, "Mr. Downing, please tell me the truth. We have several witnesses that overheard the row."

"Witnesses." He snorted. "Surely you're not going to take the testimony of a couple of servants seriously."

"I assure you, sir, we take it very seriously, especially when one of the men involved in the quarrel ends up dead." Barnes pulled out his notebook, flipped it open, and laid it on the desktop. "What's more, the servants have no reason to lie about such a thing. Unless, of course, you're claiming that they would deliberately make up a story because they disliked you for some reason."

"Don't be absurd, of course they don't dislike me, they're complete strangers . . ." His voice trailed off as he realized what he was saying.

"In which case, I hardly think they're making up tales. Now why don't you just tell me the truth?"

Downing flattened his lips into a thin, disapproving line. "Alright, we did argue, but it was about something very personal, something I'd prefer not to speak about."

"Mr. Downing, I assure you, if your dispute with Mr. Edison has nothing to do with his murder, we'll be very discreet about the matter. But you must tell me the truth or, if you prefer, I can question your household and friends . . ."

"No, no, don't do that," he said hastily. He pulled a white handkerchief out of his pocket and mopped his forehead. "Please, I'm sorry, but that's the last thing I want to happen. I'll tell you. Our dispute involved a domestic matter."

"Go on."

"Women found Orlando Edison very charming." He looked down at the floor. "My wife found him attractive and he, in turn, seemed to find her equally so. Cecily is my second wife and she's a great deal younger than myself."

"And you suspected she and Edison were having a relationship?" Barnes probed.

"No, they weren't involved and that's what the quarrel was about: I wanted to make sure it stayed that way."

"Had he been making improper advances to her?" Barnes asked.

Downing grimaced. "He claimed he wasn't, but I'm not a fool, I could see what he was doing. He was trying to seduce her. Cecily was flattered, of course, but then she's a foolish young woman whose head is easily turned by the kind of nonsense he spouted."

Barnes wondered if Downing realized he'd just admitted to having one of the oldest motives for murder in the world: jealousy. "Could you be more specific, sir?"

Downing's eyebrows rose. "I am being specific. I told you what the blackguard was trying to do. He was in love with her. Two weeks ago at the Harrimans' dinner party, he cornered her in their drawing room and spent half an hour listening to her prattle on about some silly novel."

"And because he spent time actually listening to what she might have to say about a book, you decided he had feelings for her?"

"That wasn't the only reason." Downing flushed angrily. "Every time he was around her, he watched her and smiled at her. He was in love with her, I tell you, in love with her, and I told him I wasn't having it."

"How did he respond when you accused him of this?"

Downing shrugged. "He denied it, but that's to be expected from someone like him. He'd no honor, no breeding—he was nothing but a jumped-up little jackanapes."

"But you did business with him," Barnes reminded him.

Downing crossed one leg over the other. "We should never have trusted him. It was a terrible mistake. One that we were doing our utmost to rectify."

"How?"

"We met this morning to determine if we had any legal recourse against him over this wretched Granger Mine problem. But before we could even discuss it properly, Cecily interrupted us with the news that he'd been murdered. She'd heard the news from our housekeeper."

"And how had your housekeeper found out? The murder wasn't reported in the morning newspapers."

"She heard it from a neighbor. Naturally, we were skeptical about the truth of it, which is why we came rushing over here."

"On the day that you quarreled with Mr. Edison, what time did you arrive?"

"It was about ten o'clock," he replied. "As I told you before, I dropped by to invite him to dinner and then he asked after my wife and before I quite realized what was happening, we were arguing."

"Why were you inviting him to dinner if you thought he had designs on your wife?" Barnes asked.

Downing said nothing. He merely pursed his lips and looked down at the floor.

"Mr. Downing," Barnes prompted, "please answer the question."

"As I told you, I hadn't planned on quarreling with him, it just happened. The dinner wasn't going to be just for him. All the directors for the Granger Mine were going to be invited. It wouldn't have been right to ignore him."

Barnes didn't believe him, but he decided to let it go for the moment. "Mr. Downing, exactly where were you at six o'clock yesterday evening?"

*   *   *

Smythe stopped just inside the door of the Dirty Duck Pub. The place was quiet, with only a couple of day laborers at the bar and a bread seller sitting alone at the side bench with her empty baskets piled next to her. Blimpey Groggins, the owner of this fine establishment, was the only one sitting at a table.

Blimpey spotted him just then and gave a cheerful wave. He was a ruddy-faced, ginger-haired, portly man wearing a checked coat and trousers, a cream-colored shirt that had once been white, and a faded brown waistcoat.

"Good day to you," Blimpey said as Smythe sat down on the stool opposite him. "I was expecting you."

"So you've 'eard," Smythe commented. It wasn't a question. Blimpey made his living by knowing everything that went on in London and, if truth be told, there were times when he thought the fellow knew everything that went on in the whole of England.

Blimpey Groggins had once been a thief. He'd been an accomplished second-story man but a nasty fall from a bedroom window accompanied by a painful bite from an enraged mastiff had convinced him to find another source of employment. Being a smart fellow, he'd realized the only skill he had that didn't involve substantial risk to life and limb was his exceptional memory. So he'd put it to good use and become a buyer and seller of information. Blimpey had sources working for him at the newspapers, police stations, insurance firms, shipping companies, the Old Bailey, the Inns of Court, and every major hospital. He also had a network of low-level men who kept him informed about the activities of London's less-than-honest citizens. But Blimpey had standards and would not deal in information that harmed women or children.

"Don't be insultin', of course I 'eard," Blimpey said. He tapped the cup of coffee in front of him. "You want something? Tea, coffee, or a pint?"

"Nothin', thanks."

"Right then, we'll get down to business. Like I said, I was expectin' you'd be by this morning and I've already got a few bits and pieces."

"That's why I always give ya my business." Smythe did much of his investigating through Blimpey. "Even though ya charge an arm and a leg."

"You can afford me."

Smythe chuckled. "True." Years earlier, he'd been a coachman for the inspector's late aunt, Euphemia Witherspoon. He'd saved his wages and gone to Australia, where he'd made a fortune. When he'd come back to England, he'd stopped in to pay his respects to his former employer and found her dying and surrounded by thieving servants. A very young Wiggins had valiantly been trying to nurse the ailing woman. Smythe had sent for a doctor, tossed all the servants but Wiggins out on their ear, and prayed for a miracle. But Euphemia Witherspoon was too far gone to save and her last request of him was that he stay on at Upper Edmonton Gardens and make sure her nephew, Inspector Witherspoon, was settled at the house with a staff he could trust. But by the time the household was established with people Smythe felt were honest and reliable, they'd started solving murders and he'd fallen in love with Betsy. He'd never told the others about his wealth but, as the years passed, he found himself in a very awkward position. Mrs. Jeffries had figured it out on her own and he'd told Betsy before they'd married, but he'd never told Wiggins or Mrs. Goodge. Now he worried that if they found out, they'd feel he'd deliberately deceived them, and that wasn't the case at all. But he'd worry about that problem some other time. Right now he had to do his part to get this murder solved. "What 'ave you got for me?"

"First of all, your victim, Orlando Edison, he's made a lot of money the past few years in the City." Blimpey took a sip of his coffee. "No one seems to know where he comes from but he's done so well for himself and his clients, I don't think the money men much care."

"Clients?" Smythe repeated.

"Well, he styles himself a stockbroker, but my sources tell me he's more of a promoter, leastways he was until the last couple of years. Then he started doin' serious investin'. He even got the Merry Gentlemen to sit on the board of his last venture, not that it's doin' them any good, considering the mine is now in bankruptcy court. But I don't want to mention too much about his business—I'm not all that certain my source knew what he was goin' on about," Blimpey admitted. "Give me a couple of days and I'll have reliable information. Now, you got any other names for me?"

"Yancy Kimball," Smythe said. "He's Edison's cousin and the only known family of the dear departed." He gave him the details Mrs. Jeffries had learned from the inspector.

Blimpey nodded. "Right, anyone else?"

"Them 'Merry Gentlemen' might 'ave a part in it. Two of 'em might 'ave been arguin' with the dead man in the days before the murder."

"Ezra Amberly's been in a sickbed for months now, so if he was involved, he'd have had to hire it done," Blimpey told him promptly, "and the Merry Gentlemen aren't the only ones with a motive for sending Mr. Edison to meet his Maker. I've got another source that's sayin' Edison was a bit of a ladies' man."

"You're thinkin' it was a woman that coshed him over

the head." Smythe looked doubtful. "That'd take a bit of strength."

"There's plenty of strong women out there." Blimpey grinned. "But I was thinkin' it would be more like the lady's husband. My source also said Edison liked to fool about with married women."

Constable Griffiths rapped on the drawing room door and then stepped inside. "You wanted to see me, sir?"

"Yes, Constable," Witherspoon said. He was standing by the fireplace. Constable Barnes was sitting on the sofa, rubbing his knee. "I've finished speaking to Mr. Ralston and Constable Barnes told me you'd finished interviewing Mr. Bagshot. What did he have to say?"

Griffiths took his notebook, a twin to the one Barnes carried, out of his pocket and flipped it open. "Mr. Bagshot was upset, sir, but I couldn't tell whether that was because he was just nervous about knowing someone who'd been murdered or whether he was trying to hide something. He answered my questions readily enough, but he kept his replies very short."

"Yes, I'm afraid that's often the case. Most people aren't used to dealing with the police, especially about homicide. Does Bagshot have an alibi for the time of the murder?" Witherspoon asked.

"Not really, sir. He said he was at the stock exchange until half past four and after that, he took a hansom to Oxford Street to do a bit of shopping. He doesn't recall seeing anyone he knew."

"It was the same thing with Downing," Barnes said. "He claims he was on his way home as well but that he got out of his hansom at Marble Arch because he wanted some fresh air so he walked across Hyde Park home." He grinned at Griffiths. "Strange, isn't it, how much alike their alibis are."

Witherspoon sighed. "If they are telling the truth, it's not surprising. Both men worked during the day and then went to buy presents." He glanced at Griffiths. "What did Mr. Bagshot say when you asked him about the quarrel he had with the deceased the day before the murder?"

"At first he tried to make light of it—he said whoever had overheard the supposed argument must have misunderstood the situation—but when I pressed him, he admitted their discussion had gotten heated and that it was about the Granger Mine bankruptcy hearing. He admitted he lost his temper and blamed Edison for the whole mess. But he claims that before he left, he apologized for losing control and that they'd parted on good terms. That's about it, sir." He shut the notebook and put it back in his pocket. "Shall I carry on with reinterviewing the servants?"

"Please do and when you go downstairs ask Mrs. Clarridge to come up here."

"Yes, sir." Griffiths nodded smartly and hurried off.

As soon as he'd gone, Barnes said to Witherspoon, "Charles Downing had a personal reason to dislike Orlando Edison." He gave Witherspoon a quick report on his interview. "And as I've already said, Downing's alibi is essentially the same as Bagshot's. He was on his way home. If it's all the same to you, sir, I'd like to go and have a word with the vicar at St. John's Church. Constable Sanderson reported that when they were doing the house-to-house looking for witnesses, one of the housemaids said that the carolers who were here last night always finished up at the church."

"That's certainly good news," Witherspoon said. "Perhaps

we'll get lucky for once and one of them will have seen the murderer."

"Let's not get our hopes up, sir." Barnes smiled ruefully as he got to his feet and headed for the door. He reached for the handle but just then it opened and Mrs. Clarridge stepped into the room.

Barnes nodded respectfully and closed the door softly behind him.

"I take it you're ready for me now, sir?" Her eyes were red from weeping and she held a handkerchief to her nose. "Sorry." She tried a weak smile as she came toward him. "It's just so sad planning his funeral reception."

"Mrs. Clarridge, please sit down and have a rest. This must be very stressful for you and the rest of the staff," Witherspoon said sympathetically.

She held up her hand. "No, sir, I'm alright. I must carry on, there's much to be done. Now, sir, what else do you want to know?"

"When you overheard the argument between Mr. Downing and Mr. Edison, was it your impression they were quarreling over business or something else?"

She hesitated and then said, "I thought it must be about business. I very clearly heard Mr. Downing shouting that Mr. Edison better be careful, that people wouldn't take kindly to losing their money. But that one comment is the only thing I heard, sir. I went upstairs to fetch a clean tablecloth from the linen cupboard."

"I see," Witherspoon said. "When Mr. Ralston stopped by yesterday afternoon, he wasn't expected, is that correct?"

"That's right. I answered the door and had him wait in the foyer while I announced him. Even though he'd finished work for the day, I knew Mr. Edison was busy. Right after luncheon, he said he had an important letter to write and that he'd need Kitty to post it for him as soon as it was finished."

"What time did Mr. Ralston arrive?"

"It was half past one," she replied. "I remember because I'd just noted the time and I was wondering if I ought to pop in and ask Mr. Edison if he was ready for Kitty to post his letter. He'd had an early lunch, you see, and he'd been in the study for almost an hour, which seemed to me plenty of time to write a simple letter. Generally, I'd not have interrupted him, but as we were going out that evening, there were a number of household tasks that needed to be done before we left." She crossed her arms over her chest. "Frankly, when Kitty goes out with the post, she takes her time coming back. But you're not interested in our domestic problems. I went into the study and told Mr. Edison Mr. Ralston had stopped in. He said to send him in."

"How long was Mr. Ralston here?"

"I'm not sure," she said. "But I don't think it was too long because when I came back fifteen minutes later, he was gone."

"So he stopped in, spent a few minutes with Mr. Edison, and then left rather quickly," Witherspoon asked. Her statement was very much the same as what Ralston had already told him, but it never hurt to double-check.

"I'm not sure of the exact time he left, but I can ask Kitty or Mary. They said he suddenly appeared downstairs and asked them to get him a headache powder and a glass of water."

Mrs. Goodge grabbed her shears out of the drawer and snipped the string wrapped around her package. She slipped her fingers under the stiff brown paper and pulled it open. She gasped in pleasure as she saw what lay before her.

Unable to believe her eyes, she blinked, but when she looked
again, she saw she'd not been mistaken. Someone had sent
her a copy of the famous American cookbook *Mrs. Lincoln's
Boston Cook Book.* She laughed in delight, picked it up, and
ran her fingers over the gold gilt lettering on the spine.
Opening the cover, she saw a folded piece of notepaper. She
put the book down on the table and flipped open the note.

Dear Mrs. Goodge,

I do hope you are well and still living at Upper Edmonton Gardens.
   This cookbook came into my possession recently and
I thought I'd pass it along to you. You once did me a
great service and I've always wanted to say thank you.
I'll always remember your kindness to me when I arrived
unexpectedly on your doorstep. I'd just been sacked and
you took the time and trouble not only to listen but to
give me some excellent advice about my future endeav-
ors. Currently, I have two very genteel ladies lodging
with me and because all of us prefer simple English fare
a foreign cookbook will do me absolutely no good. I
hope you'll accept this small gift in the spirit in which
it is meant and make good use of it.

Your friend,
Mollie Dubay

Surprised, because she'd not heard from Mollie in two
years, Mrs. Goodge sat down and dug deeper into her trea-
sure. Within minutes, she was so deeply engrossed in reading recipes that she forgot about the notes she'd intended to
send to three of her old colleagues inviting them to tea, old

workmates who might know something about Orlando Edison and who might have wanted him dead. Her only interruption was Mr. Sears when he delivered the laundry but she soon got rid of him, forgetting that he was generally one of her better sources when it came to neighborhood gossip.

Her concentration was broken when Samson butted his head against her shins. Startled, she glanced down at the fat, orange-colored tabby cat. "Oh dear, sweetness, you want your sardines, don't you." Samson loved his afternoon treat. Yawning, she glanced at the clock. "Good Lord," she exclaimed. "It's almost four o'clock. The others will be here any minute and I've not even started dinner." Samson butted her again, but she ignored him, grabbed her book, and tucked it into the top drawer of the pine sideboard.

"Good day, ma'am. I'm so glad you're home." Lena, Ruth's maid, opened the door wider. "Mr. Everton's gone out to the wine merchant's, and the minute he left, a lady showed up and said she has to speak to you. She won't leave, ma'am."

Ruth slipped off her coat as she stepped inside and crossed to the coat tree. "Oh dear, I don't have time for a social call now, Lena. I only came home to change my shoes and then I've got to go."

"I'm sorry, ma'am, I tried to tell her you might not even be coming home, but she insisted on waiting. Here, ma'am, let me take that." She reached for the heavy garment and hung it up.

"Who is it? Not one of Lord Cannonberry's relatives, I hope."

"I don't think so, ma'am. I know most of them and I've never seen this lady before. She won't give her name but she's nicely dressed and very insistent on seeing you." Lena lowered her voice to a whisper. "I'm sorry if I did wrong by letting her in, ma'am, but Abigail and I are the only ones here."

"Don't fret, Lena, you didn't do anything wrong. I'm sure it will be fine. I'll just pop in and see what this woman wants." Ruth was actively involved in the London Women's Suffrage Alliance and it wasn't outside the realm of possibility that her visitor was a strong, upper-class woman who wanted to lend her support for women's rights without revealing her identity to anyone, even a housemaid.

She opened the doors to the drawing room and gasped in surprise. A woman rose from the red and gold striped satin empire chair. Despite being well into middle age, she was as slender as a reed and still beautiful enough to turn heads on the Kensington High Street. Her black hair was coiled in a knot at the nape of her neck, her complexion was as smooth and unlined as a girl's, and her brilliant blue eyes perfectly matched the peacock blue hat and dress she wore under her cloak.

"Good gracious, Lady Mortmain—Lydia—it's you! I'm so glad to see you. It's been ages." Ruth hurried across the room.

"It's no longer Lady Mortmain." She grinned impishly. "Now it's just plain old Mrs. Alexander Grappington and I couldn't be happier. Forgive me for barging in like this, but it's important."

Ruth motioned her back into her chair and sat down across from her. "Mrs. Grappington, is it? I take it you've remarried?"

"To an American. He's a wonderful man and I'm so lucky to have met him." She grinned again. "And he's rich as sin but believe it or not, we're actually in love."

"I do believe it—you're positively glowing," Ruth said.

The last time they'd met, Lydia was the impoverished widow of a nobleman and she'd made no bones about the fact that the only path open to her was to find a rich husband.

"Unfortunately, we're leaving for New York tomorrow and this was the only time I had to see you."

"Don't apologize, please." She smiled ruefully. "I will have to leave shortly, but do let's visit for a few moments."

"This won't take long. I've got some information for you."

"Information?" Ruth stared at her curiously. "What do you mean?"

"Let's not be coy, Ruth, I know you help your inspector when he's got a murder case and I also know he's investigating Orlando Edison's murder."

"You knew Orlando Edison?"

"Very well," she replied. "One could say we were more than friends, but he was never a serious contender as husband material. Sometimes he was rich but just as often, he didn't have two pennies to rub together. But that's neither here nor there. The point is, I was fond of him and I want to make sure his killer hangs. Like all of us, he had character flaws, but he didn't deserve getting his brains bashed out and dying on his own doorstep." She glanced at the clock on the mantelpiece. "Now, I don't have much time, so please, listen carefully to what I'm going to tell you."

Witherspoon nodded his thanks as the housekeeper escorted Orlando Edison's solicitor into the drawing room. "Mr. Lofton, it was good of you to come today."

"Of course I'd come," Henry Lofton replied. He was a short, red-haired man with freckles. "Mr. Edison wasn't merely a client, he was also a friend. I want to see his killer caught."

Surprised, because in his experience lawyers were rarely

this cooperative, Witherspoon gaped at the man. "Thank you, sir. I appreciate your assistance. Uh, er, can you tell me what is the value of Mr. Edison's estate?"

"Just off the top of my head, I'd say it was approximately fifty thousand pounds split equally between property, a large stock portfolio, and cash."

Witherspoon frowned. "Property? But his housekeeper said he was leasing here."

"The lease on this house expires at the end of March," Lofton explained. "But he had plenty of property in America. He told me that once his testimony in the bankruptcy trial concluded, he'd be moving to New York. He'd recently purchased a town house there and he's owned a farm in Virginia for a number of years."

"He was leaving the country?" Witherspoon muttered. "His staff hasn't mentioned that."

"They probably didn't know," Lofton replied. "He didn't want their Christmas ruined by the knowledge they were soon going to be unemployed. Last week, he instructed me to set aside funds to pay all of them their salaries for the first quarter in the upcoming year."

"That was very generous of him." Witherspoon prided himself on seeking justice for murder victims regardless of who they might have been in life; he'd worked hard to stay as detached as possible from the emotional turmoil that often accompanied homicide, but he realized he was genuinely sad that this man had been so cruelly taken. Orlando Edison cared about his servants and to Witherspoon that spoke volumes about the kind of man he must have been. He remembered his mother always saying that you could judge the measure of an important person by how he treated the little people who surrounded him. Orlando Edison had treated the people who served him with respect and concern.

Lofton shrugged and looked away, but not before the inspector had seen a sheen of tears in his eyes. "He was a good man, I don't care what anyone says, he was a good man." He turned back to the inspector. "I met him five years ago. He'd just come back to England from Africa and needed a solicitor." Lofton broke off and took a deep, ragged breath. "I had been having some difficulties. I'd made a mistake in a commercial property conveyance my firm was in charge of and it had gone very badly. Needless to say, I was sacked. As my prospects had dimmed substantially, my fiancée left me and I was barely able to keep a roof over my head."

"Couldn't you find another position?"

Lofton smiled bitterly. "The principals in the company that suffered because of my error were very vocal in their criticism, and in London, commercial real estate transactions inhabit a very small world. So even though I'd had an exemplary record of success prior to my mistake, no one wanted to give me a chance. Then I met Orlando Edison."

"How did you meet him?"

"At a pub on Throgmorton Street. I don't recall why I'd gone there, but nonetheless, that's how I became acquainted with him. He was such an easy person to talk to and before I knew it, he'd heard the whole story. He invited me to supper at a restaurant and I accepted. That was the beginning. He took me on as his solicitor and as the months passed, he recommended me to more and more of his colleagues. I've now got a thriving business because of him, so I assure you, Inspector, I'll do everything in my power to help you catch his killer."

"His household servants have said much the same thing. Now, I take it he had a will?"

"He did. Orlando had several beneficiaries. I'll begin with the smallest first. His servants were each left a bit of money. Mrs. Clarridge got the most; he left her three hundred pounds. She's been with him the longest, you see. The housemaids are each getting a hundred pounds."

"So they're receiving a very generous legacy on top of his instructions to pay their next quarter's wages?" Witherspoon pressed.

"I wouldn't exactly put it that way," Lofton said. "The legacies are to go to them directly as part of his will; the salary for next quarter was because he wanted them to stay on and continue working here."

The inspector was now thoroughly confused. "So he was leaving, but he wanted them to stay here and run the house?"

Lofton raised his finger. "There is a reason for his actions, Inspector. I'll get to it in a moment. Let's get to the other legacies. Orlando left his property in Virginia to his cousin, Yancy Kimball."

"Did Mr. Kimball know he was a legatee?"

"I've no idea, Inspector," Lofton replied. "I can try and find out for you. I believe Mr. Kimball is now in London, so contacting him won't be difficult. The rest of the estate is to go to Mrs. Madeleine Flurry. She's in a small flat in Shepherd's Bush and I've brought her address with me."

"Good, we're all here." Mrs. Jeffries swept into the kitchen and took her seat at the head of the table. "Shall we get started? Who would like to go first?"

"I will," Luty volunteered. "But I don't have much to report, though I did find out a few bits and pieces." She told them about her meeting with Angus Fielding. "My source knows a lot about money," she concluded, "and he's of the opinion that the Merry Gentlemen weren't all that much smarter than anyone else on Throgmorton Street, they was just luckier."

"Throgmorton Street?" Phyllis repeated.

"She means the financial center of the City of London." Hatchet gave his employer a frown. "Really, madam, must you resort to modern slang to make your point?"

"Don't be such an old stick-in-the-mud," she shot back. "At least I found out that the Merry Gentlemen were a bunch of jailbirds."

"Being arrested as a form of civil protest against outdated rules and regulations hardly makes those men 'jailbirds,'" he returned. "A number of decent people were arrested at that time and if you'll recall, public sentiment was on the side of the protesters. Honestly, telling people they can't buy and sell their own property, their own shares . . ." He broke off as he realized everyone was staring at him. "Sorry, but I do feel very strongly about this matter."

No one said anything for a moment. Then Phyllis said to Luty, "I know you've told us before. But I don't understand why the 'Merry Gentlemen' are so important."

"They're important because every investor in the City watches what they buy and sell. They've got the kind of influence that can make or break a company's shares."

"I understand that, but how did they get to be so important?" Phyllis persisted. She was determined to make up for her negligence today by at least understanding the situation properly.

"Well, it's like this. A few years back, the Merry Gentlemen started investin' in minin' stocks."

"You mean the mines in South Africa?" Smythe helped himself to a slice of bread.

"Not just them, but minin' stocks from around the world. They hit it big on a stock everyone else had said was a dog. It was a gold mine in California and it made 'em a fortune. I guess it must have been Christmastime two or maybe three years ago, but all of a sudden, everyone and their brother thought these fellers knew everything there was to know about investin', especially in gold mines. After the riots on Throgmorton Street, they'd already formed their little club and been right successful by poolin' their resources and buying foreign stocks. They were written about in the financial press and, from what my source said, they all four pushed the idea that they were financial geniuses. So when they wanted to start investin' in the Transvaal gold mines, Edison asked them to be on the board of directors of the Granger."

"Because if they were on the board, investors would take them seriously," Betsy added. She was very intrigued by the idea of buying and selling shares in exotic stocks from faraway places. But her husband seemed to think they already had enough money.

"But that one is goin' bankrupt," Wiggins reminded them. "So maybe these Merry Gentlemen weren't as clever as everyone thought."

"Or maybe they were victims," Hatchet suggested. "It's not unknown for some mine owners to exaggerate the potential of the mine. It's quite possible that these men were innocent victims."

"Which would probably make 'em mad," Luty said. "In which case, they'd have a motive to want Edison dead."

"Now, now, let's not get ahead of ourselves," Mrs. Jeffries warned. "We've no idea whether or not anyone felt themselves a victim of fraud. We've no idea why Orlando Edison was killed. His murder might have nothing to do with his professional life. But time is getting on and we must go ahead. Wiggins, would you care to go next?"

Wiggins shrugged. "I don't really 'ave much to say. I 'ung about on Throgmorton Street and tried to find someone who knew the deceased, but I didn't 'ave much luck." In truth, he felt a bit guilty, like he'd not done his fair share today. Once he'd finished talking about football with the two lads at the pub, he'd gone to Smithfield's to have a quick word with his friend Tommy, who was an apprentice there. Tommy's guv was out with the flu so he and Tommy had gone for a quick pint at the local pub and discussed the upcoming Millwall match. By the time he'd finished, it was so late he barely had time to get back for the meeting. "But I'll go out again tomorrow and maybe I'll 'ave better luck."

"Don't worry, lad." Mrs. Goodge patted his arm. "I didn't find out anything today, either."

"I didn't find out very much, either," Phyllis added quickly. "But I did hear a bit at the greengrocer's." She told them what she'd heard from Dulcie Prescott. When she was done, she grabbed her teacup and took a quick sip. She was sure that Mrs. Jeffries would take one look at her face and know that she'd done something terrible. After she'd left the greengrocer's, instead of making the rounds to all the shopkeepers in the neighborhood, she'd found herself on the omnibus and heading toward the Gaiety Theater. She hadn't understood what had come over her, it was as if she was under a spell, but she'd not been able to resist the urge to go back. Once there, she'd stared at the playbills out front, memorizing the names of the actors and wishing with all her heart that she could go inside and, for just a moment, be a part of the magic. "But I'll go out tomorrow and I'll try the neighborhoods where those Merry Gentlemen live."

"But they're not the only suspects," Ruth blurted out. "Edison's murder might not have anything to do with stocks and shares. The man was rich, attractive, and enjoyed the company of women and, according to my source, the lady in question didn't have to be single."

CHAPTER 5

"Has my goddaughter gone already?" Witherspoon asked as he handed Mrs. Jeffries his bowler. "I got home as quickly as possible." He knew that Betsy usually brought the baby over at teatime.

"I'm afraid so, sir." Mrs. Jeffries smiled sympathetically. "She waited as long as she could because Amanda does love to see you. But the little one started fussing so Betsy decided it would be best to get her home."

Witherspoon's face fell in disappointment. "Oh well, perhaps I'll get a chance to see her tomorrow." He started down the hall toward the study. "Let's go have a nice glass of sherry, that will cheer me up."

She hung his hat on the peg above his overcoat and followed him. A few moments later, he was ensconced in his favorite chair as she poured both of them a drink.

"How is the case going, sir?" She handed him his glass. "Any new developments?"

She knew she was perfectly welcome not only to have a drink with her employer, but to talk freely with him about his work. They'd established this custom years before, when she'd first come to work as his housekeeper. Unlike most wealthy men, Gerald Witherspoon had been raised in very modest circumstances and only inherited his fortune and this house later in his life. Consequently, having not been raised with servants, he treated them as human beings.

"Actually, we've learned a number of interesting facts which may have a bearing on this case. Mr. Edison's solicitor gave us some information which may prove to be very useful." He took a sip of sherry and then told her the details of his day.

Mrs. Jeffries listened closely, occasionally asking a question or nodding her head in agreement. When he'd finished, she said, "Gracious, sir, you did cover a lot of territory."

"Unfortunately, despite everything we learned, there's still much that we don't know," he muttered. "We've done two house-to-house inquiries looking for witnesses but all we found out was that the carolers might have some sort of association with St. John's Church. Constable Barnes immediately went to have a word with the vicar, but he wasn't there."

"That's unfortunate, sir. One of those carolers might have seen something."

"We're not giving up. The constable was going to stop in again on his way home. He's going to time it so he arrives at the church a few minutes before the start of evensong. The vicar has to be there for that."

"Very clever, sir." She chuckled.

He grinned. "I'd like to take the credit but it was Constable Barnes' idea. Mind you, I did find out that Edison wasn't the only one with the murder weapon."

Surprised, she raised her eyebrows. "What does that mean, sir?"

"Oh dear, I didn't mean to sound flippant, not when someone's been murdered. But what I meant was that the victim wasn't the only one with a bronzed shovel. The entire board of directors for the Granger Mine had one—they were given out as souvenirs at their first meeting."

"Is that a customary sort of gesture in the business world?" Mrs. Jeffries asked. She wasn't sure what this information might mean, yet she had a feeling it could be important.

Witherspoon tapped his finger on the rim of his empty glass. "I'm not certain. I suppose it's the sort of thing that would be dependent on the personality of the people involved and, from what we've learned, a generous gesture is very much in keeping with Mr. Edison's character."

"He seems a strange mixture, doesn't he," she commented. She had to be careful here. She couldn't let on that she knew anything other than what he'd told her about the victim, yet at the same time, she wanted to push him to delve a bit deeper into Edison's life.

"In what way?"

"Well, as you said, sir, on the one hand, he was well liked by his staff and he seems to have genuinely cared about them." She broke off and took a sip of sherry in an attempt to clarify her own thoughts on exactly what she was trying to tell him. But she wasn't really sure herself; it was more a feeling about the victim rather than anything factual she could put her finger on. "Yet at the same time, he was planning on leaving the country and hadn't said a word about it to the people who would be directly affected by his actions."

"True, but he didn't leave them without wages or a roof over their heads. As I told you, he made arrangements for all the servants to stay on in the house through the first quarter of next year."

"But he's also giving them a new mistress," she pointed out. "Isn't this Mrs. Flurry moving into the premises and taking over the household during this very same period?"

"Well, yes."

"Who exactly is this Mrs. Flurry?" Mrs. Jeffries asked.

"Mr. Lofton doesn't really know. All he could tell us is that Edison added her as a resident to the property in a codicil to his will two weeks ago. When Lofton tried to question Edison about her"—Witherspoon put his glass down on the table and leaned forward—"all he would say was that she was a friend."

"Two weeks ago," she repeated. "Was that when he made the arrangements for the servants to stay on in the house until March?"

"No, he made those arrangements the previous month."

"So he knew even then that he was going to be leaving the country," she murmured.

"So it would appear."

Mrs. Jeffries had no idea what to make of any of this. Thus far, they had all sorts of hints about Edison's character but they had very few facts. "Did the solicitor know where Mr. Edison was going?"

"New York," he replied. "But we'd guessed that already."

"Yes, of course you had, sir, you told me that last night. When you searched his study, you found the newspaper where he'd circled sailings from Liverpool to New York. How silly of me to forget."

He started to get up, but she wasn't having that. She

snatched his glass off the table. "Would you like another sherry, sir? It might help you get a good night's sleep."

"That would be lovely, thank you." He relaxed back into his seat. She got up and went to the cabinet. As she poured the drinks, she tried to marshal her thoughts into some kind of order. "So everyone on the board had one of those bronzed shovels?" she said as she returned to her seat.

"Oh yes. Mrs. Clarridge said Mr. Edison had five of them made."

"Five?" She handed him his glass.

"One for every member of the board," he replied. "The four Merry Gentlemen and one for himself."

"Then all of the Merry Gentlemen would have known he had such an object."

"Not just them. Anyone who'd been in his study would know. It was sitting out in plain sight. Mrs. Clarridge said he used it as a doorstop."

Artemis Lund, vicar of St. John's Church, blinked in surprise as Constable Barnes stepped out of the narthex and into the sanctuary. "Goodness, why, you're a policeman," he sputtered. "Is there something wrong? Has something happened to my verger or Mrs. Cobb?"

"No, sir," Barnes said quickly. "Not as far as I know. I just wanted to ask you a few questions." The vicar was a short, balding man with a fringe of brown hair circling the back of his head.

Apparently relieved that nothing had happened to either the verger or Mrs. Cobb, he turned and darted up the aisle toward the altar. "Then you'd best come along while I put on my robes and stole," he called over his shoulder. "Evensong is going to start soon."

"But it doesn't start for another half hour." Barnes scrambled after him, noting with some surprise that for such a portly fellow, he was fast on his feet.

"Yes, yes, I know that." The vicar reached the end of the aisle and turned right, racing past the pulpit and through a small door.

Barnes followed him down a short, dimly lighted hall into another room at the back. There was a desk and two chairs in one corner, and rows of shelves filled with books, stacks of paper, ledgers, and what looked like several moldy cushions lined one wall. On the other wall was a large wardrobe with ornate carvings along the top and a beveled mirror on the front door. The vicar dashed in that direction, nearly tripped on the faded Oriental rug, and managed to right himself before he tumbled to the floor.

"Are you alright, sir?" Barnes cried.

"I'm fine. Really, I must ask Mrs. Cobb to do something about that rug, that's twice this week I've nearly tripped." He yanked open the wardrobe door and pulled out a long, white garment. "Please, do go ahead with your questions, though in all honesty, I can't imagine why on earth you wish to speak with me. I told the verger not to bother the police with such a trivial matter but apparently he took it upon himself to ignore my instructions. But really, I shall have a word with him about this."

"What matter would that be, sir?" Barnes asked.

"Didn't he tell you? As I said, Constable, it's such a silly thing I hesitate to even mention it. After all, people have a right to change their minds."

"Change their minds about what, sir?" Barnes forced himself to be patient.

"About donations, sir. Sometimes people bring us their old clothes, things they don't use anymore, and we hand them out to those less fortunate than ourselves. It's not a formal sort of system, but we do what we can, especially this time of the year. It's so very cold at night and not everyone has a warm bed or even a coat that isn't threadbare." He flipped the white robe over, unfastened the clasp at the neck, and spread it open. "Was it yesterday or the day before . . ." He cast his eyes heavenward as though he were seeking divine guidance. "Oh dear, I can't seem to recall—no, I tell a lie. I can remember it was most definitely yesterday."

"Yesterday?" Barnes repeated. "Are you sure?" He was interested in anything out of the ordinary that happened on the day of the murder.

"I'm sure, but there's no reason to make a fuss, it was only a matter of some old clothes, and then the fellow that was going to donate them obviously changed his mind. I tried to tell the verger that there was nothing criminal in that, but as always, he wanted to argue with me. He said that once the man put the bundle of clothing down on the back pew, it became church property. But then he must have changed his mind about leaving it, because all of a sudden, he grabbed the bundle and left."

"Would you recognize him if you saw him again?" Barnes asked.

"Of course not, I didn't see him," he replied. "It was Mr. Benson who saw it and reported it to the verger. I was in here getting ready for evensong."

"Do you have a choir here, sir?" Barnes asked. "Or any carolers?"

"We do indeed have a choir and quite a fine one, I might add, and some of them have gone caroling. As a matter of fact, Mr. Idlicote and Miss Parsons took a small group out a couple of nights ago."

*   *   *

The house was quiet as Mrs. Jeffries came down the back stairs toward the kitchen the following morning. The inspector and Constable Barnes had left an hour earlier, they'd had their morning meeting, and she'd made sure everyone now had the complete names and addresses of everyone involved in the case thus far. Armed with that information, they'd all gone out to ferret out what they could and she sincerely hoped they'd come back with more this afternoon than they had yesterday.

After a cursory dusting of the drawing room, she'd been so restless she'd decided to see if Mrs. Goodge might have some ideas on how to proceed. She simply wasn't sure they were moving forward in the least. True, it was early days still, but yesterday afternoon's meeting had been so lacking in information that it bordered on dismal. No one had really learned anything. Had it not been for all the information she'd gotten out of the inspector last night, they'd have very little to go on. Constable Barnes had added a few details this morning, the most important of which was that the vicar at St. John's had supplied the constable with the names of several possible witnesses.

She came into the kitchen and stopped in the doorway. The cook wasn't there. Fred was asleep on his rug next to the cooker and Samson was perched on the stool by the sideboard. He broke off cleaning his paw to give her a glare.

From the hallway, there was suddenly a scraping sound that pinpointed Mrs. Goodge's location. She was in the dry larder. Mrs. Jeffries moved into the room and thought about making a cup of tea. But perhaps that wasn't wise; the cook might be expecting one of her sources to arrive soon. But even if she was expecting someone, perhaps she could spare Mrs. Jeffries a few moments. She wanted to discuss the case.

There were now too many motives and not enough suspects. True, the Merry Gentlemen might have been angry with Edison, but surely as professional investors they knew all investments had risks. What was more, would one of them have used the mining shovel as the weapon? Would any of them have been that stupid? Besides, just because they'd lost money on the Granger Mine didn't mean they were destitute. Most people didn't put all their eggs in one basket, so it was quite possible that despite losing money in the bankruptcy, the Merry Gentlemen were still rich. Luty had promised to try to find out about their individual finances today.

And what about this mysterious Mrs. Flurry? Who was she and why was Orlando Edison leaving her most of his fortune? What was her role in this drama? Could she have been the woman fighting with Edison in the mews or perhaps the one who was crying? Or maybe she wasn't either of them. Mrs. Jeffries sighed. She had a horrible feeling this case was going to drag on for ages, ruining everyone's Christmas and Boxing Day.

She was also suspicious about Yancy Kimball. He'd told the inspector he and Edison didn't keep in close touch, but he'd shown up in London shortly before Edison was murdered and he was inheriting a good part of the estate. What, if anything, did any of this mean?

Outside, the sun must have gone behind a cloud because the room suddenly darkened. As her eyes adjusted to the dim light, she noticed a book on Mrs. Goodge's worktable. Curious, she went over and took a look. *Mrs. Lincoln's Boston Cook Book*. Picking it up, she noted that it was brand-new and one she'd never seen before. She was so engrossed in the book that she didn't hear Mrs. Goodge shuffling up the hall.

"Good gracious, what are you doing here?" the cook exclaimed. She held a bag of flour in her arms.

Mrs. Jeffries jerked in surprise. "I was looking for you and then I spotted this lying on the table. Is it new?"

"It was a present." The cook dumped the bag onto the worktable. "It came yesterday. I've been so busy, I've not had much time to even look at it. But that's alright; one of the few nice things about aging is that you learn patience. I'll have a nice sit-down with it when the case is over. Did you need something?"

"I just wanted to discuss the case."

"But it's only been two days," Mrs. Goodge said. "Surely you didn't expect to find the truth of the matter this quickly."

"Of course not. But it's already confusing and talking it over with you is always useful. Honestly, I've got the feeling that this one is already ridiculously complicated."

"You always feel that way at the beginning." Mrs. Goodge ducked down to grab a bowl from the shelf underneath.

"Admittedly, that's often the case," Mrs. Jeffries protested. "But you heard what Constable Barnes said this morning: We don't know if any of the carolers saw anything and none of us seems to be making any headway."

Mrs. Goodge interrupted. "Stop worrying so much, Hepzibah. You'll sort it out. You always do. Now, if you don't mind, I need to get busy."

Mrs. Jeffries blinked in surprise. Clearly, she was being dismissed. "Alright, I'll leave you to it."

The cook gave her an embarrassed smile. "Sorry, that sounded rude and I certainly didn't mean for it to, but, well, I agree with you, it is a complicated case so all of us need to do our part to sort it out and I've a source coming by soon." The cook looked toward the window and cleared her throat.

"And I'd like to get this batch of scones made up first. Come back later and we'll have a nice long chat."

"I'm going to go back to St. John's this evening," Barnes said as he swung out of the cab. "The vicar says that both Mr. Idlicote and Miss Parsons should be there."

"Excellent, Constable. Perhaps we'll get lucky and either of them or one of the other carolers will have noticed something useful." Witherspoon pushed his glasses up his nose and fixed his gaze on the three-story redbrick town house while Barnes paid the hansom driver. "Shepherd's Bush isn't Holland Park, but this seems a very decent place."

"And it's close enough that it wouldn't take more than ten minutes to walk from here to the victim's home," Barnes said.

"True, but we mustn't speculate this early in the case. Let's just hope Mrs. Flurry can help us shed light on this situation," he warned.

"Right, sir, but you must admit, money is a powerful motive and she stands to inherit the bulk of his estate," Barnes reminded him as they started up the concrete walkway. They climbed the short flight of steps leading to the shallow portico. The house was divided into two flats, each with its own front door. Barnes banged the brass knocker of the one on the left.

They waited a few moments, the constable leaning close to see if he could hear any movement from within. He reached for the knocker again but just then the door opened a few inches. "What is it? What do you want?"

"Are you Mrs. Flurry?" Witherspoon asked quickly. "Madeleine Flurry?"

"I am." She opened the door wider and stared at them,

her expression somber. "And I know why you're here. It's about Orlando, isn't it?"

"Yes, ma'am, I'm afraid it is," Witherspoon replied softly. Though not in the first flush of youth, she was a beautiful woman with deep, rich brown hair, hazel eyes, an ivory complexion, and high cheekbones. She was dressed in a frumpy, oversized gray jacket and a black day dress with a high collar.

She glanced at Barnes' uniform and then motioned for them to enter. "Please come in, I've been expecting you."

Witherspoon nodded and he and the constable stepped inside.

She closed the door and leaned against it with her eyes closed for a brief moment. Then she seemed to get ahold of herself. "Let me take your coat and hat, sir," she said to Witherspoon. "Then we'll go into the sitting room. I expect you've questions for me."

Witherspoon did as she asked and she put his outer garments on the pegs hanging from the back of the door. She led them down the narrow hallway and into a small sitting room.

There was a fireplace on one wall; two windows with white lace curtains; a nice green, gold, and bronze patterned rug on the hardwood floor; and a tall bookcase filled with colorful china and porcelain figurines, a shelf of books, and a stack of magazines. A green horsehair sofa and two matching chairs were the only other furniture.

"Please sit down." She waved them toward the couch while she took one of the chairs.

The inspector introduced himself and Barnes. "I'm sorry to trouble you, ma'am, but as you appear to know why we've come to see you, I'm hoping you can help us in this matter. I take it you know that Mr. Edison has, uh . . ."

"Been murdered," she finished for him. "Yes, Inspector, I'm aware of it. His housekeeper notified me about what happened and it's been in all the newspapers." Her voice broke and she looked away.

"I take it you and Mr. Edison were more than just acquaintances, ma'am, and I'm sorry for your loss," he said.

She nodded and gave him a wan smile. "We're old friends." She pulled a white handkerchief out of her pocket and dabbed at her eyes. "And he acted as my financial adviser. My late husband left me a small legacy and Mr. Edison managed to invest it well enough so that I won't have to worry about my future. He was very dear to me and I'm going to miss him terribly. I hope you catch who did this to him."

"We'll do our best, ma'am," the inspector replied.

"When was the last time you saw Mr. Edison?" Barnes asked.

"Last Friday. We had dinner together at Marconi's."

"Marconi's," the inspector repeated. "Exactly where is that?"

"It's just off Shepherd's Bush. It's a small, family-run place that both of us enjoyed. Afterward, Orlando walked me home."

"You haven't seen him since then?" Witherspoon clarified. He noticed there was nothing in the room that hinted she knew Christmas was almost here. There was no holly, no ivy, no greenery or decorations of any kind. But perhaps there had been and, out of respect for the dead, she'd taken them out.

"No. I haven't."

"When you had dinner with Mr. Edison, was he upset or worried about anything?" He pushed his glasses up his nose and noted that Barnes had taken out his little brown notebook and pencil.

She shrugged and her jacket fell open. "He wasn't looking forward to going to court. I assume you know he was to testify in a bankruptcy matter. But he wasn't unduly upset and he certainly gave no indication he was in fear for his life." She grabbed the edges of the material and pulled them together, closing up the gap.

"We're aware he was to testify, ma'am," Witherspoon said. "Did you know that Mr. Edison was planning on leaving the country?"

"Yes. He told me when we were at dinner that he was going to New York," she said. "The news didn't make me happy, but he was free to do as he liked."

"Did Mr. Edison say why he was leaving England?" the inspector asked.

"He did; it was the court case. He was afraid the Granger bankruptcy was going to ruin his reputation in the City. He wanted a fresh start in New York."

"He owned property in New York, didn't he?" Barnes looked up from his notebook.

"I believe so."

"Were you aware that you're one of the beneficiaries to his estate?" Witherspoon asked softly. Even though he wasn't good at reading faces, nonetheless, he watched her expression and saw the quick, hard flash of pain in her eyes.

"Yes, I was. When he had the will done, Orlando told me I was one of the major beneficiaries. I believe his cousin is also going to inherit part of the estate." She lifted her chin a notch. "But I assure you, Inspector, I'd much rather he be alive than dead."

"I wasn't implying anything untoward, ma'am," Witherspoon said. "But as you are someone who directly benefits from his death, I have to ask these questions."

"Benefits?" She gave a short, hard laugh and looked down at her hands. "Believe me, I'd benefit far more if he were alive rather than gone." When she lifted her gaze to meet the inspector's, her eyes were glazed with tears. "Money doesn't replace people, Inspector, and as I told you before, we were very good friends."

"Of course it doesn't." Witherspoon smiled sympathetically. He had the feeling they were a bit more than "friends" but he'd leave that till later as he couldn't see what, if anything, the relationship might have had to do with Edison's death. Both the victim and the lady were single, so there shouldn't be any reason they couldn't be together if they so chose.

"When I last saw him, he asked me to move into his home and take over the household."

"What did you tell him?" The inspector was a bit confused. He wondered whether this had been put in the dead man's will or if it was simply one of the instructions he'd given his lawyer. Drat, he should have paid a bit more attention to the solicitor.

"I told him I wasn't sure that would be appropriate, but he told me not to be ridiculous, that he wouldn't be there and he wanted someone to oversee packing his things and shipping them to New York."

"Mr. Edison owned the furnishings in the house?" Witherspoon asked. Neither Mrs. Clarridge nor Henry Lofton had mentioned that Edison owned furnishings.

"Not all of them, but he wanted his files, his books, and what furniture that was his packed and shipped to America. He gave me a list."

"So you had agreed to move into the house," the constable pressed.

She lifted one shoulder in a shrug. "It was hard to refuse, Constable. He's done me many services over the years and this was the first time he'd asked anything of me."

"When you met Mr. Edison for dinner on Friday evening,

did the two of you walk through Holland Park at any time in the evening?" Barnes asked. He was aware that the inspector gave him a fast, curious glance. Perhaps he should have passed this tidbit along to Witherspoon on the way here, but he'd not had time. But he could tell by the surprised look on Mrs. Flurry's face that his salvo had hit its mark.

"How did you know that, Constable?"

"We have a witness that saw the two of you together," he replied. He knew that Witherspoon would understand that when he said "witness" he really meant "informer."

She seemed to deflate into the chair. "Then I'm sure you already know that we were having a terrible argument. That was the last time I saw Orlando and I said awful things to him, things I'll never be able to take back."

"We don't mean to distress you, Mrs. Flurry." Witherspoon flicked a quick look at the constable, who gave a barely perceptible nod, before he continued speaking. "But it's important we know what the quarrel was about."

"Why? It hasn't anything to do with his murder! It was personal. Very personal."

"You were seen, ma'am," the inspector pointed out, "and if you were seen together, it's possible your discussion was overheard."

"But even if it was, it's nothing to do with anyone else," she cried. "I've told you, it was between us."

Witherspoon looked at Barnes and then back at Madeleine Flurry. "Did Mr. Edison have any enemies?"

"Of course he did, Inspector." She laughed harshly. "A lot of men in the City were jealous of him. He was very successful at what he did and there were those that resented him."

"I'm sorry, I don't quite follow." Barnes knew exactly what she meant, but he'd found that playing the dullard often got people saying more than they realized. "Why should they resent him just because he was good at what he did?"

She laughed cynically. "Isn't it obvious? Orlando came from nothing; he educated himself by his own efforts and learned decent manners by observing those he served as a child. He was intelligent, strong, and decent and he earned a fortune. Of course there were many in the financial community who hated him." She suddenly leaned forward and fisted her hands on the arms of the chair. "Orlando wasn't like them, he had none of the advantages most of the men in the City have. Yet he achieved a great deal. Most of his colleagues were handed life's opportunities on a silver tray and they've not done half as well."

"Do you know of any specific people who might have resented him enough to murder him?" Witherspoon asked. He noticed the more she spoke, the more agitated she became.

She flopped back against the cushion. "No, I'm afraid I don't."

"Mr. Edison didn't discuss his business with you?" Barnes pressed.

"Oh, but he did. I just don't recall any one person who considered him a genuine enemy."

The constable wasn't going to give up so easily. "What about his testifying in the Granger bankruptcy matter? Surely some of those investors were angry."

"Naturally, Constable, but hundreds of people have lost money in the Transvaal. This is only one of many mines that didn't have any gold in it and it certainly isn't the first one to go bankrupt."

Barnes nodded. "Did you invest in the Granger Mine?"

"No."

"Why not? You said Mr. Edison was your financial adviser."

"He was and that's exactly why I didn't." She smiled coldly. "He advised me not to."

"That one walks about with her nose up so high it's a wonder she don't trip." Enid Carter pointed to the woman walking out the front door of number 8 Hanover Villas. "No matter how expensive them clothes are, it don't hide the fact that she's fat as a pig and looks like one to boot!"

Phyllis swallowed uneasily and hoped they were far enough away that the lady in question wouldn't hear or, for that matter, even see them.

"Stop lookin' so worried, the likes of her won't take any notice of the likes of us—it'd be beneath her to even look this way. What's more, she's half-deaf." Enid grabbed Phyllis' elbow. "Now come on, you promised to buy me a drink at the Blackbird Pub on the Uxbridge Road."

"Who is she?" Phyllis had the presence of mind to ask as she was tugged toward the busy street in the distance.

"That's Miss Waterson, Mr. Ralston's fiancée, and she's as mean as they come. Her father's Sir Thomas Waterson. Come on, hurry up, I've got to get back in time to scrub the vegetables for supper."

Phyllis kept her gaze fixed on the woman, who was now stepping into a brougham carriage. Enid was right; she wasn't very pretty. Miss Waterson had a face as round as a china plate and a short stubby nose that turned straight up. Her lips were thin and her complexion blotchy. Her mousy brown hair was tucked up beneath an expensive sable hat that matched the fur muff she carried, and her navy blue cloak came all the way to the ground.

"Come on, with Laura gone I can't stay out too long." Enid gave her hand a good yank.

"Yes, alright, I'm coming." She took one last look at the

tall, elegant white-fronted house that belonged to Paul Ralston. Determined to make up for her negligence of the previous day, she'd come to Notting Hill after the morning meeting. She'd spent the first part of the day on the high street, chatting up shopkeepers, and to her delight she'd learned a snippet or two about Paul Ralston. But she'd really hit pay dirt at the fishmonger's when she'd brought up Ralston's name.

"That's who I work for," a voice exclaimed.

Startled, because Phyllis had thought she was alone with the clerk, she looked over her shoulder. A thin, thirtyish woman stood there staring at her. "Why are you asking about Mr. Ralston? Who are you?"

Flustered, Phyllis had stammered the first thing that came to her mind. "I heard there was work there."

"How'd you hear that? Laura only left yesterday and I know his nibs hasn't advertised the position yet." Enid had eyed her suspiciously and turned to the clerk. "A pound of haddock, please."

Embarrassed, but sure that she could learn something, Phyllis had bobbed her head politely at the lad and hurried outside. But she didn't go far. She turned left and went a half dozen yards down the pavement until she found a recessed opening between two shops. She wedged herself in the space and waited. When Enid emerged, she gave her a head start and then hurried to catch up. "Please wait, I really do need a job. A friend of a friend told me that Miss Laura had quit . . ."

Enid stopped and turned to her. The two women were of the same height, but Enid's threadbare green and gray plaid coat hugged a body so thin as to be almost skinny. Beneath her white maid's cap, her hair was brown and her face, though still young, was already lined with worry brackets on each side of her lips. "Then your friend got it wrong because she didn't quit, Ralston sacked her when she tried to give notice, and if I'm late getting back with this fish, I'll get the sack as well." She whirled on her heel and continued down the street.

Phyllis took a deep breath and then raced after her. "Wait, wait. I need to talk to you."

"What for?" Enid continued walking. "I've told you, I can't be late getting this fish back. Cook will have my guts for garters. She's already in a nasty state because there's so much work and Laura's gone."

"I have to find out about Paul Ralston."

Again, Enid stopped. "Why do you want to know anything about him?"

She was ready for that one. "I work for a private inquiry agency and his name has come up in the course of an investigation we're conducting." She'd used this ruse on previous occasions and, to her surprise, found that it worked.

"Are you claimin' you're one of them detectives?"

"I'm merely saying I work for a private inquiry agency, and I know you're in a hurry, but if you can slip out later and spare me a few moments, I'd be pleased to buy you a cup of tea," she replied. Her heart was beating a mile a minute. This was such an outrageous lie she was sure that she'd been caught out, but she felt she had to play it to the end. The worst that could happen was that she'd have to turn and make a dash for it.

"I can slip out," Enid said thoughtfully. "But it won't be later, it'll be now, and it won't be for a cup of tea, it'll be for a drink. Cook might bark a bit, but she's not stupid. I'll take her the fish and then tell her I'm meeting a friend who's going to recommend me for a housekeeper's position. That'll put the fear of God in the old cow; she'll not want to be left alone to do all the work so she'll not go tattling to Mr. Ralston. If you've a bit of coin, we'll go to the Blackbird Pub. It's decent enough for the two of us."

"A pub?" Phyllis had done this before, but walking into a drinking establishment still took every ounce of courage she possessed.

Enid nodded and grabbed her arm. "That's right, but we've got to go by the house first so I can get rid of this fish."

They'd hurried toward Hanover Villas and Phyllis had waited while Enid slipped inside and then returned. As they were leaving, the front door had opened and that was when they'd seen Miss Waterson.

On the walk to the pub, Enid had complained mightily about Anne Waterson. She was still carping about the woman as the barman slid their drinks in front of them.

"Ta." Enid picked up her gin and knocked it back.

The pub wasn't crowded and Phyllis hadn't wanted anyone she might know to spot her. She'd made sure they were close to the shadows at the far end of the bar. She tapped the side of her own glass. She wasn't much of a drinker, but she had the feeling that the best way to keep Enid chatting was to play along with her. "If this Miss Waterson is so objectionable, why does your master want to marry her?"

"Why do men usually want to marry someone like her?"

"Money?"

"That'd be one reason." Enid drained her glass and set it on the polished bar.

"But I've seen his house, it's beautiful, so it doesn't look like he's hurting for money."

"No one ever has enough of that." Enid looked pointedly at her empty glass and Phyllis waved at the barman. She handed over her coins and waited silently while he poured.

Enid took a sip. "Ah, that's good. Cook claims he's not

just marrying for money, he wants a leg up on the social ladder, if you know what I mean."

Phyllis did, but she wanted to make sure she understood exactly. "He wants to be in the upper class? But isn't he already one of them?"

"Not likely." She laughed. "His father was an accounts clerk at Deptford and his mother once took in laundry for the neighbors. He made his money in the City and, from what Miss Carlisle across the road says, a generation back he'd not even have gotten his foot in that door. No, his nibs wants to do it the easy way. He wants to marry up, as my old gran used to say. He's not just after money, he's wantin' a ruddy title, and taking Sir Thomas Waterson's homely, ill-tempered daughter as his wife is his first step." She took another drink. "Mind you, he's in for a big surprise if he thinks he can have her and keep a bit of fluff on the side."

"Fluff on the side?" Phyllis was fairly sure she knew what that meant as well. "You mean a mistress or a paramour. Well, lots of rich men do that."

"Lots? You mean most of 'em." Enid cackled. "But the Watersons are different. Sir Thomas would walk barefoot over hot coals before he ever broke his marriage vows and I expect that once his nibs married into that bunch, he'd better watch his step. Miss Carlisle from across the road told me that Sir Thomas disowned his older daughter."

"Disowned? Why?"

Enid shrugged. "All Miss Carlisle says is that it was because her husband had done something wrong, something dishonorable, and the old man wouldn't have it that the woman insisted on staying with her husband."

"She must have been deeply in love with her husband," Phyllis murmured. "By the way, who is Miss Carlisle?"

"She's the housekeeper at number eleven." Enid burped

softly. "You can't let her catch you when you're in a hurry because the woman can talk the paint off a fence. But she knows what's what, I'll give her that. I swear she has the sight. She was standing outside waiting when Laura left yesterday morning. I don't know how she knew the girl had gotten the sack, but she did."

"Does she have someplace to go?" Phyllis asked. She knew she should keep asking about Ralston, but she had to know the girl wasn't on the streets.

"You mean Laura? Oh, she'll be alright. She's gone to her family in Clapton. She's getting married next month." Enid laughed. "That's why she lost her job. Mr. Ralston got so angry that she was only giving two weeks' notice that he sacked her on the spot."

"And this was yesterday."

"Nah, it was the day before. Mr. Ralston was in a foul mood that afternoon. He's never very nice, but he was really miserable that day when he come home and it only got worse when Miss Waterson come by and nagged him into tryin' on his new overcoat. She likes to take over, she does, and right now, she's the one with the upper hand, if you know what I mean."

Phyllis wasn't sure she did, but she nodded in agreement.

"Truth is, he doesn't much like the woman." Enid snickered. "But that don't stop his kind from marryin', does it."

CHAPTER 6

"Now, I ain't askin' you to spill any secrets," Luty said earnestly. "But surely, considerin' your position, you've heard gossip about one of this bunch."

"I know a number of things about all of the gentlemen." John Widdowes grinned broadly, leaned back in his chair, and crossed his arms over his chest. "But I'm not sure I ought to repeat them; they're not the sort of things for a delicate lady's ears."

Luty put her hands on her hips. "Oh, come on, John, how much scandal can there be about four stockbrokers?"

She'd come to the offices of Widdowes and Walthrop, Merchant Bankers, because John Widdowes, one of the two founding partners, was both a good friend and one of the smartest men she'd ever met. With a full head of dark honey-colored hair only starting to gray at the temples and a burly physique that was muscle rather than fat, he was a man in the prime of life. He knew the London financial community like the back of his hand but getting information out of him wasn't easy, as he had an annoying tendency to be discreet. He was also someone she admired a great deal, though she'd die before she'd ever let him know that.

"Five, if you include Ezra Amberly."

"I thought he was real sick."

"Not just sick, but at death's very door." John shrugged. "But he's been meeting the Grim Reaper every winter for the last ten years, so no one is readying themselves to attend his funeral just yet. As for the others, the only one of the lot that I cared anything about was Orlando Edison. He was a decent man, for a stock promoter."

"Are you sayin' the others ain't?"

"That depends on one's point of view," he replied. "My assessment of a man's character is often at odds with the way the rest of the world might regard him."

"I'll take your opinion over anyone else's." She knew he'd been raised in poverty and had worked hard to get where he was today. He judged others on character, not wealth, social position, or title, and he certainly didn't suffer fools gladly. "Come on, tell me what you think."

His grin broadened. "Surely you're not asking me to spread gossip."

"You ought to be ashamed of yourself, John, a grown man like you toyin' with a poor old lady like me. You're enjoyin' this too much."

"I always enjoy your visits, Luty. I just wish you'd occasionally drop by when you're not snooping for information about some killer or other. It hurts my feelings and makes me feel used."

Outraged, she gasped. "That's not fair. I've invited you to dinner three times and you've not come even once, so don't you go actin' like I only want to see you when I'm on the hunt."

He burst out laughing. "You're so easy to rile and it's so entertaining. I've already sent for tea so sit down and let's have a nice long chat."

She tried to glare at him, but she couldn't help it, she laughed as well. "I'm glad I'm a source of amusement for you." She flopped down in the padded straight-backed chair in front of his desk.

"For goodness' sake, woman, this is a bank. Getting someone to crack a smile around here takes an act of Parliament. So when you show up, I can't help myself—you're too much fun." He looked up as the door opened and his secretary, a dark-haired lad, came into the room carrying a tray.

"Set it down on the desk, Jeremy. I'll pour for us."

"Yes, sir." He put the tray down, nodded respectfully, and disappeared.

As soon as they were alone, John got up and moved close enough to manage serving. He reached for a pair of dainty silver tongs and picked up a lump of sugar. "Do you still take one lump and a dash of cream?"

Luty was inordinately flattered. "You remembered that?"

"Naturally. You're one of my favorite people." He put the sugar in the cup, added the cream, and then poured. "Before we get down to business, I want to assure you that the only reason I declined your dinner invitations was because I had no choice. The first two times you invited me I had to go out of town and the last time I had influenza." He leaned in her direction and put the cup on the edge of the desk, close enough for her to reach it.

"Don't worry, I know you'd have come if you could." She took a sip. "This is good. I was thirstier than I thought."

"You promise you'll invite me again?" He picked up his tea and went back to his chair. "Because if you don't, I won't tell you one ruddy thing about Orlando Edison or the Merry Gentlemen."

"'Course I'm goin' to invite you again." She tried to look stern. "I didn't come here today just to pester you for gossip about murder victims and suspects. If you don't have other plans, I'd like you to come to dinner on New Year's Eve. It'll just be a small group of people, but they're all nice and I think you'd have a good time."

"I don't have plans and I would be delighted."

"Good. Now that we've settled that, what do you know about Edison? Did he have a lot of enemies?"

"No, for someone in his line of work, he was remarkably well regarded."

"What does that mean?" she asked.

"You must understand, he was a stock promoter," John said. "They're considered somewhat less respectable, I guess one could say, than a stockbroker or a financier."

"But I thought he was a broker."

John shook his head. "No, I don't think so. From what I understand, he was hired by other people to raise money to buy into their concerns. Take the Granger Mine, for instance—three years ago the original claim was sold to a consortium of investors, but in order to work the mine, they had to raise a lot of capital. That was Edison's specialty. He was very good at getting others to part with their money. The first thing he always did was to ensure he had an impressive board of directors."

"You mean the Merry Gentlemen." Luty was a good

businesswoman and considered herself quite knowledgeable about the financial world but she wasn't sure she understood this completely. "So he didn't actually buy or sell shares."

"No, once he had the board of directors he wanted, in this particular case, the Merry Gentlemen, other investors begged to buy the stock."

"But surely even with the Merry Gentlemen on the board, smart investors would want to see a surveyor's report before they parted with their hard-earned cash. I know I wouldn't buy anything unless I did. Mining is tricky. I know—my late husband and I mined for silver in Colorado."

He smiled wanly. "You give people too much credit, Luty. Put an aristocrat and a couple of supposed financial geniuses on the board and they'll stand in line to buy the stock without even reading the prospectus carefully." He took a sip of tea. "But, personally, I liked Orlando Edison and I don't think he had any idea that the Granger didn't have gold in it. His other ventures had certainly been successful and many in London had made a great deal of money because of him."

"Sounds like you genuinely liked him."

"I did. He was affable, good-natured, and could actually talk about something other than finances. Most importantly, he treated everyone he met with dignity and respect. That's something I notice."

"What do you mean?"

John looked past her with a faraway expression his face for a long moment before he continued. "Did you know I was born at the Limehouse?"

"The workhouse in the East End?"

He nodded. "My mother died giving birth to me. My

father had been killed working on the railways before I was born. It was a miserable place, but I was one of the lucky ones. I was intelligent and came to the attention of one of the board of governors, who saw to it I was educated properly. But I've never forgotten how we were treated, how people look down on those who serve them and assume they're less than human." He suddenly shook himself. "But that's a tale for another day. The reason I brought this up is because I want to do anything I can to help catch whoever murdered Edison. Last summer, I saw him step between an enraged man and the poor bootblack who'd just gotten polish on the fellow's trousers. Orlando didn't hesitate; he grabbed the man's arm and kept him from thrashing the lad. As I once was in the same position as the bootblack, my admiration for Edison went up a thousandfold. But you're not interested in why I want to help, you want to know if I've anything useful to tell you." He smiled smugly. "And I do."

"You're not interested in me, you're trying to find out about Mr. Kimball," Penelope Freeman, chambermaid at the Larchmont Hotel, poked Wiggins on the arm as she spoke, then turned on her heel and stalked off.

"That's not true." He hurried to catch up with her. "I was just curious because my guv mentioned his name."

"I don't talk about our guests," she snapped as she turned out of the tiny mews onto Stanley Street. "And I don't for a minute believe you work for a newspaper. If I see you sniffing around here again, I'll sic the manager on you."

Wiggins gave up as she disappeared into the crowd heading toward Paddington Station. He slumped against the side of the redbrick hotel and felt like kicking himself. He'd handled this badly; he should have realized that, despite his best efforts, she hadn't believed a word of his story. But usually pretending to be a reporter worked, and it was just his ruddy luck to find the one person who saw right through it. He pulled his coat tighter as a blast of cold wind slammed into him. What was he going to do now? He didn't want to risk going back into the hotel and trying with someone else—he couldn't be sure that Penelope hadn't pointed him out to the manager when she went to fetch her hat and coat. But, if he didn't find someone else willing to talk, he'd have to go back to their afternoon meeting with nothing. So far, the only thing he'd discovered about Yancy Kimball was what the fellow looked like!

Discouraged, he trudged down the street without having come to any conclusion about what to do next. Out of habit, he watched the front of the hotel as he walked. The establishment was a small place catering to passengers going to and from Paddington Station who couldn't or wouldn't pay the exorbitant rates at the opulent Great Western Hotel around the corner. The pavement in the front was crowded with people—men in business suits and bowlers, two women trying unsuccessfully to stop a group of street lads from carrying their cases, and an elderly porter that was helping a frail old woman out of a hansom.

Just as Wiggins came abreast of the front door, it opened and his quarry stepped out. Kimball dodged around the two women and then stopped on the bottom step. Wiggins kept on moving. When he was far enough away to deem it safe to look back, he turned and saw Kimball heading in his direction. He stopped, bent down, and pretended to tie his shoelace.

Kimball went past and Wiggins waited a few moments before he followed. He was sure the man was going to Paddington, so he stuck his hand into his pocket and made certain he had plenty of money in case he had to buy a train ticket. But he was wrong. When Kimball got to the corner, instead of turning toward the station, he turned the other way and went toward Praed Street. Wiggins went after him. There were so many pedestrians crowding the pavement, he didn't bother to stay back, but he did slow his steps when Kimball reached the corner, stopped, and turned. Wiggins didn't break his stride, but kept on going as Kimball's gaze swept the faces of those on the streets. He'd almost reached him when Kimball suddenly whirled on his heel and started down Cambridge Place.

Wiggins didn't have to dawdle in order to stay behind the fellow; he was moving so fast he was almost running. Kimball was now a good twenty yards ahead of him when he turned and disappeared. Again, Wiggins continued walking. He saw that Kimball had gone through a dilapidated wooden lych-gate into a churchyard and was now standing with his back to the road. He'd didn't think Kimball had spotted him, but he couldn't be sure. He went to the corner and then turned in to a mews, praying that it circled back to the rear of the church building. It didn't, so he retraced his steps.

When he reached the lych-gate, he craned his neck around the structure but couldn't see Kimball anywhere. Blast a Spaniard, he thought, maybe he's gone into the church. He opened the gate and stepped through, wincing as the rusty hinges creaked.

The church proper was directly ahead of him at the end of an old paved walkway. He moved cautiously over the broken bricks, taking care where he stepped so he wouldn't trip on the chunks of crumbling mortar.

There was a narrow yard that went from the front to the right side of the building. It was choked with weeds and filled with ancient tombstones covered with moss and leaning haphazardly in all directions. Dead leaves lay in windswept mounds against the weathered stone of the building and, overhead, the weak winter sun went behind a bank of clouds, dimming the already gloomy day even further.

He was almost at the stairs leading to the entrance when he saw the chain and lock on the handles and realized the church was shut. Kimball obviously wasn't inside, so where had he gone?

"Let me go!" The voice was American and came from around the corner of the church. "Damn you, punching me in the face isn't going to get him his money."

Wiggins' heart leapt into his throat and, for a moment, he was tempted to make a run for it. He wasn't a coward, but he wasn't a fool, either. But then he remembered his duty and flattened himself against the wall. He edged to his right, moving quietly and hoping the noise from the street would mask any noise he made. When he got to the end of the building, he sank to his knees and peeked around the corner.

Yancy Kimball was there with two other men. A stocky man with stringy blond hair and dressed in a long brown coat had Kimball by the lapels. The other, a giant of a fellow with a black mustache and wearing a blue wool hat, pinned Kimball's arms behind his back.

"Blast a Spaniard," Wiggins murmured. "What the ruddy 'ell do I do now?" He looked toward the street, hoping against hope that someone would miraculously appear.

"There's no need for the rough stuff. Let me go," Kimball pleaded. "I told you I was good for it."

"You've been tellin' us you're good for it for weeks now," the blond snarled. "And Gedigan's sick of waitin'. He wants what you owe and he wants it now."

"He'll get nothing if I'm dead," Kimball cried.

"Yeah, and we've heard that one before, too. But at least if you're dead, Gedigan'll have the satisfaction of knowin' you paid for cheating him. People who can't pay their debts shouldn't gamble." He tightened his grip on the lapels while the man holding Kimball's arms jerked them hard.

Kimball squawked in pain.

Wiggins balled his hands into fists as he frantically wondered what to do. If he left to find a policeman, by the time he got back, Kimball could be beaten to a bloody pulp. He took a deep, ragged breath and forced himself to calm down. He wouldn't do Kimball any good by standing here like a terrified schoolboy. But he wasn't stupid, either. He was no match for either of those brutes; they were professional hoodlums who made their living collecting gambling debts. But all he needed was for them to be distracted enough for Kimball to make a run for it.

He scanned the ground and spotted what he needed lying beside a crumbling headstone. Moving quietly, he stood up and walked the three feet that stood between him and what was probably a very stupid idea. He reached down and picked up a handful of the broken stone. It felt funny using bits of someone's gravestone for this sort of thing, but he wasn't about to let these two hooligans murder Kimball.

He took a deep breath and put the largest chunk in his right hand. Going back to the wall, he peeked around the corner. Wiggins swung around the building, aiming the stone just as the ruffian raised his fist.

"Don't be a fool," Kimball yelled. "Gedigan will be a lot more satisfied with his money rather than me being dead. If you've half the brains God gave a weasel you'll listen to what I have to say. Something's happened. I've got money coming."

"Quit playin' about and take your medicine like a man." He drew back his arm. "Why should we believe you now when you've done nothin' but lie for weeks?"

"Because I'm getting a huge inheritance from my cousin. For God's sake, you must have read about it. Orlando Edison—it's been in the newspapers—he was the financier who was found murdered. I'm his only heir and, believe me, he had plenty."

The man lowered his fist and eased off Kimball's lapels. "Go on, keep talkin'." He nodded and the other thug stepped back. Kimball was now free.

Wiggins sagged in relief and ducked back behind the corner. He kept them in sight, though.

"Orlando Edison was my cousin. He's got no other family so I'm going to get it all. He's got plenty of money as well as property both here and in America." Kimball straightened his coat. "Tell Gedigan to be patient and he'll get his money with interest."

"When?" Baldy demanded. "Gedigan's not goin' to be put off any longer."

"I'll not have the money in my possession until the estate's settled." Kimball shrugged. "But as I've got lots coming my way, I can get a proper loan now. There's nothing a bank likes more than giving money to someone with prospects. I'm going to see my banker this afternoon. Tell Gedigan I'll be along this evening to see him."

"I hope the lady is home," Witherspoon said as he stepped down from the hansom cab in front of the five-story brown brick home of Charles Downing. Like all the houses along the street, the ground floor had a plastered white façade and sat behind a raised black railing that enclosed a staircase leading to a lower floor.

"So do I, sir," Barnes said as he pushed open the gate and stepped through. "If she's out, when she comes home her servants will warn her that we were here."

Witherspoon pushed his spectacles up his nose as he followed the constable up the short walkway to the front door. "That's true. I'm hoping the element of surprise will get us more information."

Barnes banged the knocker against the wood.

The door opened a few inches and a young housemaid stared out at them. Her eyes grew as big as saucers as her gaze flicked over Barnes' uniform. "Uh, yes, may I help you?"

"We'd like to speak to Mrs. Downing," Witherspoon said. "Is she at home?"

"I'll see if she's receiving, sir," the girl stammered.

"This isn't a social call," Barnes interjected. "Tell Mrs. Downing if she doesn't wish to speak to us now, we'll ask her husband to escort her to the station."

"That won't be necessary." The voice was female and came from within the house. "Show them in, Grayson."

The maid opened the door and stepped back. The inspector took off his bowler as he entered the foyer. Bright Oriental rugs covered the dark wood floor, a crystal chandelier hung from the ceiling, and a wooden hall tree painted in gold and white stood against the wall opposite the door. A wide staircase led off to the right and on the bottom step stood a woman.

Blonde haired, blue eyed, and rail thin, she was dressed in a teal blue day dress with white lace trim on the cuffs and collar. She stared at them solemnly for a few moments. "I'm Cecily Downing. I understand you wish to speak to me?"

"We do, ma'am," Witherspoon said. "I'm Inspector Witherspoon and this is Constable Barnes." He glanced at the constable and saw the expression of surprise that flashed across his face before he could mask it. Downing had told the constable that his wife was a good deal younger than himself. The inspector was not an expert on ascertaining a lady's age and she did appear to be a *bit* younger than her husband. Barnes had reported that Downing described his wife as "a foolish young woman," and that was most definitely stretching the truth. Foolish she might be, but "young" had been left behind a good ten years earlier.

"I know who you are. My husband says you're in charge of investigating Orlando's murder. I suppose I'll have to answer your questions."

"That would be very helpful, ma'am." Witherspoon unbuttoned his coat.

She stepped onto the floor and motioned for them to follow her. "Come along, then, we'll be more comfortable in the drawing room." She led them down the hallway to the open doors of the drawing room and they went inside.

Christmas was very evident here. A huge evergreen, fully decorated but with the candles unlighted, stood between the emerald green loveseat and couch, and a wreath with a red velvet bow was suspended by maroon cords on the wall between the windows. Holly and ivy were draped around the bases of all the lamps and the candles, and another, larger wreath with a gold and white bow hung on the wall over the green marble fireplace and mantel.

"Please sit down." She gestured at two straight-backed chairs with embroidered seats opposite the sofa. She waited till both the policemen were seated before she spoke. "Go ahead and ask your questions, but I assure you, I don't know anything about Orlando's murder."

Witherspoon glanced at Barnes, who was taking his notebook and pencil out of his jacket pocket. He waited till the constable was ready before he answered. "I understand you and the deceased were, er, friends."

She shrugged. "He was my husband's colleague. They did business together. That hardly makes us friends, though we did occasionally frequent the same social events. I'm sorry he's dead, of course."

"If you're not friends, why did you use his Christian name and not his surname a moment ago?" Barnes looked up and stared her straight in the eyes. "For a woman of your class and stature, ma'am, that was a very odd way of referring to the deceased. Generally, when a married woman uses the first name of a handsome, eligible bachelor, that usually means they are either old friends or intimately acquainted on another level."

Witherspoon held his breath and knew he was blushing. He was a policeman so he knew it was silly to be embarrassed by delicate subjects during the course of a murder investigation, but somehow, he'd never gotten used to some of the awkward questions one was forced to ask. He didn't fault the constable; Barnes was frequently provocative and, just as frequently, it loosened otherwise recalcitrant tongues. Furthermore, Barnes was merely following up on information they had been given by the woman's husband.

"That's ridiculous," she snapped. "I made a mistake and used the wrong form of address. Do get on with your questions, I've people coming to tea soon and, frankly, I'd prefer the police not be here when they arrive."

"When was the last time you saw Mr. Edison?" Witherspoon asked.

She lifted her finger to her chin. "Last week at the Drummonds' dinner party. As a matter of fact, I was seated next to him."

"You spoke with him at length?" the inspector asked.

"Of course, Inspector—it was a social occasion and I don't generally sit like a mute statue next to my dinner companions. I spoke to everyone at our end of the table."

"How did his manner seem to you?" Barnes interjected.

Small lines appeared on her forehead as she frowned. "I'm not sure I understand. It was a festive occasion and he was like always, charming and gracious. There was nothing special about the evening."

"Mr. Edison didn't appear to be worried or upset about anything?" Witherspoon pressed.

"Not at all."

"What were you doing on Wednesday evening at six o'clock?" Barnes smiled as he asked the question.

"Wednesday evening? Why is that any of your business, Constable?" She drew back in surprise as she understood the significance of the question. "That question is outrageous. How dare you ask me such a thing."

"Ma'am, we've had it on good authority that you and Mr. Edison had more than a passing acquaintance," Barnes explained. "As a matter of fact, shortly before the murder, your husband had a terrible argument with the deceased. He warned Mr. Edison to stay away from you."

She started to get up. "I don't know where you heard such nonsense—"

Witherspoon interrupted. "We know Mr. Downing argued with Mr. Edison because he was shouting loud enough to be heard by several witnesses. Your husband told us what the quarrel was about."

"Charles told you they'd fought over me?" She eased back into her seat.

"He admitted it, ma'am," Barnes said. "Now, you do

understand why we need to know your movements on the evening Mr. Edison was killed."

She said nothing for a moment; she simply stared at her hands. "I don't know what to do. I had no idea that Charles would do something so foolish."

"Then you admit that Mr. Edison was more than just a casual acquaintance," the constable said.

She lifted her chin. "I admit nothing. I don't know what nonsense Charles was babbling about, but I assure you, Orlando Edison was nothing more than one of my husband's work colleagues."

Witherspoon noted that thus far, she'd not bothered to tell them where she'd been at the time of the murder. "Again, I must ask you, Mrs. Downing: Where were you at six o'clock this past Wednesday evening?"

"I was out shopping, Inspector. On Regent Street, if you must know. It's Christmas and I wanted a new set of household linens for Boxing Day. We're having a dinner party and the old linens need to be replaced."

"Shopping seems to be a very common pastime these days. Your husband claims he was shopping as well."

"It is Christmas, Inspector. That's often when people buy things for one another."

"Yes, of course." He inclined his head in agreement. He wished he had time to do a bit more shopping. He'd seen a lovely wooden hobbyhorse that he wanted to get for Amanda. "Mrs. Downing, while you were out that afternoon, did you see anyone you know? A friend or an acquaintance who might be able to verify your whereabouts?" Witherspoon felt a bead of sweat gather under his shirt collar. The room was stifling.

"No, I did not." She crossed her arms over her chest.

"What time did you arrive home that evening?" The

constable shifted in his seat. The embroidered padding on the chair was elegant, but ruddy uncomfortable.

"I'm not sure. I didn't look at the clock, but I imagine it was close to seven o'clock. We don't dine until eight, so I had plenty of time to rest and change for dinner."

"Perhaps one of your servants noticed the time," the inspector suggested.

"They were in the kitchen when I came home."

"Even the housemaids?" Barnes asked.

"Yes, even them, Constable. Furthermore, I went straight up to my room when I arrived home." She gave Barnes a withering look. "And before you ask, I don't have a personal maid to help me dress."

"What about your husband, what time did he get here?" Witherspoon asked.

"I've no idea, I didn't see him until dinner and I didn't ask him what time he'd come in the front door." She got up. "I'll have to ask you to leave. If you've more questions for me, you can ask me later. As I told you, I've guests coming."

"Just one more question, ma'am." Barnes shoved the notebook back into his jacket and stood up. "Can we have a look at the souvenir miner's shovel your husband owns? The one he got when he became a member of Granger's board of directors."

"No, Constable, that's not possible. I thought it an ugly piece of nonsense and I didn't want it cluttering up my home so my husband kept it at his office."

"Merry Gentlemen, my foot," Maurice Bradshaw exclaimed. "There's not a bloody thing merry about any of them. What's more, none of the four of them care one whit about the less fortunate." He took a sip of tea and eyed Hatchet over the rim of his cup.

They were in a small café on Commercial Road in the East End. Hatchet had tracked down his old friend Maurice Bradshaw, who until he'd retired had been a broker at the stock exchange.

Bradshaw had gray hair that stood up in tufts no matter how much pomade he applied, a ruddy complexion laced with wrinkles, and a nose that looked much like an eagle's beak. But his stern countenance was in direct contrast to his character. Bradshaw was a widower and, once retired, he'd devoted his life to serving others. He'd used his wealth to start the Frances Bradshaw Trust for the Poor, a charity named after his late wife and housed in property he'd purchased next to the Methodist church on Chapman Street. Mrs. Bradshaw had been a devout Methodist. The charity provided food, warm clothes, and, once a week, a medical clinic for the poor of the East End.

"You don't sound as if you like them very much," Hatchet commented.

"There's nothing to like about any of them. Amberly's a tightfisted miser who'd kick a starving kitten's bowl of milk just for the sport of it, Ralston's a social-climbing upstart who doesn't give a toss about anyone but himself, Bagshot wouldn't have a farthing to his name if he'd not gotten lucky on that Sperling Mine deal five years ago, and Downing is a blustering idiot with all the personality of a tree stump."

Hatchet laughed and reached into his pocket for his watch. Unfortunately, much as he liked Bradshaw, he'd not learned anything about the Merry Gentlemen or Orlando Edison that he didn't already know. At this point, he was simply going to enjoy Bradshaw's company until he had to leave for the afternoon meeting. He held the timepiece on his knee, flipped open the lid, and saw that it wasn't quite half past two. "But Orlando Edison seems to have been a decent man. Everyone seemed to have liked and admired him."

Bradshaw's thick eyebrows drew together. "He was liked, that's true, and he did donate generously when I was collecting money for the trust. But the only time the others ever gave so much as a farthing was for show. You know what I mean—if someone they wanted to impress was involved, they'd open their purses fast enough. Last month I was at a dinner party and Lord and Lady Medford were there, as was Martin Bagshot and his wife. Lady Medford generously offered ten pounds for the trust, as did several others at the table. Martin Bagshot, who, as I said, never opens his purse, piped in and said he'd like to contribute the same." He chuckled. "Within a few days, everyone except Bagshot made good on their donations. But I cooked Bagshot's goose. I ran into him at the Uxbridge Road Station a couple of days ago and reminded him that he'd promised to send me ten pounds for the charity. I hinted that I was seeing the Medfords over Christmas, and of course Martin immediately agreed to make good on his offer."

Hatchet's grin faded. "A couple of days ago," he repeated. "Which day, exactly?"

"This past Wednesday, the eighteenth." Bradshaw took another sip.

"What time?"

Bradshaw put his cup down. "Let me see . . . I'm not sure. My meeting had ended at half past five and it took about fifteen minutes to walk to the station. Bagshot was just coming out when I arrived so it must have been around five forty-five or ten minutes until six."

*   *   *

Wiggins sprinted through the back door and skidded to a halt as he flew into the kitchen. "Sorry I'm late," he apologized on a ragged breath. "But I found out somethin' and it took me a good while to finish it up properly." That wasn't quite the truth. He'd been so proud of himself about Kimball, he'd rushed to the pub on Throgmorton Street but, to his great disappointment, the two lads he'd met before weren't there and the only person he'd struck up a conversation with knew nothing about football. Then he'd had to race back here, using some of his precious coin on a hansom rather than the omnibus in order to get here for the meeting. He pulled out his chair and sat down.

Mrs. Goodge peered at him over the rim of her glasses. "Are you alright, lad? You look a bit flushed."

"I'm fine," he muttered. "Just a bit out of breath. 'Ave I missed anything?"

"We've just started," Mrs. Jeffries replied. "Luty was about to tell us what she'd learned today."

"As I was sayin'," Luty continued, "my source is someone who knows what's goin' on in the financial community and he give me an earful today. He told me that Orlando Edison was well liked, but considered a bit of a rogue. In other words, he wasn't above sweetenin' the pot to get what he wanted."

"Madam, what on earth does that mean?" Hatchet glared at her irritably. He'd really wanted to go first, as he thought his information was very useful, but being the gentleman that he was, he'd kept silent when it was apparent she wanted the floor.

"It means that there were rumors he got the Merry Gentlemen to sit on the board of directors of the Granger Mine by payin' them." She grinned broadly. "And though that ain't illegal, it's not exactly ethical."

"And now the Granger Mine is in bankruptcy," Mrs. Jeffries murmured.

"But that's not that important," Wiggins interrupted. "I mean, I'm sorry, but I found out something this afternoon that will 'ave us thinkin' a bit differently."

"As did I," Hatchet declared.

"You're not the only ones that learned something useful," the cook interjected. "Just because I got a new cookbook doesn't mean I wasn't doing my part. I found out some bits and pieces that will have your heads spinning."

"I've found out something as well," Betsy stated. She glanced at Smythe, who gave her a quick grin.

"Me, too," Ruth said.

Mrs. Jeffries couldn't believe her ears. What was going on here? This wasn't the way they usually behaved. "Gracious, let's settle down and discuss this in a reasonable manner."

Everyone ignored her and kept on arguing.

"Let me go next," Hatchet insisted.

"I'm not finished," Luty exclaimed.

"Then say something useful," he replied. "We've danced around this for two days now. It's time to end the waltz."

"What in the name of Hades does that mean?" She glared at her butler.

Mrs. Jeffries had had enough. She stood up. "Everyone, please, take a deep breath and say nothing for the next minute."

Stunned into silence, they all stared at her. "I'm not sure what is going on here, but it seems to me that everyone needs to be mindful that we all should be working together.

Now, let's do this as we should, one at a time." Mrs. Jeffries had no idea why everyone had suddenly become so rude to one another, but this had been building since they'd learned about the murder. It was as if they all wavered between being distracted or acting as if the case was the most important thing in their respective worlds. She had no idea what, if anything, was happening, but she knew they needed to step back and regroup with one another. "Luty, please continue with your report."

Luty straightened her spine. "Well, if everyone is listening, the last bit I picked up was that Martin Bagshot is in a load of financial trouble. He sunk every cent he had into the Granger based on Edison's recommendation and now he's just about broke."

"Thank you, Luty." Mrs. Jeffries looked at Wiggins. "Would you like to go next?"

Chastened, he nodded. "Sorry, but I was so excited about what I saw that I couldn't wait to tell everyone." He told them about Yancy Kimball and the threats to the fellow's life. "So you see, once he got the thugs to listen for a bit, he 'ad a smooth enough tongue to keep 'em at bay long enough to convince 'em 'e had a lot of money comin' his way," he finished.

"But how would 'e know that?" Smythe asked. "Kimball claimed 'e'd only been back in London for a short while, so how would 'e have found out he was one of Edison's heirs?"

"'E's the only blood relative," Wiggins insisted. "And remember, he probably didn't know that Edison made a will and that 'e's not getting the whole estate. He might not know about Mrs. Flurry so 'e's assumin' that as he's the only family, 'e'll be getting it all."

"Then he's a fool," Mrs. Goodge argued. "Everyone knows that people often ignore their relatives, especially if they've someone else in their life that's given them a bit of time and attention. Blood might be thicker than water, but the one that's right in front of the face generally gets the goods. Remember what they say, out of sight, out of mind, and Yancy Kimball has been thousands of miles away until recently."

Mrs. Jeffries had no idea what any of this meant, but she didn't worry about it. She had faith that things would sort themselves out. "Wiggins, if you're finished, we need to move along."

"I'd like to go next," Hatchet offered. "My source knew quite a bit about the Merry Gentlemen and Edison, but it wasn't much more than we'd already heard. However, he did tell me something we hadn't heard, namely, that Martin Bagshot was at the Uxbridge Road Station on the evening of the murder. My source saw him coming out of the station at a quarter to six."

"So what?" Luty challenged. "Baghsot lives just off Holland Park—he probably comes home by that train station."

"Hardly, madam. He lives on Sunningdale Gardens in Kensington and the closest station would be Kensington High Street, but where he lives isn't the point. If you'll recall, Mrs. Jeffries reported that Constable Barnes had told her that at the time of the murder, Bagshot claimed he was shopping on Oxford Street. Which means he was lying. Uxbridge Station is only a ten-minute walk to Edison's house."

Luty made a face at him. "Nell's bells, Hatchet. I hate it when you're right."

"I'll go next," Phyllis offered quickly. "I found out some information about Paul Ralston." She told them about her meeting with Enid Carter.

"Sir Thomas Waterson sounds like a mean old man—

imagine, disinheriting his own daughter because she stood by her husband." Mrs. Goodge clucked her tongue in disapproval. "I hope Paul Ralston knows that marrying into a family like that won't buy him happiness despite their wealth and position."

"He'll not be the first to marry for money and a title," Betsy said. "But it still seems such a sad way to waste your life."

"Don't waste your sympathy on Ralston," Phyllis said. "According to my source, he's no better than Sir Thomas Waterson. He's a very angry person. On the day Edison was murdered, his housemaid gave her notice and he got so furious, he told her to get her things and be out of his house by the next morning."

"That's terrible." Betsy frowned. "Where did he expect the poor girl to go?"

"He didn't care. Enid said that he'd never been a nice person to work for, but on that day, he was in a particularly bad mood. He came home that afternoon, shut himself in his study, and thumped his fist against the sofa pillows for half an hour."

"How did she know that?" Ruth asked.

"She heard him when she walked past the study. Later that day, his fiancée arrived right about the time the tailor delivered his new overcoat. Enid overheard him promising Miss Waterson his old one for some charity she collects for. When she went in to serve the tea, he was tryin' on his new coat and actin' for all the world like he was the sweetest fellow there was."

"I hope his other maid had somewhere to go," Betsy murmured.

Under the table, Smythe squeezed her hand. He hated for her to be reminded of the misery of her past. She'd once been forced onto the streets with no place to call home and he knew that hearing about it happening to someone else bothered her more than the others realized. But she suddenly gave him a quick, grateful smile and he knew she was handling it just fine.

"She'll be fine. She's goin' to her family for a few weeks before she marries." Phyllis giggled. "But Enid said Laura got back at Ralston. She saw her goin' through the pockets of his old overcoat the next morning and helping herself."

CHAPTER 7

Mrs. Jeffries stood at the drawing room window and stared out into the dark night. She focused her gaze on the gas lamp across the road and tried to think of a plan of action. The inspector was due home any minute now and she still wasn't certain of what she was going to say when they had their sherry tonight. Today's meeting had netted so much information that it wouldn't be fair to expect Constable Barnes to pass it all along. But what would be the most reasonable tidbits for her to weave into their conversation? She cast her mind back to the meeting, going over every report one by one. Surely Wiggins witnessing Kimball's altercation was something Barnes should handle. He could always say one of his informants had told him that Kimball was a gambler. Likewise, the constable and his network of sources could easily have obtained Hatchet's and Luty's information. But there was still the information from the others.

A dog barked frantically, jerking her out of her reverie. She blinked and realized that her neighbor, Mrs. Pomeroy, and her buff-colored spaniel, Sasha, were on the pavement outside the window. The dog was bounding up and down, straining against its lead and howling at a cat that darted across the empty road. Mrs. Pomeroy, on the other hand, was staring straight at her with a curious, bemused expression on her face. Embarrassed, she gave the woman a smile and quickly drew the curtains. The barking faded as Mrs. Pomeroy resumed her walk. Drat, she thought irritably, her train of thought was completely ruined.

But Mrs. Jeffries didn't have time to marshal her thoughts again because, almost immediately, she heard the distinct sound of a horse's hooves and the jangle of a harness. She peeked through the curtains just as a hansom cab pulled to the curb and the inspector got out. It was pointless to try to plan what might or might not be possible to convey to him, she decided; she'd just have to do her best.

She went to the foyer and opened the door as Witherspoon mounted the top step. "Good evening, sir. Gracious, you must be exhausted. You're home so very late."

"I'll admit that I am a bit tired." He smiled wanly as he took off his hat and coat.

"Of course you are, sir. You do work so very hard when you're on a homicide case." She took the inspector's garments and hung them on the coat tree.

"I don't suppose Amanda is still here?" he asked hopefully as he unwound his scarf and tossed it on the top peg.

"No, sir, I'm sorry, but Betsy did say she was going to bring the baby around tomorrow morning. She said she'd try to be here before you left for the day so you could see how well Amanda is walking."

"That's the best news I've had all day. I know Christmas is only a few days away, but I had so hoped to see the little one before then. I wanted to ask Betsy if she and Smythe would have any objection to my getting Amanda a hobby-horse. I know she's a bit young, but it's a beautiful toy and she would so enjoy it."

"I'm sure Betsy and Smythe will think that's a lovely idea, sir," she said. "Would you care for a sherry before dinner? Mrs. Goodge says it won't be ready before seven o'clock."

"That would be splendid." He started down the hall toward his study.

"Any new developments in the case, sir?" she asked as they entered the room. She went to the liquor cupboard and pulled out a bottle of Harvey's Bristol Cream. Opening it, she poured the fragrant sherry into the small, cut crystal glasses she'd put out earlier.

"We clarified a number of things." Witherspoon sat down in his overstuffed chair. "But it's all rather confusing."

She laughed as she handed him his drink. "Now, sir, you know very well that the jumble in your mind is part of your method. It happens with every case. It's very much a necessary step in the way you develop your case, sir."

"That's very good of you to say, Mrs. Jeffries," he said and smiled gratefully, "but sometimes it doesn't feel that way. I don't mean to complain, but I'm not sure of solving this one. No one has an alibi—I mean, people have alibis but they're all the sort that can neither be proved nor disproved."

"You mean like the Merry Gentlemen, sir?" she asked. "They apparently were all out shopping for Christmas when the murder took place."

"Not just them. Cecily Downing and Madeleine Flurry were also out between the hours of four and six on the day of the murder and, like the others, they claimed to be Christmas shopping." He shook his head in disbelief. "Honestly, Mrs. Jeffries, I wouldn't think there was that much shopping to be done for the holidays."

"I take it you spoke with Mrs. Downing and Mrs. Flurry today?" she pressed. She didn't want him sidetracked on the subject of the upcoming holiday.

"Yes, but Mrs. Downing wasn't very forthcoming." He frowned. "And if you ask me, she wasn't as young as I thought she'd be."

Surprised, because the inspector never made ungentlemanly remarks about a woman's appearance, she stared at him. "What do you mean, sir?"

"Mr. Downing led me to believe that his wife was hardly more than a girl but honestly, and I don't mean to be unkind, she seemed no more than a few years his junior. What's more, she wasn't in the least concerned that her husband had a vicious argument with the victim shortly before the murder. All she said was that Downing was acting foolish but he wasn't the sort to bash someone's head in in a jealous rage. She also maintained that Edison was nothing more than her husband's business acquaintance."

He took another sip of sherry and told her about his interviews with both Cecily Downing and Madeleine Flurry. Mrs. Jeffries listened to his recitation carefully and in the expectation that something he said might give her an opening to convey *some* of the information from today's meeting. But as he talked, her hopes dimmed.

When he paused to take a breath, she said, "Did Mrs. Flurry know she was one of Edison's heirs?"

"She did. Edison told her when he did his will that she'd inherit. I suppose they must have been very good friends."

His comment gave Mrs. Jeffries a fighting chance. Now she could convey the tidbits that Betsy had picked up. "From what Betsy heard, they were more than friends, sir."

"What?"

"Don't be alarmed, sir, Betsy isn't in the habit of discussing your cases, but you've become so very famous and everyone in the neighborhood knows she worked here, so"—she broke off and shrugged—"even when she's out shopping people pass along gossip."

"But how would anyone know that Mrs. Flurry had anything to do with the victim? That's not been in the papers and the details of his estate have most certainly not been made public."

"It wasn't his will the gossips were discussing." To give herself time to choose her words, she sipped her sherry. "It was Edison's relationship with Madeleine Flurry. Betsy was at the butcher's on Shepherd's Bush Road and, well, to make a long story short, she heard a rumor that Madeleine Flurry and Orlando Edison were lovers." That wasn't quite all the gossip that Betsy had heard, but she needed to tread carefully here and not say too much. If she was lucky, sowing a few seeds might do the trick and have him looking a bit closer at Mrs. Flurry.

Witherspoon's eyebrows rose. "That would certainly explain why he'd left her the bulk of his estate."

"And a roof over her head for the next quarter," Mrs. Jeffries added.

"Mrs. Flurry claims he wanted her to oversee packing his things and shipping them to him," he murmured.

"That's certainly one explanation, but you yourself said

that his housekeeper, Mrs. Clarridge, struck you as an emi-
nently capable woman," Mrs. Jeffries said. "And let's face it,
not every woman is going to be reasonable when she finds
out she's being left behind."

"You think she might have killed him because he was
going to New York?"

"It's possible, sir. After all, as you pointed out, the murder
weapon was one of opportunity, not planning." She wasn't
sure if he'd made this assertion or not, but to her way of
thinking, it never hurt to bolster the inspector's confidence.

"She might have grabbed it and bashed him over the
head in a fit of rage," he speculated. "Yes, that's very possible. And like the others, her alibi is very weak. As a matter
of fact, when I asked her where she was shopping at the
time of the murder, she couldn't say with any certainty, just
that she'd been on the Kensington High Street."

"Now that I'm telling tales out of school, I might as well
pass along another tidbit from around the neighborhood."

"My goodness, there's more? Poor Betsy, she must hate
going shopping when I'm on a murder case."

"This one isn't from Betsy," Mrs. Jeffries replied. "It's
from Lady Cannonberry. Now please understand, she was
most reluctant to mention this to me, it's just something
she heard at one of her women's meetings. Lady Cannonberry is most certainly not a gossip and would never indulge
in any behavior that might reflect negatively upon you or
impede one of your cases."

"Of course she wouldn't," he agreed. "She is the most
wonderful woman and her character is above reproach. Uh,
exactly what did she hear?"

"Apparently, her source was someone who once knew
Edison quite well. But that's neither here nor there. What is
important is that she told Lady Cannonberry that Orlando

Edison didn't keep all his money in the bank," she said. "Supposedly, he always kept a substantial amount of money close at hand. 'One should always have some cash hidden close just in case one needs to bolt.' Supposedly, those were his exact words, sir."

"But we searched his house thoroughly and there was no money found." Witherspoon frowned in confusion. "But perhaps we ought to have another look. If Lady Cannonberry's acquaintance knew what she was talking about, perhaps the killer was looking for money and Edison's death was a robbery gone wrong."

Mrs. Jeffries knew exactly what she'd been talking about; her source had told Ruth that she and Edison had been "far more than friends before he took up with that Flurry woman."

The house was quiet as Mrs. Jeffries came up the hallway to the kitchen. She'd checked that all the doors were locked and then, realizing she wasn't in the least bit sleepy, decided to make herself a cup of tea before going upstairs to bed.

She put the kettle on the cooker, then got down the teapot and her mug. As she waited for the water to boil, she stared across the room toward the small window over the sink that faced the street. A carriage trundled past and she listened; in the darkness, she couldn't see it well, of course, but that didn't matter, she was simply trying to empty her mind and let the ideas come and go as they would.

All the new information she'd learned both at their meeting today and from the inspector this evening just left her more confused. But no matter how she looked at what few facts they had, she couldn't make heads nor tails out of any of them. They seemed to be long on gossip but woefully short on cold, hard facts.

For once, concentrating on the victim to find the reason for the crime didn't seem to be very helpful. Edison's murder could have been a robbery that went wrong or he might have been killed by a woman furious at being abandoned while he went off to America or even by a lady whose advances he might have spurned. It could also just as easily have been an angry shareholder who'd lost everything because of the bankruptcy or someone who was convinced that Edison had defrauded them. But which was most likely? Which made the most sense?

Edison's murder had been a particularly brutal one, which brought up another question. Why kill him with a shovel? Why hadn't the killer used a different method? According to Constable Barnes, the postmortem revealed that there had only been two blows struck. So did the killer know exactly where to hit the skull or did he or she just get lucky? And if your aim was to murder, why risk that weapon? Surely a gun or even a knife would be far more effective, because it was quite possible to survive even the most horrendous head injuries. A hard stab through the heart would guarantee death and a knife was the most accessible weapon there was; every kitchen in London had one.

Because the killer had no choice. The thought came unbidden into her mind. The kettle whistled and she turned to grab a tea towel.

Mrs. Goodge was standing in the archway. Despite the lateness of the hour, she was still fully clothed. Samson sat by her feet.

"Gracious, I'm sorry." Mrs. Jeffries snatched up the towel and grabbed the kettle off the stove. "I didn't mean to disturb you."

"You didn't. I knew I couldn't sleep yet. I'll get us a jug

of milk for our tea." She trudged down the hall toward the wet larder. Samson trotted after her.

Mrs. Jeffries let the tea steep while she got down Mrs. Goodge's mug, two dessert plates, a bowl of sugar, and the biscuit tin. By the time Mrs. Goodge came back with the milk, she had everything nicely arranged.

"Let's the two of us have a little chat." Mrs. Goodge handed her the jug. "I can see you're worried about this one."

"Good, I could use your advice." Mrs. Jeffries added the milk, poured the tea, and put the cook's cup in front of her.

"I'm sorry I wasn't very helpful earlier when you tried to talk to me," Mrs. Goodge said. "And I think that's part of the problem with this case."

Mrs. Jeffries helped herself to a shortbread biscuit and put it on her plate. "So you've noticed there's a problem."

"There's a problem, alright, but I don't think it's the one you think it is." Mrs. Goodge grabbed the tin and reached in for a gingersnap. "You always get muddled at this point in the investigation and, I will admit, this time it's a bit worse. But what's really worryin' you is that you've a good idea why we're not makin' much progress and you don't know what to do about it. Some of us has been distracted by our own interests and you're not sure we're getting our bits and pieces right."

Surprised, because she'd noticed but had deliberately pushed the idea firmly to one side, she said, "I wouldn't exactly say that, but I have sensed that at times some of us have seemed to be a bit preoccupied and not really paying attention at our meetings. I suppose it's the time of the year, the holidays—"

Mrs. Goodge interrupted. "Nonsense, the holidays have nothing to do with it. Some of us are bein' selfish." Her cookbook was on the table so she reached over and tapped it on the cover. "This is what has stopped me from doin' my duty and I'm heartily sorry about it."

"But you have done your duty, Mrs. Goodge. You came up with a very valuable piece of information at today's meeting."

"I heard the same rumor that Betsy did, only Betsy went out and hunted it down, I just happened to stumble across it when I ran into Mrs. Bird out in the garden. As a matter of fact, I was downright annoyed the woman had caught me out there. I'd slipped out to look up a recipe for something called Brunswick stew."

"I don't know what to say, Mrs. Goodge."

"Don't say anything, I'm ashamed enough as it is and I need to get this off my chest." She glared at the cookbook. "Much as I'd like to blame this book, it's my own fault. I've been so het up with reading these recipes and dreamin' about trying this, that, and the other, that I've neglected my real duty. Good, plain English cooking is what I do and I shouldn't have let my head get turned."

"Mrs. Goodge, you're being far too hard on yourself! You do your fair share," Mrs. Jeffries said. "You always have."

"Not this time. I've not sent out notes to my old colleagues inviting the ones that might know something about the suspects to tea, I've not baked enough decent treats to get my kitchen sources to sit more than fifteen seconds, and when I have gotten someone in here, I was in a hurry to get them out so I could read that wretched thing. But no more. Starting tomorrow, I'm getting in the thick of it."

"Mrs. Goodge, honestly, it hasn't been that bad—"

"Yes, it has, and I'm not tattlin' on the others, but as I said, I'm not the only one that's been distracted," the cook interrupted. "I'm not the only one that's been shirking lately. Phyllis has been moonin' over that play she saw and Wiggins has his head in the clouds over that ruddy football team he likes."

"But they've both contributed."

"True, they had something useful to say this afternoon and maybe I'm bein' unfair, but I've the strongest feelin' they only went out on the hunt today because they were feelin' a bit guilty."

"But they shouldn't feel guilty, even if they did pursue their own interests." She held up her hand as the cook opened her mouth to argue. "They're under no obligation to help investigate the inspector's cases."

"True enough, but answer me this, how many cooks or housekeepers or maids or footmen have ever had the chance to do something this important? We might never be recognized for what we've done, but we've helped keep innocent people from being hung and made sure the guilty, no matter how rich or powerful they might be, weren't above the law. For the first time in my life, I did something other than just struggle to survive or worry about keeping a roof over my head. When you get to be my age, there aren't many Christmas dinners left to cook, so you start taking stock of your life and how you've lived it. When my time comes, I can go with no regrets because my being here made a difference. *You* made it possible for me to do something extraordinary, something that no one can ever take away from me. I served the cause of justice and I did my bit to make the world a better place." She paused and took a breath. "Maybe the others aren't obligated to help, but I am."

Deeply touched, Mrs. Jeffries felt her eyes fill with tears. "No one has ever said anything that nice to me before," she murmured.

"Yes, well, sometimes we need to speak what's in our

hearts." Mrs. Goodge sniffled, glanced away, and then took a quick drink from her cup. "Now that we've got that settled, let's get on with this."

Mrs. Jeffries wasn't sure what she meant, but she didn't want to spoil the moment by asking what might be considered a stupid question. "Uh, yes, let's."

"Why do you think we've so few real facts in this case?"

"As you said, some of us have been distracted."

"Yes, and that's made us accept pure poppycock as if it's the gospel." She held up her hand and spread her fingers. "First, we should have sorted out everyone's silly alibis. That Mrs. Downing, she claimed to be on Regent Street shopping for linens for a Boxing Day dinner, but have we confirmed that with any of her servants? We bloomin' well have not." She ticked off that finger. "And secondly, that Mrs. Flurry, she said she'd not seen Edison since the previous Friday, but did we ask anyone about that?"

"Who could we have asked?"

"For her, considering the number of people who know gossip about the woman, any number of people. Who do we usually ask when we're checking on someone's whereabouts? Shop clerks, street lads, and neighbors." She ticked off her second finger. "And those Merry Gentlemen, they all claimed to be out shopping for Christmas." She snorted derisively. "Not bloomin' likely. Men of that class hate shopping unless it's for themselves. They'd have had their wives or secretaries or clerks out fetching the bits and pieces they were buying as presents. But we didn't bother to find out, did we? But that's going to change. I'm going to be sending out notes to every old colleague I have in London, I'm going to bake enough treats to feed an army, and I'm going to make sure they all sit here long enough so that

I can find out what we need to know for you to solve this case."

Mrs. Jeffries said nothing for a moment. "What about Phyllis and Wiggins? Should I talk to them?"

"Oh no." Mrs. Goodge grinned. "I've got a much better idea. Let's have another cup of tea and I'll tell you all about it."

The two women talked for another hour and by the time Mrs. Jeffries went up to bed, she was feeling much better about the prospect of solving this case by Christmas.

She was the first one up the next morning. She'd lighted the cooker when she heard Mrs. Goodge shuffle into the room. Samson, mewing piteously for food, was right on her heels.

The cook ignored the cat and headed for the sideboard. "I've written to three of my old colleagues and if I get the letters mailed by the first post, I might have one of them around for tea." She pulled the tea tin off the top shelf.

Mrs. Jeffries grabbed the kettle and headed for the sink as Mrs. Goodge spoke, and suddenly she felt a familiar tug at the back of her mind. She stopped dead in her tracks and stood in the middle of the floor.

"What is it, why are you just standing there? What's wrong?" Mrs. Goodge looked at her, her expression worried. "Are you havin' a fit? Should I get the inspector?"

"No, no, I'm fine." She laughed self-consciously and continued to the sink. "But something you said just now nudged me, you know, in the back of my mind and I was trying to figure out what it was."

"Well, if it's any help, I'll repeat myself." She opened the tin and measured the tea into the pot. "I've written to three of my old colleagues inviting them to tea. I picked the ones that I think might be the most useful. They all live in London and if I'm very lucky and Phyllis gets these letters in the first post, one of them might be around this afternoon."

Mrs. Jeffries gave a negative shake of her head. "It's no use. I just hate it when that happens. Something pokes the back of my mind and then, poof, it's gone in the blink of an eye." She finished filling the kettle and brought it back to the cooker.

"If you ask me, it's a good sign; it shows your mind is working on the problem," Mrs. Goodge said. Samson meowed again and she got his food from out of the wet larder. She took his food to the sink, filled his bowl with scraps, and put it on the floor just as they heard a faint knock on the back door.

"That'll be Constable Barnes," Mrs. Jeffries said. "I'll let him in."

Betsy arrived with the baby just as Constable Barnes sat down with Mrs. Jeffries and Mrs. Goodge. She took Amanda out of her pram and started toward the table, but the cook waved her back. "Take my darling upstairs to see her godfather. I'll have my chance to cuddle her during our meeting. You just make sure I get her on my lap before Luty gets here."

"You will, I promise." Betsy laughed and Amanda waved her chubby fists in the air as they disappeared up the staircase.

The three of them had so much to share, the meeting went on longer than usual, but luckily, the inspector so enjoyed his time with his goddaughter that he either didn't notice or didn't care that his constable was a good fifteen minutes later than usual.

But once the two men had gone, the women got the kitchen tidied up and made a pot of fresh tea for the morning meeting. When they were all assembled, Mrs. Jeffries waited till everyone was in their usual seats before she started speaking. "We've a lot of territory to cover this morning, so I'll get right to it." She glanced at Hatchet. "I told Constable Barnes about your source seeing Martin Bagshot at the Uxbridge Road Station. He's going to have another chat with him about where he really was at the time of the murder."

"It'll be interesting to hear what Bagshot has to say for himself." Hatchet grinned.

Luty snorted faintly. Her nose was out of joint because Amanda was sitting on the cook's lap and Mrs. Goodge didn't seem inclined to share. "I hope you told him what my source said."

"I most certainly did," Mrs. Jeffries replied. "I passed along everything we know thus far and he returned the favor. His information, coupled with what I learned from the inspector, should give us plenty of avenues for investigation." She repeated what she'd heard from Witherspoon and then nodded for Mrs. Goodge to continue the narrative.

"Constable Barnes had plenty to say as well," the cook said smoothly. She gave them a few details that the inspector had forgotten to mention when he and Mrs. Jeffries were chatting over their sherry the previous evening. "But the exciting bit he told us was that he found two of the people who organized the caroling group. Neither of them reported seein' anyone hanging about at Edison's house, but he's got the names of the rest of the bunch and he's goin' to be sending Constable Griffiths to question all of them. So there's a good chance that if someone saw the killer, we'll know it within the next day or so."

"Good, then maybe we'll be able to 'ave us a nice Christmas," Wiggins muttered. He glanced at the clock. Today was the football match.

"Let's hope so," Mrs. Jeffries said cheerfully. She looked at Luty. "You're probably bored with bankers, but as you found out Bagshot is not only broke but in desperate financial trouble, do you think you can find out about the rest of the Merry Gentlemen?"

"I think so. I've got a few sources I ain't tapped yet," Luty said. "You want me to find out about this Madeleine Flurry and Cecily Downing as well? Or should I just concentrate on anyone involved in the Granger mess?"

"Find out as much as you can about all of them and anyone else you hear of who might have lost a substantial sum because of the bankruptcy." She looked at Hatchet. "And if you're free today, I'd like you to undertake a task as well."

"Of course, Mrs. Jeffries, what is it?"

"You have some very influential friends, people who know everything about the London social structure." She paused, not certain of how to phrase what she needed. "What I want you to do is hard to put into words, but we need to understand the place that everyone involved occupies in society and, more importantly, who wants to move up and who is in danger of moving down."

"I'll do my best." He looked puzzled by her request. "But I may not be able to learn much about all the actors in our drama."

"Yes, I understand that." Mrs. Jeffries was aware that Hatchet wasn't the only one staring at her with a confused expression on their face; the others didn't understand what she wanted, either. Well, truth be told, neither did she. But since this morning, she'd had this nagging feeling that she ought to look deeper.

She smiled at Smythe. "I've a task for you as well. Can you use your sources to get us information on this Gedigan person, the one Yancy Kimball apparently owes a gambling debt?"

"You're a mind reader, Mrs. J—that's exactly what I was goin' to do today." Smythe chuckled. He'd already planned on seeing Blimpey this morning and Groggins knew every gambler in London. "I was also figurin' on findin' out exactly how long Kimball's been in town. Gedigan sounds like a pro and they don't let people they don't know gamble without seein' their money."

"So Kimball must 'ave been 'ere long enough for Gedigan to trust him," Wiggins said eagerly.

Mrs. Jeffries nodded approvingly at Smythe and then flicked her gaze to Betsy. "And there's something I want you to do as well. Remember our conversation this morning? Well, I want you to make contact with Madeleine Flurry and see if you can get her talking." She'd waylaid Betsy before the meeting started, to pass along an idea that had occurred to her in the wee hours of the night.

"But what about the baby?" Phyllis interjected. "What are you goin' to do with the little one while you're out on the hunt?"

"She'll come with me." Betsy grinned. "As a matter of fact, she might be what loosens Mrs. Flurry's tongue."

Mrs. Goodge suddenly shoved back in her chair and got to her feet. "Speaking of our darling, I think I've hogged her enough." She moved around the table and handed the baby to Luty.

"Why, thank you." Luty cuddled the child close, grinning broadly as Amanda giggled.

"Ruth, I've a task for you as well and it might not be easy."

"Do tell, I love a challenge," Ruth said.

"You had a friend who made the comment that Edison's, uh, paramours were often married women, right?"

"But she's left town," Ruth reminded her.

"But isn't there someone else you can ask?" Mrs. Jeffries persisted. "Someone who would know whether or not Cecily Downing was once romantically involved with Orlando Edison?"

Ruth thought for a moment and then smiled. "Oh yes, I've several sources that would know that."

Mrs. Jeffries beamed in approval.

Mrs. Goodge got up. "I don't like to be rushin' you all, but I've got several sources droppin' by this morning and I want to get my sweet buns baked."

"That's fine, Mrs. Goodge, I think we're done." Mrs. Jeffries rose from the table, as did everyone else except for Wiggins and Phyllis.

Wiggins looked a bit put out. "Is there anythin' special you want me to suss out? You've given everyone else a special job."

"And you've not given me one, either." Phyllis crossed her arms over her chest.

By this time, Betsy had tucked Amanda into her pram and the others had all grabbed their coats, mufflers, hats, and gloves. Mrs. Jeffries waited till she heard them trooping down the hall to the back door before she spoke. "I'm sorry, I didn't mean to offend either of you."

"I'm not offended," Wiggins said quickly. "I'm just curious as to why you've left me—er, us—out."

Mrs. Jeffries flicked a quick, covert glance at the cook, who grinned broadly before turning and yanking her biggest bowl out from under her worktable.

"Frankly, the reason I didn't give either of you a task is very simple." She smiled sweetly. "Both of you seem to have

been very distracted and I assumed that you each had something important going on in your own lives."

Phyllis' jaw dropped. "Distracted? But I found out ever
so much from Enid Carter yesterday and, at other times, I've
tried my best to find things out, but sometimes you just
can't."

Behind her Mrs. Goodge snorted. "Especially if instead
of gettin' out on the hunt, you spend your time hangin'
about the Gaiety Theater and moonin' over a silly play."

Phyllis gasped.

"Maybe she's been playin' about, but I've done my bit,"
Wiggins charged.

"That's not true," Phyllis cried. "You've spent more time
worrying about that silly football game you might miss this
afternoon than doin' your share for the case. I'll admit I've
gone back to the theater a time or two, but I've at least
tried."

"It's not a silly football game," he argued. "It's important
to me. I don't do much for myself and you've no right to
make me feel like I'm lettin' everyone down."

"No one is letting anyone down," Mrs. Goodge yelled.
"And both of you have a right to enjoy your own interests.
I'm no better than either of you. Since I got this new cook-
book, I've not done right by this case, either."

The room fell silent and for a brief moment, Mrs. Jeffries
thought perhaps they'd gone too far. "Forgive me, both of
you. You have every right to spend your time as you wish
and we've no right to expect you to give up the things that
make you happy just to work on the inspector's case."

Phyllis bit her lip and her eyes filled with tears. "Are you
sayin' you don't want us working on the case?"

"No, of course not. I'm saying you have every right to
live your life as you please—"

"Then I want to work on the case," Phyllis interrupted. She swiped at her cheeks and lifted her chin. "Mrs. Goodge is right, I let that silly play turn my head. But I want to stay on the case. Nothing in my whole life has ever made me feel as proud as helping to catch killers." She stood up. "So if it's all the same to you, I'm goin' to get out there now and find out as much as I can."

"Thank you, Phyllis." Mrs. Jeffries was relieved. She would never have gone along with the cook's idea if she'd known it might make Phyllis cry. "But you must believe me, I didn't bring this up to make you feel badly, I simply wanted to know if you wanted to help with this one."

"You can count on me," she declared.

"And you can count on me as well." Wiggins got up, grinned broadly, and shrugged. "I'll admit, I love football, but this is more important. Come on, Phyllis, grab your coat and hat. I'll walk you to the corner."

As soon as they'd gone, Mrs. Goodge looked at Mrs. Jeffries. "I told you it would work."

"And you were right, but honestly, when Phyllis started to tear up I felt lower than a snake."

"Don't be silly, young people need a bit of guilt now and then."

Witherspoon paused at the top of the fourth-floor landing to catch his breath. He and Constable Barnes were at the Larchmont Hotel, which, unlike the Great Western around the corner, didn't have a lift.

"Let's hope Mr. Kimball is in his room," the inspector said as he started down the corridor. He glanced at Barnes and shook his head in admiration. "You do have a very extensive network of informants, Constable. Despite all my years on the force, I was never very good at that sort of thing."

"You didn't walk the beat as many years as I did, sir." Barnes looked at the room numbers as they passed the first door. As planned, he'd told the inspector that one of his sources had tipped him that Kimball was being hounded by debt collectors over his gambling. "Here it is, sir, number 304." He rapped sharply on the door.

"Come back later." Kimball sounded half-asleep.

"Open up, Mr. Kimball, it's the police," Barnes called.

They heard a scuffling sound and then the door opened. Yancy Kimball, his hair disheveled and his eyes bloodshot, peered out at them. "What do you want? I've told you everything I know."

"We're sorry to disturb you," Witherspoon said politely. "But we do have some questions we must ask."

"You can either let us into your room or accompany us to the station," Barnes added.

Kimball sighed irritably, stepped back, and waved them inside. "Make yourselves comfortable," he said sarcastically as they stepped over the threshold. He was dressed in a pair of trousers, an undershirt, and a pair of socks with a giant hole in the big toe of the right foot.

The bed was unmade, dirty clothes were scattered over the floor, and on the table by the window was an open bottle of whiskey, a glass, and a half-eaten Cornish pastie. A pair of boots was on one of the two chairs and a stack of newspapers on the other one. Kimball grabbed the boots in one hand and scooped up the newspapers with the other. He dumped them on the foot of the bed and flopped down on the mattress. "There, I've made you a place to sit."

They sat down and Constable Barnes whipped out his

notebook. He pulled out his pencil and then looked at Witherspoon.

"Mr. Kimball, we'll be as brief as possible, but we do have to ask you more questions," Witherspoon said.

"Go ahead." Kimball rubbed his forehead. "But make it quick. I've a killer of a headache."

"On the day your cousin was killed, you said, you didn't leave here until half past seven that night. Is that correct?"

"That's right. We planned on meeting for dinner at eight. It only takes half an hour to get to Barnaby's from here."

"Then why, sir, do several staff members recall seeing you leave here at half past four?" Barnes said. They'd stopped and interviewed some of the hotel staff before coming to Kimball's room.

"I don't know who you spoke to," Kimball snapped, "but they're mistaken. I was here taking a nap until after six."

"Mr. Kimball," Witherspoon said patiently, "the desk clerk on duty that afternoon saw you leave at four thirty and the housekeeper brought fresh linens up to your room at five o'clock. You weren't here. So where were you?"

"I went for a walk."

"Why didn't you tell us that originally?" the constable pressed.

"Because my cousin had his head bashed in and I was afraid you'd think I had something to do with it," he snapped. "For God's sake, I was scared, can't you understand that?"

"Why would we think you'd want to hurt your cousin?" Witherspoon asked. "According to your previous statement, you wouldn't have even seen your cousin if you'd not run into him outside Thomas Cook's."

"That wasn't true." He sighed. "I saw Edison as soon as I arrived here."

"Which was when exactly?" Barnes asked.

"November fifteenth." Kimball sighed again. "I was hoping he'd ask me to stay at his house, but he didn't, so I asked him for a loan to put myself up here. When I found out he'd been murdered, it put the fear of God in me."

"Why?" Witherspoon shifted on the hard chair.

"Why? Are you daft? I'm his heir, Inspector, the one who'll inherit his worldly goods, the one who benefits from his death."

"How did you know you were his heir? Had he told you that?" the inspector asked.

"He didn't have to. He was a young man so I doubt he had a will, and I'm his only living relative so I expect it all comes to me."

"It doesn't." Witherspoon smiled kindly. "But that's beside the point. Where exactly did you walk on the evening he was murdered?"

Kimball's jaw dropped in shock. For a moment, he said nothing, he merely stared at the floor. Finally, he looked at the inspector. "What did you just say?"

"I asked where you were walking when your cousin was murdered?"

"No, before that. You said I don't inherit?" Kimball's face was whiter than the bedsheets.

"That's correct," Barnes said. "You're getting part of his estate, but the bulk of it is going to someone else. I expect Mr. Edison's solicitor will be contacting you shortly. We've given him the name of your hotel. Now, please answer the inspector's question. Where were you walking?"

"Oh, my God, this is a calamity." He buried his face in his hands. "What am I going to do? They'll kill me now."

"You mean the gamblers that you owe money to, is that who will kill you?" Barnes said conversationally.

Kimball looked up. "You know about this? You know that I owe them money?"

"We have informants, sir," Barnes said. "And we know you're deeply in debt and were probably counting on your cousin's estate to save your neck."

"But I didn't kill Orlando to get my debts paid," he cried. "He was my family. I wouldn't do such a thing."

"Yet you must admit that it's a powerful motive," Witherspoon said. "If you only arrived here in mid-November, how could you get in debt so quickly?"

"It doesn't take long, Inspector. Besides, I've been here before and I knew exactly where to go. But Lady Luck hasn't smiled on me lately and, within two weeks, I was up to my neck and dodging Gedigan's thugs." Kimball stopped.

"You told us originally you met your cousin outside Cook's because you'd just booked passage to New York—" Witherspoon began.

Kimball interrupted. "I didn't have the money to leave town. The day I ran into Orlando I'd gone to a jeweler's and sold a gold ring so I could pay my hotel bill. I invited Orlando to dinner to ask him for help."

"He'd already given you money," Barnes pointed out. "Was he such a generous soul that he'd keep funding you?"

Kimball glared at the constable. "I was his only family."

"And you were being hounded by thugs. From what we've learned of Edison, he was a decent man, but he wasn't a fool, and giving a habitual gambler more money is like pouring cash down a rat hole."

"I wasn't asking for money," Kimball snapped. "I wanted a ticket to New York and when he said he was sailing there himself, I was sure I could talk him into helping me. But when he didn't show that night, I panicked. That's why I went to his house. So you see, Inspector, the last person to want him dead would be me. I needed him alive."

"Not if you were expecting to inherit," Witherspoon said softly. "And you still haven't told us where you were when he was killed."

CHAPTER 8

Betsy wheeled Amanda's pram around the corner and onto the high street. "That's 'er," the street lad guiding her said, pointing at a tall woman swathed in a heavy gray cloak going into the greengrocer's at the end of the street.

"You're sure that's Mrs. Flurry." She eyed the lad skeptically. As she hadn't known what Madeleine Flurry looked like, when she'd reached the woman's neighborhood, she'd procured the services of a local street boy, one of many poor children who hung about the high streets hoping to earn a few coins running errands or carrying shopping baskets.

The boy wore a filthy black cap and a brown coat that was two sizes too big, and he had the look of one who'd not had a decent meal in days. Betsy fully intended to pay him more than they'd agreed, but she wanted to be sure he was telling the truth. "'Course I'm sure." He crossed his arms over his chest. "I've done for her lots of times. She lives on Gopler Grove in Shepherd's Bush."

"Done what for her?" Betsy asked. Now that she had the woman in her sights she'd not lose her, and the lad might have some valuable information.

"What do ya think? I've carried her packages home from shoppin', taken notes to a big house over on Holland Road, and fetched the evening papers, that sort of thing. She's a nice lady."

Betsy kept her attention on the greengrocer's. "When was the last time you took a note to the house on Holland Road?"

He didn't reply and she flicked a quick glance his way. He looked to be deep in thought. "It were last Monday," he finally said. "She give me a note for the master of the house and I give it to the housekeeper."

Two days before the murder, Betsy thought. She dug a handful of coins from her pocket and handed them to the boy. "Here, make sure you buy some decent food with this."

His eyes widened as he saw she'd given him ten shillings, ten times more than they'd agreed. "Thank you, ma'am, thank you." He grinned broadly. "Mum will be so happy. This means we might be able to have a proper Christmas dinner. If you need me again, ma'am, I work this street every day."

She bit her tongue to keep from telling him he ought to be in school instead of out working but she knew all too well the plight of the poor and that they had to do whatever it took to survive. He scampered off and she glanced down at her sleeping baby, bundled in thick, warm blankets and riding in an expensive pram. She thanked God every day that she and Smythe would never need worry about their baby starving and she heartily wished for a world where no child went hungry. A blast of cold wind whipped past, scattering dead leaves along the pavement and jerking her out of her reverie.

Betsy wheeled the pram toward the greengrocer's shop and went inside. There was only one clerk and he was serving Madeleine Flurry. She stood at the edge of the vegetable bins watching as he dumped potatoes onto a newspaper spread beneath a hanging scale.

Betsy shoved the pram to her left and edged up to her quarry. Without being obvious, she glanced at Mrs. Flurry's midsection, but the woman's cloak was closed and she was holding her shopping basket in front of her.

"Will there be anything else, ma'am?" the young man asked.

"Nothing, thank you." Mrs. Flurry put the basket on the counter while the clerk wrapped her potatoes and took out a small black change purse from the inside of her cloak. She unsnapped the top, took out her money, and handed it across the counter.

Betsy wanted to scream in frustration as the woman finished her business and started for the door. There was nothing for it but to get out of the greengrocer's as quickly as possible and follow the woman in the hopes that her cloak would blow open and that she'd put that stupid wicker basket down.

"May I help you, ma'am?" The clerk smiled at Betsy.

"A pound of carrots, please." She looked toward the door, determined to see which way Mrs. Flurry turned when she left, but the woman had stopped and was staring at Amanda's pram.

Betsy put a friendly smile on her face just as Madeleine Flurry glanced her way. "Your baby is beautiful," she said.

"Thank you. You're very kind." Betsy flicked a quick

look at the clerk and saw that he was almost finished wrapping her carrots. Good, she wanted to be ready to pursue her quarry if need be.

"Do you mind if I ask where you got your pram?" She lowered her shopping basket to her side and leaned to one side as she studied the brass joints holding the frame together. As she moved, her cloak opened, exposing her dress.

Betsy smiled widely. "Hitching's Baby Store on Oxford Street."

"It's lovely. How old is the little one?"

"Just over a year," Betsy said. Amanda was sleeping like an angel. "Before long, she'll be too big for the pram."

"Here's your carrots, ma'am." Betsy handed over her money, took the vegetables, and tucked them under her arm. She heard the shop door open but now she was in no hurry. She'd found out the most important thing that she needed to know and verifying the rest should be dead easy.

"The house and the furnishings have got to be worth a fortune," Barnes said to Witherspoon as they waited in the drawing room of Martin Bagshot's Georgian-style Kensington home.

Witherspoon nodded as he surveyed the huge room. The walls were done in alternating strips of pale blue and lilac silk paper, heavy blue damask curtains framed the three windows overlooking the garden, and at each end of the room was a white marble fireplace. Sofas, love seats, ottomans, and wing chairs were upholstered in pale greens, blues, and lavenders. The parquet floor was covered with colorful rugs and the cabinets and tables hung with fringed runners. Paintings covered the wall and a huge Christmas tree, decorated so heavily some of the branches drooped, stood next to a grand piano in the far corner.

The double doors opened and Martin Bagshot charged inside. "What the devil do you want now?" he demanded as he stalked toward the two policemen. "I've told you everything I know and now my wife tells me you're here demanding to see me."

Barnes fixed Bagshot with a hard glare, stopping him in his tracks.

"We're sorry to disturb you," Witherspoon said. "But we've come across some new information and it's imperative we speak with you."

Bagshot looked from the constable to Witherspoon. "You'll need to be quick about it, then. I've an appointment soon and I don't intend to be late."

"Would it be more convenient coming to the station after your appointment, sir?" Barnes asked politely. He managed to keep most of the sarcasm out of his tone.

For a split second, fear flashed across Bagshot's face but then he forced himself to smile. "No, no, that won't be necessary. I'm sure this is something we can clear up quickly. Go on, ask your questions."

Witherspoon looked at Barnes and gave a barely perceptible nod. "Mr. Bagshot," Barnes said, "we'd like to know if you want to change your statement about where you were at the time of the murder?"

"I've already told you, I was shopping on Oxford Street."

He was going to try and bluff it out, Barnes thought. Stupid fool. It was as obvious as the nose on his face that if they'd come all the way here to confront him, they knew he was nowhere near Oxford Street. "Are you certain, sir?"

"Of course I'm certain." Bagshot tried to look outraged, but the fear was still there, lurking in his eyes. "I know where I was."

"Mr. Bagshot." Witherspoon sighed heavily. "We have a

witness who saw you at the Uxbridge Road Station at five forty-five that day. Now, we both know the Uxbridge Road Station isn't anywhere near Oxford Street so you could hardly have been in two places at the same time."

"I don't care who claimed to have seen me." Bagshot's voice rose higher. "They're wrong. They've mistaken me for someone else."

"Our witness knows you personally," Witherspoon explained.

Bagshot's mouth dropped open and he stared at them for a long moment before moving to the nearest chair and flopping down. "It was Bradshaw, wasn't it? I should have known that self-righteous do-gooder wouldn't keep his mouth shut."

"It's about time you showed up," Blimpey said as Smythe slipped onto the stool opposite him.

"You said it was goin' to take a couple of days to find out anything," he explained. "And it's a busy time of the year. I've been all over tryin' to find something for my Betsy."

"Get her some jewelry," Blimpey advised. "My Nell loves pearls. You'll have a Christmas drink with me."

It was a command, not a question. "I'd be honored." Smythe knew Blimpey well enough to know that he only drank with those he considered friends.

"Good." He signaled the barmaid by holding up two fingers. "While we're waiting for our grog, I'll tell you what I've found out. First of all, Yancy Kimball is a gambler and not a very good one."

Disappointed, Smythe fought to keep it from showing on his face. He didn't want to offend Blimpey but this was old news. "Yeah, we'd 'eard that already."

"He's in deep to Mickey Gedigan," Blimpey continued.

"In case you've never 'eard of him, Gedigan is a nasty thug from Stepney who isn't patient with them that owes him money. He's been known to chop things off, if you get my meanin'."

"Chop what off?"

"Not what yer thinkin'." Blimpey chuckled. "Even Gedigan's not that brutal. But in the back rooms of certain pubs there's more than one punter playin' poker without their pinky finger."

"'Ow deep is Kimball in the muck?" Smythe asked.

"My man says over five hundred quid." Blimpey paused as the barmaid arrived with a bottle of whiskey and two glasses. "Ta, Susie, just leave it, I'll pour," he told her.

"Five hundred. That's a lot of money. Why'd this Gedigan fellow let him go so deep?"

Blimpey uncorked the whiskey and poured a shot into each glass. "He usually cuts them off if they get too far into debt to 'im. 'E's a mean bastard but he's a businessman and he'd rather get what's owed him than hack off a bit of bone and gristle. My man says Gedigan kept extendin' 'im because Kimball claimed his cousin would be good for it. But he was wrong about that. Edison had made it pretty clear that he wasn't goin' to be givin' Kimball any more handouts."

"When was this?"

"Last week. Kimball nabbed him at the exchange and asked for a loan." Blimpey grinned. "Knowin' his sort as I do, Kimball went there thinkin' his cousin would be afraid he'd make a fuss in front of his colleagues, but he was wrong about that, too. Edison told him in no uncertain terms, and in a loud enough voice for my source to overhear, that enough was enough. That he'd given him all he was goin' to get. Apparently, the argument got heated and Kimball trotted out that old chestnut about blood bein' thicker than water. But Edison wasn't swayed. He just said he had other obligations and walked away."

"But the day of the murder, Kimball was supposed to 'ave dinner with Edison," Smythe mused. "That sounds like they made it up."

Blimpey snorted in derision. "I'm sure they did. Kimball's sort never stays on the bad side of a rich relative for very long. Edison was a decent fellow and I don't imagine it took too much grovelin' on Kimball's part to get back in his cousin's good graces."

"He must have thought he could talk his cousin into payin' his passage back to New York," Smythe said.

Blimpey shook his head. "Nah, he'd not be wantin' to go there."

"Why not?"

"Because Kimball 'as an even bigger gamblin' debt on those fair shores. That's why he come to England this time. He was on the run from a gambler name Fenton Clegg, an even nastier piece of work than Gedigan. If Kimball so much as sets foot in New York, he'll be cut to ribbons."

"So what was he up to, then?" Smythe drummed his fingers on the tabletop. "Why was he wantin' to meet Edison for dinner that night at Barnaby's Restaurant? Edison wasn't going to give him any more money so if he wasn't goin' to 'it him up for a ticket 'ome—"

"'E probably just wanted a free meal," Blimpey interrupted. "Kimball was skint so he was probably hungry. He'd spent what little coin 'e had knockin' back gin at the Crown and Scepter. That's a pub on Napier Road, just around the corner from Orlando Edison's house." He pushed a glass of whiskey across the table.

Smythe nodded his thanks for the drink. "Bloomin' Ada,

you are good. How did your source know to keep an eye on Kimball? Edison wasn't murdered until six that evenin'."

Blimpey threw back his head and laughed. "It wasn't me keepin' an eye on him, it was one of Gedigan's boys. But, for a bit of discretion on my part and, of course, a hefty fee, he was willin' to share what he knew. He watched Kimball drinkin' at the pub until almost six o'clock, but then he 'ad to answer nature's call and when he got back, Kimball had scarpered."

Smythe nodded slowly. He was fairly sure Mrs. Jeffries didn't consider Kimball a strong suspect. But this put a whole new slant on the murder.

"That's all I've got for you now," Blimpey said. "You still want me to keep on it?"

"Yeah, see what else your sources can dig up for me."

"If we're through with business then let's 'ave a Christmas toast." He raised his glass. "Here's to good cheer, good people, and a happy Christmas for one and all."

As soon as Bagshot's door closed behind them and they were out on the street, Witherspoon said to Barnes, "How did you know that Bagshot was lying?"

Barnes couldn't say an informant had told him because he'd already used that when he'd told him about Kimball's gambling problems. So he decided to try a different tactic. "Well, sir, as I told you before we saw him, I had a feeling about the man. But I've followed your example in such matters and I've learned to trust my instincts."

"And I'm very glad that I trusted you to take the lead on questioning him," the inspector said. "Telling him we had a witness was very clever of you."

Relieved, Barnes shrugged modestly. "No, sir, I wasn't being clever, I was trusting everything I've learned from watching you. You're always saying we need to rely on our . . . uh, how do you put it, sir, uh . . ."

"Our inner voice," Witherspoon finished. "Yes, yes, that's very true and I suppose that's precisely what an instinct is. Well done, Constable, your ruse worked and of course tricked Bagshot into admitting where he really was at the time of the murder."

"Yes, he was on Holland Road gaping at Edison's house."

"Look, there's a hansom." Witherspoon pointed at a cab dropping off a fare farther down the road. He rushed to the curb and waved his arms until he caught the driver's attention. "I know Downing's house isn't far, but it's too cold to walk."

Barnes waited till they were in the vehicle before he said, "Did you believe Bagshot?"

"I don't know. He claims he panicked when he got to Edison's house and saw the police everywhere and the body lying across the doorstep, and that's certainly understandable, but his explanation for going there in the first place sounded very weak. He said it was to talk to Edison about the bankruptcy trial, but whether Edison testified or not wouldn't have made any difference to Bagshot's finances. By his own admission, he'd invested all of his money in the Granger Mine and now it was gone. So what was there to talk about?"

"Losing everything is a powerful motive for murder." Barnes looked out the window as the cab swung around the corner to the crowded high street.

"But he was very clear that though his money was gone, his wife still had substantial holdings of her own. The house and all its furnishings belong to her, and he implied there was plenty of money from that source."

"And I imagine her family was clever enough to make

sure he can't get his hands on anything they don't want him to." The constable turned to Witherspoon. "It's not like the old days, sir. Now women with property usually control it themselves."

He nodded in agreement. "True. But tell me, Constable, did you believe Bagshot? Do you think he just went there to talk?"

"I'm like you, sir, I don't know. All I do know is that once you catch someone in a lie, it gets harder to believe anything else they tell you."

"This is ever so nice of you." Kitty Long smiled shyly at Wiggins as he came back from the counter with their tea. "It was just an accident; you didn't hurt me."

Wiggins had gone directly to Edison's house after leaving their morning meeting. He'd kept a sharp eye out for constables who might know him as he'd meandered up and down the road, waiting for a servant to emerge. He'd known that, sooner or later, someone would appear. Orlando Edison may have been a good master, but he was dead and Wiggins knew that meant household discipline was relaxed or even nonexistent. He'd been proved right. Within twenty minutes, Kitty Long had stepped out of the servants' door and trotted off toward the high street. She wasn't carrying letters or a shopping basket and he'd hoped that meant she wasn't running a household errand but had slipped out on her own. He'd been proved right about that as well.

He'd let her get ahead of him and then pulled one of his old tricks. Naturally, that had led to his offer to buy her a cup of tea. Now he had to decide whether to pretend to be a reporter, a private inquiry agent, or someone looking for a position. But he had to be careful as well; this was his local neighborhood and, from the information they'd already learned, he knew she would be around the area until the end of March.

"You're bein' kind, miss. I bumped into you so hard I almost knocked you over. I feel ever so bad." He put the cups down on the small, rickety table, pulled out his chair, and sat down.

They were in a workingmen's café off the high street. He'd picked it carefully as it was close enough to Edison's house so she'd feel comfortable but far enough away so that someone he knew wouldn't recognize him and come barging in asking questions about the inspector or the case.

"My name is Albert Jones, what's yours?"

"Kitty Long."

Wiggins decided to take the bull by the horns. "I noticed you came out of Orlando Edison's house. Is that where you work?"

She drew back and stared at him warily. "How do you know whose house it is?"

"It's my job to know such things," he said softly. He had to tread carefully here; his experience with the chambermaid at the Larchmont had made it clear that not everyone was easily fooled. "I work for a newspaper and my guv sent me round to find out what I could about poor Mr. Edison."

"Is that why you bumped into me?" she demanded.

"No, I'm just clumsy. I'll admit I was tryin' to catch up to you, but the actual bump was an accident and I really did feel bad about it. My mum said that I'm like a bull in a china shop."

"I'd better go." She pushed back her chair and started to get up.

"Please, no, at least finish your tea," he pleaded. "Honestly, I'm just wantin' to ask a few questions about Mr. Edison's friends and acquaintances."

She sat back down and picked up her cup. "Alright, but you've got to tell me something. What paper do you work for?"

"The *Evening Sentinel*," he replied, naming the first one that flew into his head. "But I don't write the articles or anything, I just give my notes to my guv and he does all the rest."

"I've never heard of it," she said. "But I'll talk to you. Mind you, I'm not going to say anything nasty about Mr. Edison. He was a good man and it's a crying shame that someone killed him."

"That's what I've 'eard as well," he said. "I've also 'eard that he had three or four visitors the day he died." This was patently untrue, but Wiggins had learned that the best way to loosen a tongue was to pretend to know more than you really did. People loved to correct your ignorance.

"You've heard wrong. He had one visitor that day—well, two if you count Mr. Dempsey, but he weren't really visiting, he was just dropping off the theater tickets that Mr. Edison had ordered for us. The only other person who was there that day was Mr. Ralston and he weren't there very long. Mind you, he was there long enough to be a nuisance."

"What did he do?" Wiggins asked.

"Oh, it sounds silly, but Mary and I were in the downstairs hall looking at our tickets and chatting because we were so excited about going out that night. Mr. Edison had come downstairs with Mr. Dempsey and handed them out himself. Then he'd gone back up to his study, where Mr. Ralston was waiting for him. All of a sudden Mr. Ralston appears and demands a headache powder. Guests aren't supposed to do that, just show up belowstairs like that, they're supposed to tell Mr. Edison if they need something and then he can ring for one of us. But instead of doing it proper like, he come down himself and asked for his bloom-ing headache powder."

"That doesn't sound very considerate." Wiggins hoped this line of inquiry was going somewhere, but he now had his doubts.

"It blooming well wasn't," she exclaimed. "I had to go all the way up to the third floor of the house where Mrs. Clar-ridge was airing out one of the guest bedrooms. Mary went to the kitchen to get him some water. Mrs. Clarridge got me the powder and I went back downstairs. Mary had just come back from the kitchen with a glass of water and a spoon, you know, for mixing the powder with the water. We gave him the powder and then waited while he took it."

Wiggins nodded as if this were the most interesting piece of news he'd had all day. He had the feeling that he'd handled this badly. Maybe he ought to try a different tactic. "Did any-thing else happen that day, anything out of the ordinary?"

"Not really. It was a day like any other."

"Oh, come on, Miss Kitty, a smart girl like you must 'ave noticed something. Come on, do us a favor. If I go back to my guv with just this, he'll have my guts for garters."

"There's nothing else to tell," she insisted, but she smiled as she spoke. "Except for getting our tickets and going out that night, it was an ordinary day like any other."

"Did Mr. Edison do anything different?" He wasn't going to give up.

"He did what he always did if he was home. In the morn-ing he did his business letters and I took them to the post just before lunch. Afterwards, he went back to his study to write another letter but instead of giving it to me to take to the post, he must have taken it himself." She paused, her face frowning in confusion. "But that doesn't seem possible. He didn't leave the house that afternoon."

"Maybe he gave it to the housekeeper . . ."

"I supposed he could have. But she doesn't like to go out in the cold. But I know he gave it to someone," she insisted. "The letter was important, because he said as much when he went into the study after lunch. I heard him tell Mrs. Clarridge that he'd need me to take it to the postbox as soon as he was finished."

Phyllis came out of the railway station at Clapton and looked down at the address written on the slip of paper in her hand. She didn't know if her instincts were right or if she was on a fool's errand. But time was getting on and she had to get moving if she was going to make it back to London for their afternoon meeting. It had taken twenty minutes to convince Enid Carter to give her Laura's address and then another hour and a half to get here. She spotted a policeman at the corner and hoped he'd be able to point her in the right direction. She didn't have time to wander around Clapton looking for Beech Lane.

Ten minutes later, she gathered her courage and went up the short path to the front door of small, faded redbrick terrace house at number 15 Beech Lane. She banged the knocker and waited.

The door was opened by a gray-haired, gaunt-looking woman wearing an apron and holding a butcher knife. "Yes, what do you want?"

"Does Miss Laura Hemmings live here and, if so, may I speak with her? It's very important."

"She lives here. I'm her stepmother." The woman raked her with a skeptical glance. "What do you want to see her about? Who are you?"

Phyllis straightened her spine and looked the woman directly in the eye. "My name is Millie Barret," she said, using the same alias she'd given Enid Carter, "and I work for a private inquiry agency." They stared at one another for a few moments and then the woman shrugged and opened the door wider. "I've never heard of a woman doing such work, but come inside."

"Thank you, ma'am." Phyllis nodded respectfully as she stepped inside. The entrance was a small space with a faded blue rug lying just inside the door and set of wooden pegs holding coats and jackets on the wall. Directly ahead was a steep, narrow staircase, and a hall on the right led to the interior of the house.

"Laura's in here." The woman went to the first door on the corridor and stuck her head into the room. "There's a woman here to see you. She claims to be a private inquiry agent."

"No, ma'am," Phyllis said quickly. "I'm not a real agent, I just do a bit of work for them."

The woman ignored her and continued down the hall. Phyllis took a deep breath and pushed open the door. A woman with red hair and wearing a dark blue housemaid's dress sat in the chair by the front window. She was sewing the top of a white pillowcase that was spread across her lap. A small wicker case with the lid opened was on the sofa next to her. It was half-filled with what looked like folded linens. She regarded Phyllis curiously. "I'm Laura Hemmings. Who are you?"

"I'm Millie Barret. I got your name and address from Enid Carter."

"Do you really work for a private inquiry agency?" She cocked her head to one side and studied Phyllis from head to toe.

"I do," she lied. "And I'm hoping you can help me. I need some information about Paul Ralston."

"What about him?" She started sewing again. "He's not a nice man. He sacked me when I tried to give my notice so I had to come home." She shoved the needle through the fabric so it was clearly visible and draped the pillowcase over the wicker box. She pointed toward the back of the house. "My stepmother hasn't welcomed me with open arms but as I'm getting married in January, she'll just have to put up with my being here."

"Why did he sack you?"

"Why do you think? He was angry I was goin' and he didn't want to pay my wages." Her mouth flattened into a thin, angry line. "He's as cheap as they come and I can't say that I'm sorry to be gone from that miserable house. But why do you care about Ralston sacking me? What's it got to do with a private inquiry agency?"

Mrs. Goodge's source left the kitchen only ten minutes before the others began returning for their afternoon meeting. But despite having to hurry and make the tea, she was in good spirits. She'd not heard from any of her three colleagues yet, but she had faith that she would and she had had a bit of luck today. It was only a tidbit of gossip, but she'd worked hard to get it.

She put a plate of brown bread and butter next to the scones that were left and waited for the kettle to boil.

Betsy and the baby were the first to arrive, quickly followed by Luty, who commandeered Amanda and plopped her on her lap while Mrs. Goodge and Mrs. Jeffries huddled with Betsy at the foot of the stairs. Hatchet, Smythe, Wiggins, and Ruth came in within minutes of one another and took their usual spots around the table.

Mrs. Jeffries glanced toward the back door. "Phyllis is late." She knew it was ridiculous to be worried about the girl—she was sensible and perfectly capable of taking care of herself—yet nonetheless, she was concerned. Perhaps she and Mrs. Goodge had overplayed their hand. Perhaps Phyllis had gone off and done something foolish simply to prove she wasn't neglecting her duty.

"She'll be here soon." Mrs. Goodge fixed Mrs. Jeffries with a hard stare. "So let's get on with the meeting. If no one objects, I'll go first as I've a lamb stew on the cooker and a pudding in the oven and both will need close watching."

Mrs. Jeffries gave an affirmative shake of her head, indicating not only that the cook could have the floor but that she'd received and understood her message.

"I had three sources come by today. Two of them were utterly useless and didn't even know that there had been a murder in the neighborhood, but Mr. Megan shared an interesting tidbit."

"Who is Mr. Megan?"

"He's the builder that came to look at the wall in the wet larder. It's crumbling something terrible and that's not a problem now because it's winter, but come spring we'll have spoiled food if we don't get it fixed. But that's neither here nor there. What is important is that . . ." She stopped as they heard the back door opening and then footsteps pounding up the corridor.

Tearing off her hat as she moved, Phyllis raced into the kitchen. "I'm so sorry to be late. The train from Clapton was fine—it was the traffic here that was so awful." She tossed the bonnet onto the peg and unbuttoned her coat. "The high street was so crowded with shoppers, I got off the omnibus and ran the last quarter mile."

"Sit down and catch your breath." Mrs. Jeffries gave her a warm smile. "We've just started."

"You can listen while you take off your coat," the cook told her. "Now, as I was sayin', Mr. Megan's a builder and last week he was rehanging the drawing room doors at a house on Belden Square when the young lady of the house received a visit from one of her friends. The two of them went into the smaller receivin' room next door to have their chat and he couldn't help but overhear." She paused for a breath. "Now, this is the interestin' tidbit. They were chattin' about Anne Waterson's upcoming marriage to Paul Ralston and both of them were of the opinion that Ralston was a fool for marryin' into that family because Anne Waterson wasn't like her sister, she'd not be loyal to a fiancé or husband if the man didn't live up to her father's standards. One of them said that it was obvious Sir Thomas didn't like Ralston very much."

"Then why did he approve of the engagement in the first place?" Betsy asked.

Phyllis giggled and then clamped her hand over her mouth. "Sorry, but I've seen Anne Waterson and, well, there's no nice way to say this, but she's not very pretty."

"Looks ain't important to that class of people." Luty dropped a quick kiss on Amanda's head. "Money is."

"I expect he approved because he had no grounds for rejecting the man," Mrs. Goodge continued. "Ralston is well educated, rich, and he's not done anything wrong."

"What about being arrested during the Throgmorton riots?" Hatchet asked. "Surely Sir Thomas wouldn't approve of that."

"Maybe he doesn't know about it," the cook said. "We didn't until Luty told us. Anyway, let me finish so I can check on dinner. One of the girls said she'd heard that Waterson was just waiting for a good excuse to force his daughter to break the engagement." She got up, went to the cooker, and peeked in the oven. "Go on with the meetin'. I can listen while I work."

"Who would like to go next?" Mrs. Jeffries asked.

"Mine won't take long," Luty offered. "I talked to a couple of sources today and, like Mrs. Goodge's, two of mine were useless, but I hit pay dirt with the last one. Accordin' to him, Bagshot's investment in the Granger ruined him financially, but his wife is rich so he'll keep a roof over his head. Downing and Ralston will both be okay, too. Downing's finances will take a hit over the loss, but he's still got plenty of money, and Ralston is getting a big settlement in cold, hard cash when he marries Anne Waterson in February."

"Cor blimey, if all the Merry Gentlemen 'ave plenty of money, why would any of them want to kill Edison? Seems to me the one with real motive is Yancy Kimball. He thought he was goin' to inherit everything," Wiggins muttered.

"Let's not make any assumptions yet," Mrs. Jeffries advised.

"That's all I've got," Luty said.

"I'll go next," Hatchet offered. "I spent most of the day doing as Mrs. Jeffries requested, trying to understand everyone's place in the social world of London"—he glanced at the housekeeper—"and I must admit, I've had some very enlightening conversations. Several of my sources seemed to think that despite Orlando Edison's success and money, he wasn't considered acceptable in most social circles, but only in the financial world."

"Does that mean you'd do business with 'im, but not want 'im to marry your daughter?" Smythe asked.

"Correct, but several people told me they thought that Edison had very deliberately kept himself apart, that he didn't wish to incur social relationships or obligations among what most would call the upper classes."

"I heard the same thing," Ruth interjected. "Sorry, I didn't mean to speak out of turn."

"That's quite alright, I was almost finished." Hatchet inclined his head graciously. "The only other point I was going to make is that several people mentioned that the world is different now and the old social rules aren't enforced the way they once were. In previous generations, money alone would not give one entrée to the upper classes but that's changed and now Paul Ralston can marry a heredi-tary knight's daughter and both Downing and Bagshot are members of the most exclusive men's club in London. None of these things would have been possible even twenty years ago." He looked at Mrs. Jeffries. "I'm not sure if this is what you wanted me to find out."

"It was," she said quickly. In the back of her mind, an idea began to take shape but then just as quickly evaporated into thin air. "Thank you, Hatchet."

"My report won't take long," Ruth said. "As I said, I heard very much the same thing as Hatchet, namely, that Edison quite deliberately kept a social distance between himself and others unless they were someone he wanted to get to know."

"Like Mrs. Flurry or Mrs. Downing," Phyllis murmured.

"Not Cecily Downing," Ruth said. "No one I spoke with had heard even the slightest rumor that Edison had been involved with her. The only woman his name was romanti-cally linked with is Madeleine Flurry."

"But we 'eard he liked married women," Wiggins pro-tested. "And we 'eard that from more than one source."

"Mrs. Flurry was a married woman before she was a widow," Ruth pointed out. "And some of the gossip I heard was that the two of them were involved before her husband died. But that's difficult to confirm and I'm not sure it's relevant to Edison's murder. I hardly think the late Mr. Flurry rose from the grave to whack Edison on the head with a souvenir shovel. But that's not all I found out. Cecily Downing was on Regent Street at five forty-five on the day Edison was killed."

"So she couldn't have made it to Holland Road in time to kill 'im," Smythe muttered. "Not unless she sprouted wings and flew."

"Your source was sure it was her?" Mrs. Jeffries asked.

"She was," Ruth replied. "And that's it for me."

"I'll go next, then." Wiggins told them about his meeting with Kitty Long. He made sure he repeated everything she'd told him. "I know it's sort of bits we've 'eard before, but I figure knowin' more details of the poor bloke's last afternoon can't hurt."

"Indeed it doesn't," Mrs. Jeffries agreed. Again, she felt an idea try to take shape in the back of her mind but she didn't have time to grab the pesky imp and hang on to it. "Smythe, will you do the honors next?"

"My source had a lot to say about Yancy Kimball," he began. He told them everything he'd heard from Blimpey and, like Wiggins, he made sure he recalled every detail of the conversation.

"And he's the one who had a right pressin' reason to want his cousin six feet under," Wiggins added. "He's the one needin' money, and that pub he was drinkin' in is less than a five-minute walk to Edison's 'ome."

"But Martin Bagshot was seen close by, too," Phyllis reminded him. "And he lost all of his money. He's got a motive as well."

"Let's not jump to any conclusions yet," Mrs. Jeffries

said. "It's getting late and we've still to hear from Phyllis and Betsy."

"I'll go next," Betsy volunteered. She told them about the lad that often carried notes from Madeleine Flurry to Edison's house. Then she took a deep breath. This part was a bit more difficult than she'd imagined. But then she told herself to stop being a ninny. They were all adults here. "I got a very good look at Madeleine Flurry today and I'm pretty sure she's going to have a baby."

No one spoke for a long moment as they absorbed the news. Finally, Hatchet broke the silence. "How long has her husband been dead?"

"A bit too long, I'm afraid." Betsy shrugged. "He's been dead a year and she looks like she's a good seven months along."

"I don't understand any of this." Wiggins helped himself to a scone. "Every time we 'ave a meetin' it gets more and more confusin'. Why didn't the inspector notice the lady's condition? He didn't say anythin' about it."

"He wouldn't have," Betsy explained. "She's deliberately disguising the fact that she's pregnant with clothes. Her cloak is new and expensive looking but it's too big for her and I noticed she carried her shopping basket in such a way as to hide her stomach. I only spotted it because she was bent down to look at Amanda's pram and the cloak opened enough for me to get a good look."

"We'll just have to see what, if anything, this new development might mean," Mrs. Jeffries said. She glanced at Phyllis. "Alright, it's your turn now. You mentioned the train from Clapton?"

"I went there to have a word with Laura Hemmings." She lifted her chin. "She's the maid Ralston sacked when she tried to give notice." She told them about the conversation and as she spoke, her confidence returned in full. "Now, the interesting part is that when Anne Waterson came for tea, she made Ralston try on the new overcoat that was delivered. Laura said she could tell he didn't like being ordered about by his fiancée, but he had no choice. Then Miss Waterson asked him for his old overcoat so she could donate it to a charity and he said yes, that'd be fine, and even offered some other old things he didn't wear anymore. She told him she'd pick up the clothes the next morning. Later, after she'd left, Laura gave her notice and he sacked her and told her she had to go. But she's got a temper and wanted to get a bit of her own back. Before she left the house, she went through all his pockets."

"You mean she ransacked all his clothes?" Mrs. Goodge came back to the table and sat down. "What was she lookin' for?"

"She didn't go through his wardrobe, just the clothes he was donating to the charity," Phyllis explained. "He'd tossed them in a corner and she said they were all smelly and damp, but she found ten shillings in one of the jacket pockets."

"She was stealin' from 'im?" Wiggins asked.

"I think that was the reason she was checkin' his pockets," Luty said dryly. "And I can't say that I blame her."

"But she didn't just find money in his pockets," Phyllis said. "She found a letter and she took it with her. The envelope was addressed to Madeleine Flurry."

"Madeleine Flurry. Why would Paul Ralston be writing to her?" Mrs. Goodge exclaimed. "I didn't know they even knew each other."

"Had Laura opened the letter?" Mrs. Jeffries asked. "Did she know what it said?"

"She knew what it said." Phyllis took a quick sip of tea. "She was really, really upset about getting the sack. She was working on her linen chest when I saw her today and she needed her last month's wages to buy some sheets." She hesitated. "I'm not sure I should say this but I think she's goin' to do something with that letter, something that will hurt Ralston."

"Blackmail?" Mrs. Jeffries asked.

"I think so." She bit her lip. "Sayin' it out loud, it sounds silly, but when I asked her what she was going to do with the letter, she gave me this funny smile and said she had plans, big plans. Those were her exact words."

"I'd love to know what it says." Betsy glanced at Amanda and saw that she was falling asleep. "Luty, your arms are going to be tired, give the baby to Smythe."

Luty waved him off. "Don't let this white hair fool ya, I can still hold a sleepin' young'un, and I'd sure as shootin' like to know what was in that letter, too."

CHAPTER 9

"Mr. Downing, we know your argument with Mr. Edison had nothing to do with your wife," Witherspoon said. "So it will save a great deal of time and effort on both our parts if you'll simply tell me the truth."

Downing stared at the two policemen and then shoved away from the fireplace mantel he'd been leaning against. He flopped down in a green wing chair opposite where they sat on the sofa. "I suppose you've been talking with my lovely wife." His voice dripped sarcasm. "Are you married, Inspector?"

"No, I'm not. I've never had the pleasure." He stroked the soft wool of the muffler Ruth had knitted for him. The red and green scarf dangled around his neck and hung over his unbuttoned overcoat.

"Pleasure." Downing laughed cynically. "Disabuse yourself of that notion, Inspector. Marriage wasn't invented for pleasure but for profit. At least that's what my father always told me, and I'm sure it's true because I've had damned little pleasure in my own—"

"That's enough, Charles."

Witherspoon turned and saw Cecily Downing standing just inside the doorway. She was glaring at her husband and looked even less like "a foolish young woman" than at their last meeting. The gray dress she wore made her look skinny, not slender; her mouth was set in a thin, disapproving line; and her face was flushed an unbecoming shade of red.

"Enough what?" He leapt to his feet and scowled right back at her. "Enough love? Enough affection? Enough companionship? You tell me, Cecily—what have I had enough of?"

"How dare you speak to me in such a manner." She took a step toward him.

"I'll speak to you any way I damned well please. I'm the master of this house and don't you forget it."

"Master?" She laughed harshly and moved farther into the room. "You're master of nothing. You'd not even have a roof over your head if it wasn't for my family."

Alarmed at the turn the conversation had taken, Witherspoon half rose from his seat in case he had to step between the warring couple. He flicked a quick glance at Barnes and saw that the constable had put his notebook aside and was at the ready. From experience, both policemen knew that domestic disputes could turn ugly in seconds.

But Cecily Downing had seen the change in their demeanor so she stopped, unclenched her fists, and visibly brought herself under control. "Charles, have you been drinking?" she demanded.

Witherspoon wondered the same thing himself.

"Not nearly enough." Downing rushed to the fireplace and

reached behind the holly piled on the mantel. He pulled out a glass half-full of amber liquid and waved it back and forth like a flag. "I was just having a nice drink of whiskey before these kind gentlemen"—he bowed in their direction—"arrived to tell me that they knew good and well that my wife wasn't romantically involved with Orlando Edison. Of course, I could have told them that. My wife isn't romantic with anyone, least of all her husband."

"You're a disgusting drunk." She turned on her heel and stalked out, slamming the door behind her hard enough to rattle the windows.

Downing closed his eyes briefly and his shoulders slumped. "I'm sorry, Inspector, Constable. That was an ugly scene and you certainly shouldn't have been forced to see it." He went to the wing chair, flopped down, and stared morosely at his drink. "Orlando's murder, coupled with the bankruptcy trial, has everyone's nerves on edge."

"Of course, sir, we quite understand." Witherspoon gazed at him sympathetically.

"How much have you had to drink, sir?" Barnes propped his notebook back on his knee and pulled out his pencil.

Downing's apologetic expression disappeared and was replaced by an outraged scowl. "I don't think that's any of your business. There's no law against a man drinking in his own home."

Witherspoon winced inwardly. "The constable is only trying to determine if you're in a fit state to be interviewed, Mr. Downing. If you're not, we can come back at another time."

"I've had one whiskey." Downing put the glass down on the table next to the chair. "Which, I assure you, doesn't affect my reason or incapacitate me in any way."

The inspector wasn't sure he believed him, but then

again, a bit too much alcohol in the fellow might make him a tad more honest in his answers.

"In which case, we'll get this over and done with," Witherspoon said briskly. "As I was saying, we know that your argument with Orlando Edison wasn't about your wife."

He reached for the whiskey and took a quick drink. "No, it wasn't. It was about the trial. I went to see him to find out if he'd tell me what he intended to say."

Witherspoon frowned in confusion. "I don't understand. How could he possibly tell you that? The witness stand isn't a preacher's pulpit. When you're under oath, you're meant to answer questions, not make statements. So unless you knew in advance what kind of questions were going to be asked of him—"

Downing interrupted. "I'm not an idiot, Inspector, I know that. But there are ways of handling the situation and I wanted to impress upon him that he was under no obligation to answer more than he was asked."

"But surely his solicitor or barrister would have already given him those instructions," the inspector pointed out.

Downing shrugged. "Orlando was quite capable of ignoring legal advice. He often did what he pleased, whether it was wise or not. I wanted to make sure he understood that what he said in court could have far-reaching consequences for the rest of us. This was a civil matter, not a criminal court, and I wanted to impress upon him that there was nothing wrong with keeping his answers short and to the point."

"In other words, he should not volunteer anything even if it might be pertinent to the case." Barnes' voice dripped sarcasm.

"I wouldn't put it quite like that, Constable," Downing said defensively. "I wasn't asking him to prevaricate, only to mind his tongue. There were aspects to the company that we didn't think need be mentioned, private matters that had nothing to do with the company going under."

"I don't understand." Witherspoon stared at him curiously. "What private matters are you talking about?"

"Matters pertaining only to the board of directors." He took another drink, this time draining his glass. "We didn't see why we should be embarrassed and have our names and reputations disparaged during the course of a public trial. I went there to try and talk some sense into the man."

"In what way?" Witherspoon pressed.

"Come now, Inspector, as a policeman, you've testified in court a number of times. You know what I mean." His expression was knowing and sly.

Witherspoon knew all too well. He'd seen more than one criminal walk out the courthouse doors a free man because the crown had an incompetent Queen's Counsel handling the prosecution.

"Even when one is under oath," Downing continued, "one can be honest without blathering about matters that don't concern the court. Frankly, we didn't think that our annual compensation for serving on the board or how we'd been recruited to join had any bearing on the company going under. None of us—"

"You mean the Merry Gentlemen," Barnes interrupted.

"That's right." He nodded emphatically. "We weren't involved in the day-to-day running of the company nor should we be held responsible for the fact that the mine had no gold in it. All we wanted was a bit of restraint on his part. But Orlando didn't want to hear it. He said that he was done with shady dealings, that he'd tell the truth and answer everything he was asked honestly and completely." He grimaced in disgust. "I don't know what got into him.

We weren't asking him to lie, just to show a bit of discretion."

"I see," the inspector said. "Were the other Merry Gentlemen going to try and talk to him about this matter if you failed?"

"You make it sound like a terrible conspiracy, Inspector, and it wasn't that way at all."

"Look at it from our point of view, Mr. Downing," Barnes said. "You quarreled with him two days before he was killed and Martin Bagshot had the same kind of argument with him only one day before the murder."

"When I wasn't able to convince him to be reasonable, Martin said he'd try. But that's hardly a conspiracy. Besides, Martin had no better luck than I did."

Witherspoon leaned forward. "Paul Ralston visited him the afternoon he was killed—"

"Paul's visit to him wasn't planned and he didn't argue with him," Downing interrupted. "He stopped in on the spur of the moment; it was a social call."

"And the meeting the three of you had the morning after the murder, what was that really about?"

Downing shifted uneasily. "We've already told you, we wanted to see if we had a case for legal action."

"Stop wasting our time, Mr. Downing," Barnes snapped. "If you'd had grounds to bring a case of fraud against Edison you'd have done it well before the very day he was scheduled to testify. Now what was the meeting about?"

Mrs. Jeffries pulled on her gloves as she went down the front stairs. The afternoon meeting was done and evening was fast approaching, but she didn't care. All she'd do if she stayed inside would be to pace up and down the kitchen, driving Mrs. Goodge and even poor Fred to distraction.

Reaching the pavement, she turned to her right, heading for the high street and a chance to get lost in the crowds.

She took a deep breath, taking in the mingled scent of smoke and raw damp that was uniquely London. Her footsteps pounded rhythmically against the pavement as she walked. There was so much to understand, so much to try to make sense of, that she felt overwhelmed and, truth be told, a bit concerned. Laura Hemmings hadn't come right out and said she was going to blackmail Paul Ralston, but Phyllis had been sure the girl had implied that was going to be her next step. Was she worrying for nothing? Both Phyllis and Mrs. Goodge seemed to think so, but she wasn't so sure. Blackmail was a dangerous business.

She sidestepped to avoid slamming into an elderly woman who'd stopped in the middle of the pavement to open her change purse. She joined the crowd waiting to cross the road just as a brougham swept past, cutting the corner so much that everyone jumped backward to save their toes from being crushed by the back wheel.

"Watch it, you stupid git." A grizzled fellow waved his cap angrily at the back of the carriage, and there were angry mutterings from most of the others as well, but this happened all the time in the city, so everyone moved on.

Mrs. Jeffries continued on down the street. Tomorrow morning they were going to tell Barnes about Laura's theft of Ralston's letter and hopefully he'd know what, if anything, they should do. But what about now, what if that foolish girl decided to confront Ralston this evening? Wiggins and Smythe had both volunteered to go to Clapton and keep watch on her, but Phyllis said she thought Laura was too scared of Ralston's temper to confront him alone. If she followed through on her plan, she'd meet him in public.

But more importantly, what did this new development

mean? They'd had no hint that Madeleine Flurry and Ralston knew one another, let alone had a relationship. On the other hand, Ralston and Edison had done business together for at least four years, so there was a good chance that Ralston could have met her socially through Edison. Could their relationship and not the Granger bankruptcy be the motive for the murder? Had Edison flown into a jealous rage when he'd learned the woman he loved had betrayed him with another man? It was possible but there was something about that scenario that didn't ring true.

As she passed the baker's shop, a young woman ran out the door and almost collided with Mrs. Jeffries. "Beg pardon, ma'am," she called as she raced past. She wore an apron but not a coat and carried a letter in her hand.

"No harm done." Mrs. Jeffries watched the girl run to the postbox in front of the tobacconist's and pop her letter inside. Something tugged in the back of her mind again, and this time, she snatched the edge of the wretched imp before it completely disappeared. She went still and stood there for a good five minutes remembering bits and pieces about the case that had been shared at their meetings. A street lad bumped her arm, snapping her back to the here and now.

"Oy, Mrs. Jeffries, you alright? You've been standin' there like you're playin' statues." He stared at her curiously.

"Hello, David, I'm fine, I'm just thinking," she replied. His name was David Raymond and he was a local lad who helped support his family by doing odd jobs and errands. He was skinny, red haired, and wearing an oversized coat Wiggins had outgrown. She'd given him the garment in November and was glad he was making use of it. He was a sharp, intelligent boy and it pained her that he was out working instead of in school getting a decent education.

But she'd see to it that at least he was decently paid for his efforts. She pointed across the street to a hansom cab that had just dropped a fare. "Hurry, David, there's a florin in it for you if you get me that hansom cab before someone else grabs it."

Constable Griffiths was waiting for them outside of the Downing house when the inspector and Barnes emerged. "I was hopin' I'd not missed you," he explained. "The duty sergeant told me you were goin' to be talking to the Merry Gentlemen again. I went to the Bagshot house but the butler said you'd already left and, as this was the closest one, I figured you'd be here."

"Good thinking, Constable," Witherspoon said. "One of these days you'll be a fine detective."

"Thank you, sir." Griffiths grinned broadly, pleased that Witherspoon had noticed his abilities.

"What is it, Constable?" Barnes asked. Evening was turning into night and the temperature was dropping fast. He didn't want to stand about on the pavement breathing in the freezing air longer than necessary. "Has something else happened?"

"No, sir, but I'm goin' off duty and I knew you wanted a report on those other carolers. This area is on my way home so I thought I'd tell you what we found."

"Excellent, an oral report will save us some time." Witherspoon wound his scarf around his neck and looked at the two constables. "Constable Barnes, shall we try and see Paul Ralston before we call it a day? I'd like to hear what he has to say."

"So would I, sir," Barnes replied.

"Good. Constable Griffiths, let's hear your report as we walk."

They started off in the direction of the Notting Hill High Street. Griffiths took out his notebook and flipped it open. "There were eight carolers that night including Mr. Idlicote and Miss Parsons, and Constable Barnes had already spoken with them, so Constable Eldon and me tracked down five of the other six. We got lucky, they all live nearby. There's a Mr. Meecham, a Miss Hadley—"

"You don't need to give us their names," Barnes interrupted. "Just be sure and include them in the written report."

"Right, sir." He flicked a quick look at his superior and then went back to his notebook. "They all said much the same thing."

"Let me guess." Barnes sighed wearily. "No one saw or heard anything."

"That's pretty much it, sir, except that Mr. Meecham said the sixth caroler, a lad named Danny Wigan, had mentioned that he thought he saw someone at the downstairs door."

"You mean the tradesmen's entrance?" Barnes clarified.

"That's right, sir. Wigan wasn't home when we went to speak to him. His neighbor says he went to Manchester for Christmas and he won't be back until after Boxing Day."

"Let's hope we have this case solved by then." Witherspoon sighed. "But if we don't, we'll have a word with Mr. Wigan. Good work, Constable, this is very helpful."

Mrs. Jeffries climbed the stairs to John and Fiona Sutcliffe's Mayfair mansion and banged the knocker. Beneath her cloak, she rubbed her hands briskly up and down her crossed arms. It was full night now and the temperature had dropped sharply. She'd told Mrs. Goodge she was taking a walk, and she knew if she didn't get home before it got too late, the cook would have the entire household out looking for her.

She didn't want to worry them, but an idea was taking shape in her mind and before she could develop it any further, there was something she had to find out.

The door opened and Mrs. Sanger, the Sutcliffes' housekeeper, stared at her in surprise. "Mrs. Jeffries! I didn't know you were expected. Please come in, it's dreadfully cold out there."

"I'm not expected," Mrs. Jeffries explained as she stepped into the foyer. "And I do apologize for just barging in like this, but I must speak to Mr. Sutcliffe. Is he at home?"

"He and Mrs. Sutcliffe are in the drawing room." She hesitated, as if unsure of what to do next.

"I'll wait here while you announce me," Mrs. Jeffries said quickly. Generally, a family member wouldn't need to be formally announced but as Mrs. Jeffries' current relationship with her sister-in-law was still somewhat new, she didn't blame the housekeeper for being uncertain of how she ought to be treated.

Mrs. Sanger smile gratefully. "I'll be right back."

She didn't have to wait long before Fiona appeared. "Hepzibah, what a lovely surprise. Come in, come in, I've told Mrs. Sanger that from now on, she needn't announce you. You're family."

"How lovely of you to say that." Mrs. Jeffries hurried toward her and, impulsively, gave her a hug.

When they drew apart, she could see that Fiona was startled, but pleased.

"Now, tell me what brings you here tonight," Fiona demanded with mock severity, "and why it's John you want to see and not me."

Mrs. Jeffries laughed as they went into the drawing room. John Sutcliffe rose from his seat and came toward her. He bent down and kissed her on the cheek. "Hepzibah,

I can't tell you how delighted I am that it's me you came to visit and not my wife. Come and make yourself comfortable. I'll pour you a drink. Sherry, right?"

"I'd love a drink but I'm afraid I can't stay long." She sat down on an overstuffed chair. "My household doesn't know I'm here—they think I'm taking a walk."

"Thinking about the inspector's latest case, are you? We know that he's investigating the Edison murder." Fiona sank down opposite her. "Which means, if I'm not mistaken, that you're here because there's something we can do to help."

"There is, but I don't want you to think that I'm being presumptuous or—or—"

"Don't be silly," Fiona interrupted with an impatient wave of her hand. "When I came to you, you didn't turn me away. We're always glad to assist in any way we can and you know whatever you ask of us will go no further than this room. What do you need?"

"I believe I'm the one she needs," John said smoothly. He handed her a delicate crystal glass of Harvey's.

"That's correct." Mrs. Jeffries took a quick sip and gathered her thoughts. "When I was here for dinner the other evening, you sent off a note telling your broker to sell certain stocks."

"That's right, I wanted to get rid of my mining stocks."

"The ones in the Transvaal?" She waited until he nodded. "Oh dear, there's no right way to ask this, but I'm in need of somewhat of an expert opinion and, well, I know you're a very prudent investor. So may I ask you, did you sell them because your broker recommended you sell?"

He regarded her curiously. "I sold them because I think most people, myself included, leapt into mining stocks a bit too quickly. There's plenty of gold in the Transvaal, but not in every single mine."

"Can you explain that further?" Mrs. Jeffries asked.

"You've heard of the Witwatersrand Gold Rush?" He paused and when she inclined her head, he continued. "That was in 1886 but gold had been mined in the region since the 1850s. But as you know, it was the huge find of '86 that started the rush. Within a short period of time, the place was swarming with anyone who was able to swing a shovel. People were staking claims left and right and of course, very shortly, investors were buying anything they could get someone to sell. Unfortunately, the competition was so fierce that a number of mines were bought and developed without the proper amount of diligence as to whether or not there was actually enough gold to make mining profitable. It took a few years before all of this came to light, but there have been articles in the financial press detailing some of the frenzy that went on during the rush and, of course, the ramifications for investors. That's why I sold my shares."

"You found out that your shares were in mines without any gold?" She wanted to make sure she understood.

"I don't know whether there was gold in them or not, but after hanging on to the shares for months and seeing no return on my money, I decided to sell."

"Did the Granger Mine going bankrupt influence your decision?"

"Of course, but the Granger isn't the only mine to go under," he said. "There have been half a dozen others."

There was only one more question she needed to ask. "Was there ever any indication of fraud about the companies that have gone bankrupt?"

"You mean, did the investors who came together to buy

the claims and form the companies know how little gold there might be in any given mine?" He steepled his fingers together, thought for a moment, and then gave a negative shake of his head. "No, I've not heard any hints in that direction. It is more a matter of everyone being in such a hurry to grab a portion for themselves that they bought up any claim that was for sale."

"In your opinion, was there fraud connected to the Granger Mine?" she asked.

"Not that I've heard," he replied. "And some gold was actually found there. There just wasn't very much of it."

"It's about time you got here." Mrs. Goodge stood in the middle of the kitchen with her hands on her hips. "We were getting worried."

"'Ow far did you walk?" Wiggins hung his jacket back on the coat tree. "Good thing you showed up now, I was goin' to come lookin' for you."

Phyllis, who'd just started to lay the table, put the stack of plates down and gave Mrs. Jeffries a disapproving frown. "I'm glad you're back safely. I was havin' all sorts of horrid thoughts about what might have happened to you."

Mrs. Jeffries gazed at their worried faces and noted that even Fred looked annoyed with her. "I'm so sorry." She took off her cloak and hat. "But when I was out walking, I suddenly realized that there was someone who could answer a very important question so I went to Mayfair to see my brother-in-law." She paused as she heard a hansom cab pull up outside. "Oh dear, that's the inspector. Well, at least I got home before he did."

"Tell him dinner won't be ready for another half hour," Mrs. Goodge said.

Mrs. Jeffries made it to the hall as he came in the front

door. "Good evening, sir." She rushed forward and held out her hand for his hat. "How was your day? Any new developments with the case?"

He handed her his bowler. "We're making progress, I think, but frankly, it's very slow going. I think a sherry will be most welcome."

A few moments later, she handed him a glass of Harvey's and sat down opposite him.

"Thank you, Mrs. Jeffries." He took a sip and settled against the seat cushions. "I suppose I shouldn't be discouraged, we have found out some useful information. We began the day with a visit to Yancy Kimball and then went on to have a nice chat with Martin Bagshot. Both interviews were very interesting. By some very clever trickery on Constable Barnes' part, Bagshot admitted he wasn't shopping on Oxford Street when Edison was murdered and we also learned quite a bit about Kimball." He told her the details of their visit with Kimball.

"He actually admitted he thought he was Edison's sole heir," she commented when Witherspoon paused to take a sip of his sherry.

He nodded. "Oh yes and he was rather distraught when he found out the truth. Our interview with Martin Bagshot was enlightening as well," he said.

Mrs. Jeffries gradually relaxed as he reported what had happened with Bagshot. She'd been concerned about the burden they were forcing on the good constable. Barnes would never complain, but she knew that having to come up with one story after another about how he'd stumbled across the information they fed him must be tiresome. But in this case, it had definitely paid off. "Bagshot admitted he was at the Edison home?"

"Indeed he did, but as I said, he claimed that when he

saw the body and the police milling about the place, he panicked and ran. He said he was so upset that he went straight home and shut himself in his study with a bottle of brandy. But neither his wife nor any of the servants can confirm that."

"Do you believe him? After all, he did have a terrible quarrel with the victim the day before the murder."

Witherspoon shrugged. "At this point, I don't know. But to be fair, Charles Downing argued with Edison, and for all we know, Paul Ralston and he might have had words as well." He broke off and drained his glass.

"They were really angry about the Granger Mine going bankrupt," she commented. But somehow, even as she said it, she didn't think that was the reason Edison had died. Surprised by the notion that flitted into her mind, she blinked, but before she could figure out what her own inner voice was trying to tell her, the inspector continued talking.

"They were, but as professional investors, they know that investing in anything is risky." His brows drew together. "I think their anger at Edison was more than just the mine going under."

"Like what, sir?" She got up and refilled both their glasses.

"I'm not entirely certain but I do know that the three of them were concerned about what Edison might say when he took the witness stand—Charles Downing admitted that much to us. He told us the meeting they had the morning after Edison was murdered wasn't about seeing if the Merry Gentlemen had legal grounds to bring a fraud charge against the victim, which is what they originally claimed, but to determine if his testimony might damage their reputations. But before the meeting got started, they found out he was dead."

"Did he say anything else, sir?" She put his drink down next to him and took her seat.

"He said a number of things. He'd had a drink before we arrived and I believe it loosened his tongue." He recounted the interview with Downing, telling her everything, including the uncomfortable moment when Cecily Downing had called her husband a disgusting drunk. Then he recounted their meeting with Constable Griffiths and, finally, going to the Ralston home. "But Mr. Ralston had already left for a dinner party, so we'll have a word with him tomorrow."

Mrs. Jeffries opened the bottom drawer of the pine sideboard and took out the heavy mahogany chest that held the silverware. Grunting with effort, she lugged it to the table where a tin of silver polish, a heap of clean rags, and the previous day's *Times* were spread. She put it down, unlatched the brass hinges, and opened it before taking her seat. Reaching inside, she took out the top four spoons, laid them on the newspaper, and then pried the lid off the tin of polish.

She wanted to think, and doing repetitive, mindless chores helped her marshal her thoughts into some semblance of order. The ideas she had earlier were still very jumbled together and the only way she could sort them out was by looking at the problem logically. She readied the rag with some polish, picked up a spoon, and began rubbing it into the silver.

The first thing to try to understand, she told herself, was why Orlando Edison had been killed. But that was not an easy task. The information—or rather, gossip—they'd heard about the man was contradictory at best. The Merry Gentlemen had originally told the inspector they were concerned that Edison had fraudulently lured them into investing in a worthless gold mine, but the trouble with that point of view was that no one else seemed to think Edison guilty of fraud. None of Luty's sources nor her brother-in-law John had heard any such rumors. Tonight she'd found out that the Merry Gentlemen were more upset about what Edison might say about them in court than whether he'd cheated them.

She put the polishing rag to one side, got a clean one, and began to buff the spoon.

Secondly, there'd been talk that Edison liked married women and Charles Downing had told the inspector that Cecily Downing was one of Edison's flirtations. Downing had only admitted he'd been lying about his wife's alleged relationship with Edison when pressed. But why had he lied about it in the first place, that was the question. Added to the mix was Madeleine Flurry. How did she fit into the picture and who was the father of her baby, Edison or Paul Ralston?

"Are you polishing the silver, Mrs. Jeffries?"

Mrs. Jeffries turned and saw Phyllis in the doorway. She wore a heavy maroon dressing gown over her yellow flannel nightdress and a pair of black shoes.

"I couldn't sleep so I thought I might as well do something useful," she answered. "I'm sorry if I woke you up. I did try to be quiet."

"You didn't wake me. I couldn't sleep, either." Phyllis came to the table and sat down across from her. "Do you want me to help?"

"No, no, that won't be necessary. Why don't you have some warm milk? It might help you get to sleep." She could hardly order the girl back to bed, but in truth, she desperately needed this quiet time to try to sort this mess out.

"I don't think it'll work," Phyllis said. "I keep thinkin'

about Laura Hemmings. Maybe I should have insisted on her takin' that letter to the police. What if she is going to try and blackmail Paul Ralston? What if he's the killer and he tries to hurt Laura?"

Mrs. Jeffries was concerned about that as well. "You couldn't have forced her to hand the letter over to anyone, let alone the police. What's more, we don't know that a personal letter Ralston wrote to Madeleine Flurry has anything to do with Edison's murder."

"But she's expectin' a baby." Phyllis blushed a bright red. "And Edison left her most of his estate in his will. That means that . . . that . . ."

"Edison was the child's father," Mrs. Jeffries finished the statement. "We don't know that. Mrs. Flurry herself told the inspector that they were old friends. What's more, just because Ralston is horrible to his household doesn't mean he's a killer. And we don't even know for sure that Laura is going to try to blackmail Ralston. All she told you was that she had 'big plans' for the letter." She picked up a rag, dipped it in the polish, and slathered it on a second spoon.

"That's true," Phyllis muttered. "For all we know, Laura might just be plannin' on giving Ralston's love letter to Anne Waterson. That would cause him plenty of misery and I think she'd like that more than havin' a few pounds off of him." She pursed her lips. "I'm being silly and makin' a mountain out of a molehill, aren't I."

"You most certainly are not." Mrs. Jeffries reached for her buffing rag. "And you're right to be a bit anxious about the girl. Tomorrow morning, we're going to make sure that Constable Barnes is fully informed about the situation. But I'd not worry too much: You don't know that Ralston even knows Laura took his letter. When he finds it's missing, he might just think it dropped out of his coat pocket."

Phyllis relaxed a bit. "Mrs. Goodge says you often come downstairs in the middle of the night when you want to sort out the bits and pieces of a case. Is that what you're doin' tonight?"

"Yes," she replied. "And now that you're here, you can help me clarify my thoughts." Phyllis wasn't going back to her own bed anytime soon so she might as well make the best of it. She gave her a quick summary of her thinking thus far. "But I'm still no closer to figuring out the motive for the murder," Mrs. Jeffries concluded. "The murder wasn't a robbery gone bad."

"But how do we know that? One of Ruth's sources claimed Edison kept plenty of money hidden in his house. Maybe that was the motive for the murder."

"True, but if it was a robbery, why would the killer leave fifty pounds in Edison's pocket and, more to the point, why leave the body lying across the doorstep, where it was sure to be discovered? The window of time between the servants leaving the house and the discovery of the body was only ten minutes. Unless the killer knew where the money was hidden, he'd have had to search the house for it."

"And he or she couldn't have done that in ten minutes." Phyllis reached for a clean rag and began to help with the silver. "Nor would they have left the dead man lyin' out in plain sight of anyone walking down the road. But what about Yancy Kimball, let's not forget about him. He had a reason for wanting Edison dead. Two of them—one, Edison had cut off his money supply and, two, with Edison dead, he thought he was goin' to inherit everything. They were cousins, so if there was money in the Edison house, he might have known where it was. If you knew where to look, you could nip in and get back out in no time at all."

"And one of the carolers did tell Constable Griffiths that

another caroler claimed to have seen someone at the trades-men's door." She broke off, frowning. "No, it doesn't fit. There wasn't enough time."

"There was ten minutes," Phyllis pointed out.

"But there wasn't," Mrs. Jeffries insisted. "Not if you really think about it. The servants left at exactly six and Chief Inspector Barrows called the time of death at six ten. But that doesn't take into account the fact that the maid who raised the alarm had to notice Edison lying there in the doorway a good minute or so earlier. Then she had to go back into the house and explain what she'd seen. Barrows had to go next door, then examine the body to make sure it wasn't, as he put it, 'someone who'd had too much to drink' before he realized Edison was actually dead. At that point, he noted the time and blew his police whistle to summon the fixed-point constable. By my estimate, that whole sequence of events wouldn't have been accomplished in less than three or, more likely, four minutes. Which means the window of time for the murder wasn't ten minutes, it must have been closer to six or seven."

"I'd not thought of it like that." Phyllis pulled a butter knife out of the chest and slathered it with polish. "But you're right, there was so little time, I don't see how the murderer managed to do it."

"The only explanation is that Edison himself opened the door to his killer."

But of course, that wasn't the only explanation, but Mrs. Jeffries didn't think of the other possible solution until almost dawn.

Mrs. Jeffries yawned as she climbed into bed. She pulled the covers up to her chin, rolled onto her side, and closed her eyes. Talking the case over with Phyllis had helped enormously. She still had no idea who had murdered Orlando Edison, but she felt she'd made some progress.

She took a deep breath and relaxed. Her mind wandered into that hazy realm between waking and sleep as bits of conversation and ideas drifted in and out of her consciousness. She made no attempt to send her thoughts into any specific direction, she simply let the words come and go as they would. Wiggins grinning as he mimicked Kitty Long's words: *"I had to go all the way up to the third floor of the house where Mrs. Clarridge was airing out one of the guest bedrooms. Mary went to the kitchen to get him some water."*

She turned onto her right side as she heard Luty's words: *"Accordin' to him, Bagshot's investment in the Granger ruined him financially."* She snuggled farther into the covers as she heard her own words: *"Yet at the same time, he was planning on leaving the country and hadn't said a word about it to the people who would be directly affected by his actions."*

She fell into a deeper, dreamless sleep until the early hours of the morning, when she was awakened by a dog barking. She glanced at the window, saw that it was still dark outside, and resolutely closed her eyes. But she dozed rather than slept. Once again, she let her mind drift into something the inspector had told her: *"Mrs. Clarridge said he'd stayed home that day, that he had some personal correspondence to see to and he'd need Kitty to take it to the postbox."*

In her mind's eye, she saw the inspector sipping his sherry. *"Charles Downing admitted that much to us."* Mrs. Goodge's face appeared, her expression pleased as punch as she reported, *"Anne Waterson wasn't like her sister, she'd not be loyal to a fiancé or husband if the man didn't live up to her father's standards. One of them said that it was obvious Sir Thomas didn't like Ralston very much."*

Mrs. Jeffries moaned softly as the images and words

rushed through her hazy consciousness with the speed of a steam engine. The inspector pushing his glasses up his nose as he said, *"Oh dear, I didn't mean to sound flippant, not when someone's been murdered. But what I meant was that the victim wasn't the only one with a bronzed shovel. The entire board of directors for the Granger Mine had one—they were given out as souvenirs at their first meeting."*

She heard herself again, only this time, her voice sounded as though it were coming from far away. *"Yes, of course you had, sir, you told me that last night. When you searched his study, you found the newspaper where he'd circled sailings from Liverpool to New York. How silly of me to forget."* She flopped onto her back as Phyllis spoke again: *"There was so little time, I don't see how the murderer managed to do it."*

"The only explanation is that Edison himself opened the door to his killer."

Mrs. Jeffries jerked awake and sat up. Despite the cold, she was clammy with sweat and her heart was racing. Of course there's another explanation, she thought. But I'm going to have the devil's own time proving it. She took a slow, deep breath as she saw the murder in a whole new light. She'd been looking at it completely wrong, fooled by taking everything at face value and not looking deeper to see the crime for what it really was.

She got up, dressed, and went downstairs. She spent the next hour drinking tea and thinking about what to do next. If her theory was right, there was only one individual who could have committed the murder.

By the time the clock struck seven, she had come up with a course of action. It would take a bit of luck but if everyone was able to do their part, they'd have this case solved by Christmas.

She heard the cook's door open and a moment later Mrs.

Goodge, with Samson trotting at her heels, came into the kitchen. She stopped and stared at Mrs. Jeffries. "You've got that look on your face again."

"What look?"

"The one that says you've sussed it out."

CHAPTER 10

"I wouldn't quite say that I've sussed it out." Mrs. Jeffries laughed. "But I do have an idea. However, everything will depend on a few pertinent details we need to find today."

"What kind of details?" The cook got a cup out of the cupboard, came to the table, and poured her tea. Samson meowed and headed for the back door. "Let me put him out before we start talking." She and the cat disappeared down the hall.

Mrs. Jeffries heard the door open and then, a few seconds later, the cook returned and plopped down in her seat. "Alright, what are we goin' to do next?"

"Aren't you curious as to who I think the murderer might be?"

"Of course I am, but I know you'll not say a word until you're sure." Mrs. Goodge poured a touch of milk in her tea and reached for the sugar bowl.

"You know me too well. It's not that I want to be mysterious, it's just that I want to be certain before I start naming
names. As to what we're going to do next, I've got a task in
mind for everyone in the household. But the first thing you
and I need to do is have a chat with Constable Barnes."

"Are you worried about the Hemmings girl?"

"Very much so," she replied. "We need the constable's
advice about what to do."

"We're in a bit of a bind there, aren't we?"

Mrs. Jeffries nodded, her expression glum. "He can't
assign constables to go all the way to Clapton to watch the
girl and he can't tell the inspector. Even with the constable's
supposed network of informers, he couldn't have learned
about Laura's possible blackmail plot."

"Let's put our heads together and have a think. I know
we can come up with something that will work." There was
a muffled thump from the back of the house. Mrs. Goodge
cocked her head toward the hall. "Good gracious, he's quick
to do his business this morning."

"Samson doesn't like the cold." Mrs. Jeffries got up. "You
stay put, I'll go let him in."

"Stop in the wet larder and get his sardines. He'll want
them for his breakfast."

Despite Mrs. Jeffries' best efforts to behave and appear as
though this were a morning meeting like any other, she
must not have been successful, because within moments of
everyone sitting down, they were making comments about
the case being solved.

"You know who did it, don't ya. Don't bother to put me
off with a fib, I can tell by lookin' at yer face," Luty declared.

"Luty, really, I'm not at all certain," Mrs. Jeffries began,
only to be interrupted by Ruth.

"Oh, but I think you are." Ruth clasped her hands together. "You've got that sparkle in your eye that says you've solved it. That's wonderful, that means Gerald and I can spend Christmas Eve together."

"But you're still coming to Christmas dinner, aren't you?" Mrs. Goodge asked sharply.

A faint blush crept up Ruth's cheeks. "Of course, but Gerald and I had planned to have a quiet dinner at my home on Christmas Eve. I was concerned that he'd have to cancel because of the murder inquiry, but now that Mrs. Jeffries has got it solved . . ."

"It's not solved as yet," Mrs. Jeffries insisted. "I will admit that I do have an idea but we won't be able to put this one to rest unless all of you help."

Betsy giggled. "You say that every time." She glanced at Amanda, who was sitting on Mrs. Goodge's lap watching the proceedings curiously.

"Indeed you do, Mrs. Jeffries," Hatchet added. "However, we'll respect your rather pathetic attempt to convince us you don't know the identity of the killer, when of course you do."

She opened her mouth to protest and then burst out laughing. "I don't know whether to be offended or flattered."

"I'd be flattered if it was me," Wiggins said.

Smythe checked the time on the carriage clock and then looked at the housekeeper. "Time's gettin' on. What do ya need us to do?"

Mrs. Jeffries took a deep breath. "If my theory about the murder is wrong, then I'm sending everyone off on a wild-goose chase. More importantly"—she looked at Betsy—"some of you may have to reveal more than we like to find out what I need to know."

"Do I need to find someone to look after Amanda?" Betsy asked.

"You can leave the little one here." Mrs. Goodge stroked the baby's soft blonde curls. "Mrs. Jeffries and I will both keep an eye on her while you're out—and your task won't take too long," the housekeeper added.

"Right, then," Smythe said. "What do you want us to do?"

"The funeral is planned for December twenty-eighth, Inspector." Mrs. Clarridge's black bombazine dress rustled faintly as she led the two policemen into the drawing room. She waved at the sofa, indicating they should sit.

"The twenty-eighth." Witherspoon took a spot on the end of the couch. Barnes took the other end and dug out his notebook.

"Yes, it was Mrs. Flurry's idea and, frankly, I'm in complete agreement with her." She sat down opposite them. "The undertaker has agreed to keep Mr. Edison's body at his premises. He'll bring it in the hearse to St. John's on the morning of the service. Mrs. Flurry said that Mr. Edison wouldn't want the household's Christmas ruined with either a wake or his funeral. But I'm sure you're not here because you're interested in our domestic details."

"We do have some additional questions," Witherspoon said kindly. "According to Kitty Long, after luncheon on Wednesday, Mr. Edison was writing a letter in his study when a gentleman arrived with the theater tickets. Is that correct?"

Barnes looked up from his writing.

"That's right. He'd asked me to let him know when Mr. Dempsey got here." She smiled sadly. "He wanted to come downstairs and hand out the tickets himself. He was like that, you know, he liked making people happy."

"Was Mr. Ralston here when Mr. Dempsey arrived?" the constable asked.

"Yes, he was in the study. He'd come about five minutes earlier."

"Mr. Edison accompanied Mr. Dempsey downstairs, is that right?"

"He did. He and Mr. Dempsey waited belowstairs while I went and got the two housemaids. They were cleaning the bedrooms on the top floor. When we were all gathered together, Mr. Dempsey handed the tickets to Mr. Edison and he passed them out. We knew we were getting them, you see, so it wasn't a surprise, but still Kitty and Mary squealed when he gave them theirs." She pulled a black handkerchief out of her sleeve and dabbed at her eyes. "He was delighted with their reaction. As I said, he enjoyed making people happy."

"Mrs. Clarridge, how long was Mr. Edison belowstairs with all of you?" Barnes asked. He wasn't certain he had the inspector thinking along the lines Mrs. Jeffries had laid out that morning. She had been adamant that if her theory was correct, certain facts had to come to light, even if it meant shoving them under the inspector's nose.

"I'm not sure."

"It's important, Mrs. Clarridge," Barnes pressed. "I don't wish to cause you distress, but can you think back and recall it in your mind's eye?"

"Well, let me see, I announced Mr. Ralston and took him into the study. Mr. Edison looked up and put the letter he was writing to one side. When I left, it couldn't have been more than five minutes until Mr. Dempsey arrived and the two them went downstairs to wait while I went up and got the girls. I'd say we were gone no more than ten minutes at the most."

*   *   *

"Why, Hatchet, what a delightful surprise." Gerald Manley rose from his chair and smiled in welcome.

"Do forgive me for barging in like this," Hatchet apologized as he crossed the elegant drawing room.

"You're always welcome here." Myra Manley lifted her cheek for him to kiss and waved him into a wing chair. "We're just having morning coffee. Let me ring for another cup."

She started to rise, but just then the butler stepped back into the room. He carried a blue Wedgwood cup on a silver tray. "I took the liberty of bringing this, madam," he said to Myra as he set it next to the coffeepot. "Shall I serve?"

"Thank you, but I'll do it." She poured Hatchet a cup and handed it to him. "Now, tell me why you're here so early."

"I'll bet it's something to do with that Edison murder." Gerald Manley grinned broadly. He was a tall, muscular man on the far side of forty. His dark hair was threaded with gray and he had the kind of bone structure that still turned ladies' heads when he entered a room. He was an artist who still worked at his profession despite the fact that he no longer needed money, as he'd married Myra Haddington, an heiress. Love and marriage had come to them when they were well past the first flush of youth and they adored one another.

"You would be absolutely right about that," Hatchet agreed.

"What can we do to help?" Myra asked. She was a slender woman with a longish, rather plain face made beautiful by a lovely smile and genuine interest in her fellow human beings. As always, she was elegantly dressed, in a red skirt and long-sleeved white blouse. A garnet brooch was pinned at her throat and a string of gold beads hung around her neck.

"I'm hoping you can give me some information. Do you know Sir Thomas Waterson?" Hatchet had used the Manleys as a source several other times. Gerald knew everyone in the art world and Myra had grown up with aristocrats and royals. They were helpful and discreet, and both of them firmly believed in justice.

Myra grimaced delicately. "Unfortunately, yes. Why? What's he got to do with the Edison case? I can't see someone like him even speaking to a stock promoter, which, I understand, was how Mr. Edison made his living."

"He's not directly involved, but, well, it's hard to explain."

"What do you want to know about him?" Gerald asked. "You don't need to tell us any more than that until after the case is concluded. Then, of course, you'll be expected to come to dinner and give us all the gory details."

"I most certainly will," Hatchet promised. "There was some sort of a scandal involving Sir Thomas' son-in-law and the Foreign Office? I don't know exactly when it happened and the details are a bit vague, but supposedly, the young man had taken a bribe in exchange for a government contract."

Gerald frowned. "Sorry, old boy, but this time you're out of luck. I don't remember anything like that."

"I do," Myra declared. "I remember it very well."

Wiggins knocked softly on the back door of the Edison house. He'd ducked down the side of the building when he'd seen the inspector and Constable Barnes going in the front door. At first, he thought he'd come back later, but then it occurred to him that the best time to have another chat with Kitty Long might be when the housekeeper was otherwise occupied.

The door opened and Kitty stared at him with an expression of surprise. "What are you doin' here?" She glanced over her shoulder to the inside of the house.

"I need to speak with you—it's important."

"I'll get in trouble. There's police upstairs." She kept her voice soft and low.

"Come out just for a minute. It'll not take long, I promise," he pleaded. "Please, my guv'll sack me if I don't give 'im a bit more to write about."

She looked over her shoulder again and then slipped out the door. She closed it softly and leaned against the wood. "Alright, what is it? But I'm still not saying anything nasty about poor Mr. Edison. He was a good master."

"I just need to ask you a couple of quick bits," he said. "You said that Mr. Ralston came downstairs and made a nuisance of himself that afternoon and you 'ad to go upstairs to the top of the 'ouse to get Mrs. Clarridge to give you a headache powder."

"That's right."

"How long were you gone?"

Betsy gathered her courage, told herself not to be a ninny, and then knocked on Madeleine Flurry's front door. She wasn't sure yet how she was going to approach the woman and hoped she'd not have to reveal too much about their activities, but as Mrs. Jeffries had made clear, they weren't going to get this case solved if they didn't take a few risks.

When the door opened, she smiled brightly. "Mrs. Flurry?"

"Yes, who are you?" She stared at her blankly for a moment before her face cleared in recognition. "You're the woman from the greengrocer's shop, the one with the baby."

"That's right and I need to speak to you. It's about Orlando Edison's murder."

Her jaw dropped in shock. "What . . . what did you say? You knew Orlando?"

"No, Mrs. Flurry, I didn't, but if you're interested in helping find out who killed him, you'll let me in."

She said nothing for a moment, then she cocked her head to one side and looked Betsy up and down. "Come inside, please."

Smythe took his spot across from Blimpey. "I was afraid you'd not be 'ere. It's still too early for openin'."

"Nell's giving the house her Christmas clean, as she calls it. She's hired two girls to help and they've got the place torn apart so they can scrub every nook and corner. I ask you, who looks for dirt under a sofa or a chair? A wise man makes himself scarce when the women start washin' everything in sight. But I'm glad you come, it'll save me from sending one of my lads to your place. There's news. Yancy Kimball 'as disappeared."

"Disappeared? But I thought he and Gedigan 'ad made a deal, come to some arrangement about the money Kimball owed."

"They did, but I don't think Kimball's goin' to keep his promise to pay up. He walked out of his hotel yesterday and hasn't been seen since. He didn't pay the bill or take 'is luggage. Kimball's done a bunk. Once Gedigan finds out, he'll be lookin' for him."

Smythe frowned heavily. "That doesn't make sense. Why would 'e scarper off now? Kimball's not gettin' all of his cousin's estate, but 'e's getting a nice bit. Why would he go before the ruddy will is read?" Despite Mrs. Jeffries' refusal to name her suspect, the tasks she'd assigned everyone this morning made it clear who she had in her sights as the killer. Could she be wrong? Was Kimball the one who did it?

"Maybe he thought it safer to get out of town before it became public knowledge that 'e wasn't getting it all, if you see what I mean," Blimpey said. "His inheritance ain't goin' anywhere so maybe Kimball figured he'd steal Edison's money stash and make a run for it before Gedigan got wind that Kimball wasn't the sole heir. Inheritances don't disappear. When things quieted down a tad, Kimball could always send the solicitor instructions about his property."

"Money stash," Smythe repeated. "So you know about that? That's why I came to see ya today, I wanted to find out if it was true that Edison kept money in the house."

"That's the rumor my sources heard," Blimpey said. "Edison always wanted to be ready to leave in a hurry."

"But 'e wasn't a crook or a confidence trickster." Smythe didn't understand it.

"No, he wasn't," Blimpey agreed. "But he wasn't a toff, either. 'E'd been raised hard and had come from nothing. It could be he kept a stash of cash just to make himself feel secure, you know, like for an emergency. I know my Nell always buys more food than we can eat in a month of Sundays and our larder is always full. My Nell went hungry as a little one and she's not forgotten it."

Smythe nodded, thinking of some of the odd little things that Betsy did. She always had too many blankets on Amanda; even the past summer during the heat she'd had four coverlets at the foot of the baby's cot. They'd been neatly folded and at the ready. When he'd mentioned them, Betsy had gotten defensive and, after an argument, had admitted that she remembered being cold when she was little and no child of hers was going to suffer the way she had. He'd held his tongue after that but on warm nights he always double-checked that his overcareful wife wasn't piling too many covers on the little one. "No, ya don't forget misery like that," he agreed. "Most of us dance with them demons for the rest of our lives. Do ya think you can find Kimball?"

Blimpey shrugged. "If 'e's still in the country. But if he's got any brains, he's on the continent by now. Gedigan won't take kindly to being cheated or humiliated."

"I think 'e's still here. 'E might have gone into hiding, but I don't think he'd leave the country until he knew exactly what he was inheritin' from his cousin."

"Then I can find 'im."

"I think you're right about this, sir," Barnes whispered to the inspector as they followed Mrs. Clarridge down the back stairs to the kitchen.

Witherspoon wasn't exactly sure what the constable might be referring to, but he wasn't going to let on that he didn't have a clue why they were here or what they were doing. Barnes had been so complimentary about his ability to "see the flower amongst the weeds," a phrase that he hoped meant that his inner voice, as Mrs. Jeffries called it, was guiding his steps in the investigation of this case. It certainly didn't feel as if he knew what he was doing, but he'd go along with the constable, who seemed to understand him better than he understood himself, to see what was what. "Yes, well, I'll leave the actual questioning up to you," he replied. "Sometimes it's best if I just stand back and observe."

"Mrs. Green, these gentlemen would like to speak with you again," Mrs. Clarridge said as they came into the kitchen.

The cook, a short, gaunt woman with wispy blonde hair

tucked beneath her cap, looked up from the mound of dough she'd been kneading. She nodded. "Of course. Please have a seat." She gestured toward the kitchen table.

"I'll leave you in Mrs. Green's capable hands," Mrs. Clarridge said. "I've got to get Mrs. Flurry's quarters ready."

"She's coming right away?" Witherspoon asked.

"Yes, right after Christmas." Mrs. Clarridge smiled. "We're looking forward to her being here. All of us like her very much."

"So you've met her?" Barnes asked quickly.

"Many times, Constable. Mr. Edison and she were very, very close. Mary's changing the bed in Mrs. Flurry's room. I'll send her right down." With that, she turned and disappeared up the back stairs.

Mrs. Green dumped her dough into a bowl, draped a clean tea towel on top, and set it next to the cooker. She wiped off her hands and came to the table. "I take it you'd like to ask me some more questions," she said as she sat down.

"Yes, ma'am." Barnes hoped he wasn't making a mess of things and he prayed that Mrs. Jeffries hadn't gone off her head. "Mrs. Green, can you confirm that the door to the tradesmen's entrance is only unlocked when there's a delivery?"

"That's right." She pointed down the corridor off the kitchen toward the front of the house. "The key is kept on a hook by the door. That way, any of us can open up and Mrs. Clarridge doesn't have to worry her knees going up and down the steps."

"Was it locked when you left to go to the theater?" Witherspoon couldn't help himself. His reason was beginning to see what his inner voice might be trying to tell him.

She tapped her chin thoughtfully. "I think it must have

been. Let me see, we had a laundry delivery that morning, but I'm sure Mary locked it when the deliveryman left. She always does."

"Was that the only time the door was opened that day?" Barnes asked.

"As far as I know, yes. The grocer's order and the meat order came on the day before, on the Tuesday."

Mary came into the kitchen and went to the table. She bobbed her head politely at the inspector and then clasped her hands together. "Mrs. Clarridge said you had more questions for me?"

"Don't look so alarmed," Witherspoon said kindly. He gestured to an empty chair. "Please, take a seat."

Mary swallowed uneasily and sat down next to the cook. "Alright, I'm ready. Ask your questions, then."

"On the afternoon that Mr. Edison died, I understand Mr. Ralston came downstairs and asked for a headache powder."

"That's right. We were quite put out about it. Guests aren't supposed to come down here; they're supposed to ring when they want something. But all of a sudden, there he was, big as life"—she pointed at the corridor leading to the front of the house—"and demanding we get him a head-ache powder."

"Did he say why he'd come downstairs instead of ring-ing?" the constable asked.

"'Course not, and that's not the sort of thing we can ask." She grimaced in disgust. "But he had poor Kitty running up to the top of the house. I knew he'd need water and a spoon for mixing, so I got a glass of water and then had to traipse up two flights of stairs to the butler's pantry for a proper-sized tray."

"Where was he standing when you left? Can you show us?" Barnes got up and, as he did, the others rose to their feet as well.

"He was right over there." Mary hurried out past the back stairs and halfway down the narrow corridor. "He was right here. He said he didn't want to bother Mr. Edison so he'd come down to wash his hands and get a headache powder on his own."

"Isn't there a water closet for guests upstairs?" Witherspoon asked. An idea was beginning to form in his mind. He looked down the corridor and could see the key to the tradesmen's door hanging on the hook.

"Oh yes, and afterwards, Kitty and I both wondered why he hadn't used it. It's at the end of the front hall. But he was a guest and it wasn't our place to say anything."

The constable had one more question. "How long was Mr. Ralston alone here?"

Phyllis stood on the doorstep of the Hemmings' house and slowly turned in a circle. She'd been here for ten minutes now, knocking on the front door, but to no avail. No one was home. As she moved, she surveyed the other houses along the street. There was no activity at the place directly across from her, but as her gaze moved past the house next door, she was sure she saw the front curtain twitch. She smiled. Just as she'd hoped, there was a neighborhood snoop. She hurried over, banged on the door, and wasn't in the least surprised when it opened immediately.

A sprite of a woman, tiny with frizzy salt-and-pepper hair pulled atop her head in a bun, stared at her curiously. "Hello, can I help you?"

"I'm sorry to disturb you, ma'am, but I'm looking for Miss Laura Hemmings. She lives next door."

"I know where Laura lives," she replied. "But no one is home. Mr. and Mrs. Hemmings have gone to Colchester for Christmas."

"What about Laura?" Phyllis had a bad feeling about this. "Has she gone there as well?"

"No, she and her stepmother don't get along." She smiled as she spoke. "I think she's still here. My name is Mrs. Cole. What's yours?"

"I'm Millie Barret, a friend of Laura's. Do you know where she is now?"

"Hmm, well, I really couldn't say." Mrs. Cole put her hand over her mouth as she yawned.

Phyllis wanted to scream in frustration, but she plastered a smile on her face. "Have you seen her today?"

"Of course. I see her every day. She was here earlier, but she's not here now. I think she's gone out somewhere. She didn't look happy, but then she's always been like that, a very unhappy young woman. I can't imagine why Douglas—he's her intended—wants to marry her. She's very strong willed."

"Do you know where she went?" Phyllis persisted. Mrs. Cole was odd, but didn't appear to be completely out of her mind.

"Why would I know that?"

"I don't know, it's just that it's important I see her and I was hoping you could help me." Phyllis gave her a quick, apologetic smile. "I'll not trouble you further, Mrs. Cole." She turned and started to walk away.

"Wait, maybe I do know where she's gone. Well, not exactly where's she's gone, but she had on her good coat and gloves and she wasn't carrying a shopping basket so I reckon she's gone to meet her friend."

"Which friend?"

"I don't know her name, but it was a lady she worked with before she got sacked. They like to go to the pub together. Does that help?"

"Yes, ma'am, it certainly does."

"Aren't you going to speak to Mrs. Clarridge again?" Barnes said to Witherspoon. Despite the cool temperature, beneath his uniform he felt sweat trickling down his back. He hoped Mrs. Jeffries knew what she was about; she'd been very sure of herself, but that didn't mean her theory was foolproof. So far, it appeared she was on the right track, but Barnes knew that all it would take was one overlooked detail to derail the entire train.

They'd finished their interviews with the cook and the housemaids and were walking down the hall to the front of the house. Mrs. Clarridge stood in the foyer, waiting for them.

"Mrs. Clarridge," the inspector murmured. He looked momentarily confused and then his face cleared as they reached the end of the corridor. "Oh yes, of course, of course."

"Have you finished, Inspector?" She got his bowler, over-coat, and scarf off the brass coat tree.

"I've one more question." He took the hat from her and popped it on his head. "Did you take Mr. Edison's letter to the post, the one he was working on after lunch?"

She handed him his coat and scarf. "No, I didn't."

"Neither did Mary or Kitty," Barnes said. "And we didn't find any personal correspondence when we searched his study later that night. Is it possible he didn't write—"

"No, it's not possible," Mrs. Clarridge interrupted. "The letter was finished when I went in to tell him Mr. Ralston was here to see him. I begged his pardon for interrupting him and he told me it was fine, that he was finished and to show Mr. Ralston in. A few minutes later, when I went in to tell him Mr. Dempsey was here with the tickets, he was getting an envelope out of his top drawer. He wrote that letter."

Phyllis stood outside the Blackbird Pub and hoped she was right. It was already getting late and she ought to be back at Upper Edmonton Gardens setting up the tea things for their afternoon meeting. Instead, she was standing outside a public house hoping that Mrs. Cole wasn't crazy as a loon and that Laura would be sitting at a table sipping a drink with Enid Carter. She took a deep breath, told herself she'd done this before, she wasn't going to be scared to walk into a pub on her own. She yanked open the door and stepped inside.

The place wasn't crowded. Two men and a woman stood at the bar and only three of the tables had customers. Enid Carter and another, older woman were sitting at the one closest to the unlighted fireplace. She didn't understand it. If Laura had come to meet her friends for a drink, where was she?

She moved toward them just as Enid looked her way. "If it isn't the little private inquiry girl! Come on over and have a drink with us." She poked her companion's arm and pointed to Phyllis. "She's the one I told you about, the one asking all the questions."

"I'm sorry to disturb you, but I'm looking for Laura Hemmings. Is she here with you?"

"I told you already, she got sacked." Enid took a drink. "What do ya want with her?"

Phyllis' stomach tightened as the fear that had been following her since talking to Mrs. Cole got a hundred times stronger. "I thought she was meeting the two of you for a drink," she explained. "Isn't that why you're here now?"

"We're here because his nibs said we was to go out tonight." The older woman snorted. "Not so much as a by-your-leave did he give us—he just handed out a few bob and said we were to go and have a 'Christmas treat' and not to come back before last call. If you ask me, he's got a bit of fluff comin' for a visit and he don't want anyone to see her."

Enid cackled with glee and raised her glass. "Oh, give it a rest, we're out of the house and that's all that counts. Besides, we'll not see what he's up to, but Miss Carlisle will know what's what." She knocked back her drink. "We can ask her in the morning."

Phyllis sat down on a stool, her attention on Enid. "Did he say why you had to go out?" She just knew that girl had done something stupid.

Enid shrugged and raised her glass, waving it at the bar-maid. "It's like Cook says, he's probably wanting a bit of fun tonight and he don't want us seein' who's visiting him. Ralston's not a generous man, so giving us a few bob and chucking us out of the house wasn't because he wanted to give us a Christmas treat."

Phyllis jumped to her feet and rushed to the door. She didn't know what she was going to do, but she couldn't stay here and do nothing.

"Hey," Enid cried. "Where you goin'? Stay and have a drink."

"We can't wait any longer for Phyllis. We've got to start now." Mrs. Jeffries shifted uneasily.

"I don't like this." Wiggins glared at the clock. "She's over a half hour late."

"I don't like it, either, but I'm sure she'll be here soon. Now, why don't you tell us what you found out?"

"I managed to speak to Kitty and she confirmed that Ralston was alone in the hallway belowstairs for a good ten minutes." He looked at the housekeeper. "And I think I figured out why that's important."

"Of course you did." Mrs. Jeffries glanced at the clock again. "By now I'm sure all of you have guessed. Nonetheless, let's go over this calmly and logically. That's the only way I can understand it in my own mind."

"How about the other maid?" Luty asked. "She only had to go to the kitchen to get the water and the spoon for him to mix the powder."

"I asked Kitty about that. She said that when Mary brought the water out, it was on a silver tray and they're kept in the butler's pantry two flights up, so Mary had to go upstairs, too."

"And the key to the tradesmen's door was right there, nice and easy for him," Mrs. Goodge added. "He'd have had plenty of time to unlock the door."

"Kitty also told me that Mrs. Clarridge checks the door at night when she's locking up, but not during the day, as it's supposed to be locked up after every delivery. But there weren't any deliveries that afternoon."

"Yes, I see, it's all coming together now," Mrs. Jeffries murmured. Again, she looked at the clock. Where was Phyllis? Why wasn't she here? "Alright, Smythe, how did you do today?"

Smythe had caught the tension building around the table. He'd decided that as soon as the meeting was over, he was going on the hunt. "My source confirmed the rumor about a cash stash in Edison's house, but that's not all I found out." He told them about the disappearance of Yancy Kimball. "And I can't figure whether Kimball took off to avoid Gedigan or whether it's more than that," he concluded.

Mrs. Jeffries' heart plummeted to her toes. "Oh, my Lord, what if I'm wrong? What if Kimball is the killer?" She bit her lip and looked at the coachman. "As you've pointed out, he was Edison's cousin, they'd known one another all their lives, and he might be the one person who did know where any money Edison had stashed might be hidden."

"No, he's not," Betsy interjected. "Madeleine Flurry knew where the money was hidden. She told me so today."

The drapes at the Ralston house were tightly drawn, but Phyllis could see light seeping out of the edges of the window. An icy wind slammed into her and she shivered, but whether it was from fear or cold, she didn't know. Nor did she know what to do next. She stood on the pavement staring at the house. She knew Laura was inside, she just knew it. But what if she were wrong, what if she summoned a policeman and the girl wasn't there? Then what? She'd not only look a fool, she'd ruin everything Mrs. Jeffries and the household had worked for all these years.

But if she didn't call a policeman, Ralston was going to kill Laura and she couldn't live with that.

Think, you ninny, she told herself. Stop and think. What's the first thing you need to do? You need to find out if Laura's in there. Her heartbeat slowed and her breathing returned to normal as a great calm came over her. She turned and looked at the house across the road, at number 11, where there was a Miss Carlisle, the housekeeper who knew, heard, and saw everything in the neighborhood.

"Mrs. Flurry also said she'd only met Paul Ralston one time and that was at a dinner party." Betsy cocked her head toward the cook's quarters, listening for any sign her daughter might be waking up.

"Do you believe she was telling the truth?" Mrs. Jeffries asked. Under the table, she clenched her hands together to keep them from trembling. She was going to wring Phyllis' neck when she saw the girl.

"I do." Betsy relaxed as she heard nothing but blessed silence from the cook's chambers. "Once she realized I was trying to help find Edison's killer she talked freely. She and Orlando Edison were in love. He's the father of her baby. If he'd not been killed, they were going to get married."

"Was she the one he was overheard arguing with?" Mrs. Goodge asked.

Betsy nodded. "Yes, she got very upset when he told her he was sailing for New York as soon as his testimony was finished. They quarreled because she wanted him to stay until after the baby was born but he refused and she lost control of her tongue and said all sorts of nonsense she didn't mean. But she didn't break off the engagement."

"Did she say anything about a letter? Was she the one he was writing to on the day he died?" Mrs. Jeffries held her breath as she waited for Betsy's reply. This was the crux of her theory. If she was wrong, then she had no idea who the killer might be.

"No, she's received nothing from him."

"Thanks ever so much," Phyllis said to Miss Carlisle. "I'll go along and have a quick word with her, then. You've been a great help."

"I do hope your friend gets her position back," Miss Carlisle said. "A broken engagement is heartbreaking. Laura is lucky she's got a friend like you. It's nice that you've come to go home with her. Mind you girls be careful, it's already dark out."

The housekeeper, a stout woman with an easy smile and a sharp eye, had been very willing to talk. All Phyllis had had to do was come up with an outrageous lie. Namely, that her dear friend Laura's fiancé had run off with another woman and Laura had come back to the Ralston home to try to get her job back.

"We will," she promised. Knowing that Miss Carlisle was watching, she hurried down the steps and crossed the road. She ducked behind a hansom that had just pulled up and then went down the side of the house toward the servants' entrance. She'd found out what she needed to know. Laura was inside with Paul Ralston. Alone.

She slowed down when she could no longer be seen from across the street. She moved gingerly, taking care to be quiet. Phyllis wasn't sure what to do now. She stopped, thinking she heard voices from the front of the house, but just then a four-wheeler went past making enough noise to wake the dead. She continued moving. She couldn't just bang on the door and demand to know what was going on, that could be disastrous. Laura might just be inside chatting with the man.

She stopped at the first window. The curtains along here hadn't been drawn, but unfortunately she was an inch too short to see inside the house. She tried leaping up, but that didn't work and she was afraid the noise of her thumping the ground would alert Ralston.

She looked around, hoping to find something to stand on so she could peek inside. By now it was dark and the light from the house was so feeble she could barely see. But she wasn't going to give up. She tiptoed the length of the pathway looking for something she could use to stand on and finally spotted a circle of bricks around a flower bed by the back gate. Dropping to her knees, she pried four of them out of the hardened ground.

It took two trips to get them under one of the windows, but she finally managed it, stepped on the double-stacked bricks, and looked into the house. All she saw was an empty drawing room. Taking into account that this side of the house had at least three windows, she moved quietly to the next one, set the bricks up again, and looked inside. "Oh misery," she muttered as she stared at an empty dining room. But she'd not come this far to give up, so she moved once again, this time to the last window, stood on the bricks, and looked.

She gasped, her breath caught in her throat and her heart suddenly racing like a steam engine. Oh, dear Lord, what was she going to do?

"My source confirmed the rumor about Sir Thomas Waterson," Hatchet said. "He did disinherit his daughter. He's not seen or spoken to her since the scandal five years ago."

"But the scandal was hushed up," Ruth said. "The only thing she was guilty of was sticking by her husband. There were only rumors about what happened, so why did it matter to him so much?"

"Sir Thomas is one of those people who appear to be guided not by what society thinks of them, but by their own inner sense of right, wrong, and duty," Hatchet explained. "Apparently, he considered that his daughter violated this code when she chose to stay with her husband rather than come home to him. It may have been hushed up, but Arthur Canning did take a bribe and the fact that the government managed to keep it quiet so that a scandal was averted meant nothing to Waterson."

"He's considered a bit of a self-righteous fanatic who appears to think no one can live up to his standards," Ruth added. "My source confirmed that Waterson didn't like Ralston and was more or less looking for a reason to separate him from Anne. So what does this mean? Is Ralston our killer?"

Mrs. Jeffries was too worn out worrying about Phyllis to fob them off with a denial. They were all intelligent, intuitive people and they'd come to the same conclusion she had. "Yes, I think so. But unless the constable has managed to lead the inspector along the same path of inquiry as ourselves, we can't prove it. The evidence against Ralston is only a matter of circumstance, not fact."

Smythe looked at the housekeeper. Her shoulders drooped and her expression was clouded. "You sent Phyllis to Clapton to talk to Laura Hemmings and now you're worried about her, ain't ya."

"I've a terrible feeling that something unexpected might have happened and that poor girl might bear the brunt of my bad judgment."

"Right." He shoved his chair back from the table. He looked at Hatchet and then Wiggins. "Then there's only one thing to do. We'll go and find her."

"Can I come, too?" Luty pleaded. "I've got my peace-maker out in the carriage."

"When did you put that there?" Hatchet glared at his employer as he got up. "Madam, you know how dangerous that weapon is and you promised me you'd leave it locked in the gun case."

"It was in the gun case until I took it out today," she

replied with a shrug. "But it's there if you need it. I hid it under the seat."

"Are we going to Clapton or the Ralston house?" Wiggins hurried to the coat tree and grabbed his jacket.

Smythe looked at Mrs. Jeffries. "You tell me, where do you think she's got to by now?"

CHAPTER 11

The day had faded into evening and a cold, sharp wind blew in from the river. Barnes' knees ached, his back hurt, and he wasn't sure his careful questions or comments had done anything to lead the inspector in the right direction. What was more, as the day had worn on he'd begun having doubts. Mrs. Jeffries had an enviable record of being right but no one was perfect. What if the sequence of events she'd laid out for him that morning was missing one pertinent detail, one little thing that she'd overlooked? Something that looked inconsequential but that might have led the investigation in a completely different direction.

They had just left the Edison house but Barnes didn't know if they were going to call it a day and go home or keep at it. He glanced at the inspector. Witherspoon stood on the bottom step staring off into the distance with an intense, thoughtful expression on his face. "Inspector, should I nip out and find us a hansom?"

Witherspoon jerked slightly. "Are you dreadfully tired, Constable?"

"I'm fine, sir."

"Then let's go to the Ralston house." He headed toward the street. "I've a number of things I'd like to ask him and, more importantly, I feel I've been remiss by not speaking with his servants."

Phyllis steeled herself, opened her eyes, and looked again. Laura Hemmings was on the floor. Dressed in a dark skirt and white blouse, she lay on her left side with her right arm draped over her torso and her hand resting on the floor. There was a bloody wound on her temple and more blood on the carpet beneath her head.

Bile rose in Phyllis' throat but she fought it down. Laura was dead—the silly girl had come here thinking she was dealing with an unfaithful fiancé and hadn't realized until it was too late that the man was a killer.

From the house, she thought she heard voices again but her breathing was so loud, she couldn't be sure. She concentrated on the scene before her. A gas lamp by the closed door illuminated the room, which was small but decorated in the cheerful yellows and pinks of a morning room. She'd have to testify to this awful moment in a court of law and she was determined that Paul Ralston would pay for what he'd done, so she took her time and committed every detail to memory. Her gaze scanned the unlighted fireplace and she drew a quick breath. A miniature shovel, its end darkened by something she was sure was blood, rested next to the metal rack holding the fireplace implements.

She'd started to get down when she saw Laura's fingers

move. She went still, staring at the prone figure and hoping against hope that she wasn't seeing things. But she wasn't; Laura's hand moved again and she rolled onto her back.

Phyllis fought off a wave of panic. Oh, dear Lord, the girl was still alive. But what could she do? She had to get help. Then she heard voices from inside the house. Someone was here, someone had come, that was why Ralston had left Laura alone.

What should she do? Whimpering softly, she started up the walkway. If there was someone inside, then regardless of what it might cost the household of Upper Edmonton Gardens, she was going to raise the alarm. She was almost at the end when she slammed to a halt as two figures stepped into the darkened walkway.

Barnes' senses were on full alert before they even climbed the short set of steps to Ralston's front door. As he'd paid the hansom driver, he'd spotted a familiar carriage race past them. He'd recognized it right away because of the fancy brass and gold headlamps on the front; it belonged to Luty Belle Crookshank. He'd dallied behind the inspector, keeping his eye on the vehicle as it pulled to the curb at the end of the street.

Witherspoon, who by this time was a good fifteen feet ahead of him, had already reached Ralston's door. He glanced at Barnes and then banged the knocker.

Ralston himself answered. He frowned when he saw who was on his doorstep. "I'm afraid it's not convenient just now, Inspector." He was dressed in a white shirt open at the collar and a pair of trousers. "I've a dinner engagement in a few minutes and I'm pressed for time."

"We want to speak to your staff." Barnes fixed him with a hard stare. "There's no need for you to be here." There was something going on here, he could see. Ralston was disheveled, and there was sweat on his forehead and dark spots on his white shirt.

"My servants are gone. I gave them the night off." He started to close the door but the constable slapped his hand flat against the wood and kept it open.

Ralston's mouth gaped open in shock. "How dare you!" he sputtered. "This is a private house!"

Witherspoon edged forward. "Mr. Ralston, we'll not take up much of your time, but if you refuse to speak with us, I'm afraid I'll have to post constables here until such time as you are available for an interview."

"That's absurd," Ralston snapped, but he stepped back and motioned for them to come inside. "I assure you, Inspector, your superiors will hear of this impertinence."

They stood in the foyer. Ralston crossed his arms over his chest and stared at them expectantly. "Well, go ahead, let's get this over with."

"May we go into your drawing room and sit down?" Witherspoon asked.

"No, Inspector, this isn't a social call so you can damned well ask your questions right here," he replied sharply. "Now get on with it."

"Mr. Ralston, when you last saw Mr. Edison, it was the afternoon of his death, correct?" the inspector asked.

"You already know that, Inspector."

"While you were there, Mr. Edison was interrupted by his housekeeper and he left the room for a time, is that right?" Barnes asked conversationally.

Ralston shifted uneasily and glanced toward the back of the house. "I've already told you that as well."

"No, sir, you mentioned your visit but you were deliberately vague when we pressed you for details," Witherspoon said. "But that's neither here nor there. How long were you alone in Mr. Edison's study?"

"Two or three minutes, Inspector. He went downstairs to take care of a domestic matter but was back very quickly."

"That's not true, Mr. Ralston." Barnes held his gaze. "Mr. Edison was gone for at least ten minutes."

Outside, Phyllis spun around to make a run for it, when she heard a familiar voice say, "Phyllis, cor blimey, it's you! Thank goodness. We was worried to death."

"Wiggins, Smythe." She almost fainted in relief as she realized the two men were indeed her friends. "Thank God it's you two. We've got to hurry. Laura Hemmings is inside. She's been hurt—I think Ralston tried to kill her. We've got to do something." She started back down the pathway as she spoke and they hurried after her.

"The inspector and Barnes are inside," Smythe whispered. They reached the window and he didn't need a stack of bricks to see inside.

"What are they doing here?" she asked in confusion. "How did they know?"

"Blast a Spaniard, what did the bastard do to her? She looks dead," the coachman said.

"She's still alive," Phyllis whispered. "But I don't understand what's going on. Why are you two here?"

"Not just us. Hatchet's at the back of the house. He went round by the mews." Smythe rubbed his hand over his chin. "There's no time to explain everything. Are you sure she's alive?"

"I saw her hand move and I think I heard her moan . . ." Her voice trailed off as an idea struck her. "That's it, that's what we'll do."

"Right now we've got to suss out a way to get the inspector to find this poor girl." Smythe pointed through the window.

"We'll 'ave to own up to it," Wiggins muttered. "It'll be over for us, but we can't let 'im finish her off."

"No, no, we won't," Phyllis declared. "I'm going inside. Once I'm in, I'll make sure the inspector and the constable know she's there. Smythe, can you come with me and hold the back door open? I might have to leave in a hurry." She turned and headed for the servants' entrance.

"What are you going to do?" Smythe hissed as he trailed behind her.

"I'm going to moan. Once we know for sure they've heard me, the four of us will have to get out of here fast."

By this time they'd reached the servants' door. Phyllis turned the handle and wasn't surprised when it opened. Enid was acting true to form and had wanted an unlocked door so they could be as drunk as they liked when they came back. She'd not wanted to bother with a key.

Inside the foyer, Ralston scowled at them. "These questions are ridiculous. Your superior will hear of this, Constable. I'm not without influence in this town. My fiancée is the daughter of Sir Thomas Waterson."

"You've already told us that, sir," Barnes reminded him. "Now, back to what's important. Mr. Edison was writing a letter when you were there and when he went downstairs, the letter was left on his desk. Is that correct?"

A bead of sweat rolled down Ralston's forehead and onto his nose. He didn't appear to notice it. "He was writing something but I've no idea what it might have been. I'm not in the habit of looking through other people's correspondence."

Witherspoon's brows came together and he cocked his head toward the back of the house. "Did you hear that?"

"No," Ralston snapped. "There was nothing."

"But I distinctly heard something; it sounded like a moan."

"This is an old house, Inspector." Ralston moved to the front door and jerked it open. "You've taken up enough of my time and I'd like you to leave."

The sound came again, and this time it was unmistakable. "Ohhhh . . . ohhhh . . . help . . ."

Barnes moved first. "It's coming from down the hall. Someone's hurt." He tossed his notebook and pencil to one side and charged down the corridor.

Witherspoon was right on his heels.

"Come back here! Come back here!" Ralston screamed as he raced after them. "You've no right to invade my house, no right, I tell you!"

Phyllis stood against the wall at the back staircase and held her breath. She wasn't going to budge until she knew that either the inspector or Constable Barnes had opened the door to the morning room and seen Laura.

Her heart raced as she heard doors slamming, feet pounding, and Ralston screaming in rage. Seconds ticked by, but to her, it seemed like time moved in slow motion.

"Here, sir," Barnes called. "There's someone badly hurt."

Phyllis turned and ran down the staircase, hoping the noise of Ralston shouting would cover her footsteps. Smythe caught her as she stumbled out the door. She started to turn toward the street, but he yanked her gently in the opposite direction, where Wiggins waited. "This way, it's safer. We'll go out the mews and around the block to the carriage."

They'd reached the mews when they heard a crash and

footsteps thundering from inside the house, but they kept going. The three of them were a hundred feet up the mews when the gate smashed open and Paul Ralston flew out. He suddenly stumbled as a foot came out of the shadows, tripping him and sending him headlong into the ground. Ralston bellowed in pain. But before he had time to recover and gain his feet, Barnes charged through the gate and leapt upon his back.

"You'll be sorry about this," Ralston shouted. "I'm going to make sure you pay for treating me this way. I've no idea how that stupid girl got hurt."

Hatchet stayed in the darkness against the fence, using Ralston's nonstop threats to cover the sound of his retreat as he edged farther up the mews.

"Save it for the judge and jury." Barnes kept his knee on Ralston, keeping him flat against the ground while he blasted his police whistle. He glanced toward the darkness where Hatchet stood and nodded his thanks.

Witherspoon suddenly appeared at the back gate. "Help is on the way," he called. "I've sent the lad next door for the point constable." He hesitated.

"Go back to the girl, sir. I've got this one under control."

Mrs. Jeffries paced across the kitchen to the window over the sink. She pulled the curtain back and stared at the empty street.

"Stop frettin', Hepzibah," Luty commanded. "They'll find her."

"I'm sure she's fine," Ruth said kindly. "You're going to wear yourself out if you keep pacing."

"You don't know that she's come to any harm," Mrs. Goodge added. "Her being late could have a simple explanation."

"She might have gotten stuck on an underground train," Betsy suggested. "That happens frequently."

"Phyllis refuses to use the underground." Mrs. Jeffries turned and smiled at the four women. "I know you're trying to make me feel better, but honestly, until I see she's safe and sound with my own eyes . . ." She stopped and whirled back to the window as she heard the distinctive sound of a carriage.

"Is it them?" Mrs. Goodge asked as the housekeeper peered out the curtains again. "Yes, it's them—oh, thank goodness, Phyllis is with them." Mrs. Jeffries sagged in relief and sent up a short, silent, but heartfelt prayer of thanks. She didn't think she'd ever been so happy to see someone as she was now. If anything had happened to the maid, she'd never have forgiven herself. What the others didn't understand was that she was the one who'd encouraged Phyllis to get involved in the inspector's cases. The maid had been scared, frightened first of losing her position if the inspector found out what they were up to, and second, anxious about her abilities to contribute. "I'm going to let them in the front." She hurried upstairs and opened the door.

"I'm so sorry to have worried everyone," Phyllis cried as she came face-to-face with Mrs. Jeffries. "But it couldn't be helped."

"Come in quickly and tell me all about it," the housekeeper said. "Hurry, the inspector will be home soon."

"No, he won't." Smythe grinned broadly. "He'll be at the station for a few hours. He's just arrested Paul Ralston."

"For Edison's murder?"

"We're not sure." Hatchet swept off his hat as he stepped into the house. "But I certainly hope so."

"Then why is he being arrested?"

"'E tried to murder Laura Hemmings," Wiggins explained. He jerked his thumb at Phyllis. "But that one figured out a way to make sure 'e didn't get away with it."

She ushered them downstairs. Mrs. Goodge and Betsy had made fresh tea and Luty and Ruth were at the table. Amanda had fallen asleep and been put to bed in the cot in Mrs. Goodge's room.

"It's about time you got back," Luty exclaimed when they clambered into the room. "We was gettin' worried."

"Wait'll you 'ear what happened." Wiggins tossed his jacket onto the back of his chair and sat down. "You'll never believe it, but our Phyllis 'ere is a 'eroine."

"Don't be daft, Wiggins, I didn't do much at all," she scoffed, but her cheeks were flushed with pleasure and her eyes sparkled.

"Everyone sit down," Mrs. Goodge ordered. She put a plate of roast beef sandwiches and a bowl of pickled eggs on the table. Betsy, who was right behind her, carried a seed-cake that she placed next to the teapot. "We'll eat and talk, and do it fast before the inspector gets home."

"He'll be a while yet." Hatchet slipped off his overcoat and hung it on the coat tree along with his hat and scarf. "Paul Ralston is under arrest."

"Thank goodness." The cook laughed. "Then the inspector will not be annoyed that I only had a bit of steak for his supper. Everyone take off your coats, sit down, and tell us what's happened."

They did as directed and soon everyone was at their places helping themselves to food and in general just being grateful they were together and unharmed. Though it hadn't been discussed, they all sensed that the case had come to a satisfactory conclusion.

Mrs. Jeffries waited till everyone had time to eat a few

bites before she looked at Phyllis. "You go first. Tell us what happened today."

Phyllis swallowed the last of her sandwich. "It started out simple enough. I went off to Clapton with the intention of asking Laura how the letter was folded when she dug it out of Ralston's pocket." She grinned. "It took me a while to figure out why you wanted to know that particular detail, but I finally understood."

"I don't," Wiggins complained.

"She wanted to know if it was folded or stuffed in the pocket," Phyllis explained. "Because if it was stuffed, that meant it wasn't his letter, he stole it from Orlando Edison. You don't stuff a letter you're going to post in your pocket like it's a used handkerchief. But I couldn't ask her about it because she was gone when I got there." She told them about her encounter with Mrs. Cole and her trek across town to the Blackbird Pub. "But when I got there and Enid and the Ralston cook said that he'd sent them off for the evening, I got worried that she was there and trying to blackmail Ralston." She turned to Mrs. Jeffries. "I thought about coming here for help, but I had this feeling that I had to get there fast. I don't know how to explain it."

"Don't try," Mrs. Jeffries said. "You trusted your instincts and, in the process, you saved her life. Go on, tell us the rest of it."

"I hope she's going to be alright," Phyllis said. "But she was still unconscious when we left." She told them about how she'd peeked in the window and spotted Laura. "I couldn't believe it when Smythe and Wiggins showed up, and I almost cried in relief when I found out the inspector and Barnes were already inside the house."

"It was Mrs. Jeffries that sent us there to look for ya," Smythe interjected.

"And Mrs. Jeffries told the constable this morning what she suspected happened when Edison was killed. I imagine that he helped get the inspector thinking along those lines and that's why he went to the Ralston house," Mrs. Goodge said to the maid. "But go on, tell us the rest."

Phyllis continued with her narrative, pausing self-consciously when she got to the part where she went into the back hall and moaned loud enough to get the inspector's attention. "I thought that Ralston would keep them at the front of the house," she said. "But I knew that if the inspector or Constable Barnes heard someone moaning and crying for help, they'd search till they found her no matter what kind of shenanigans or excuses Ralston might come up with. And they did. Once we knew they'd seen her, we slipped out through the mews so no one would see us." She grinned at Hatchet. "You were the hero for this part, so you tell them the rest."

"I knew it, I knew it," Luty cried. "He got to have some fun."

"Don't be absurd, madam, Miss Phyllis is being kind. All I did was stick out my foot and trip Ralston when he tried to make his escape." But he bowed to their pleas and told them what had happened. "After that, we hurried back here as quickly as possible. But what I don't understand is, how did Mrs. Jeffries determine that Ralston was the killer?"

Everyone looked at her. "Well, are you goin' to tell us or not? Come on, Hepzibah, spill the beans," Luty demanded. "Sendin' us all out to find out the little bits and pieces that pointed at Ralston was clever, but what we want to know is how you knew to put yer sights on him in the first place."

"It wasn't a matter of cleverness at all," she protested. She reached for the teapot and poured another cup. "It was simply that I suddenly realized we were getting nowhere and I understood that the only way to get the case solved was to look at it from an entirely different angle." She added a touch of milk to the cup. "The first thing I asked myself was who really benefited from his death."

"Madeleine Flurry and Yancy Kimball," Phyllis murmured. "They're both inheriting his estate."

"True, but if you think about it, both of them would benefit far more if he were alive." Mrs. Jeffries helped herself to a spoonful of sugar.

"That's true of Mrs. Flurry," Betsy said quickly. "She and Edison were in love and they were going to get married."

"But they 'ad a row," Wiggins pointed out. "'E was leavin' her."

"All couples row," Betsy insisted. "And he wasn't leaving her. She was going to join him in New York after the baby was born. Why do you think he arranged for her to live in his house? Edison didn't want her living alone with him out of the country. He wanted her looked after by people he trusted."

"That explains why he left instructions with his lawyer for the staff to stay on until the end of March," Ruth said. "Will the baby be born by then?"

Betsy nodded. "The little one is due at the end of January."

"Right, then, so that puts Mrs. Flurry out of the runnin' for bein' the killer. What about Kimball?" Smythe asked. "Edison 'ad cut off his money supply but left 'im an inheritance, so why wouldn't he want his cousin dead?"

"That's simple. Kimball was a professional gambler, not a part-time card player but someone who made his living with cards," Mrs. Jeffries replied. "I'm not expert on how gamblers view the world, but it has been my observation that they are very superstitious. Their world revolves around a throw of the dice or the turn of a card. I don't think Kimball would risk a prolonged run of bad luck by committing the murder of his only living family member."

"But gamblers have killed before," Smythe argued. "I was in a game in Sydney and it took three of us to keep Billy Harold from killing a Frenchman we caught cheatin'."

"But that was in the heat of the moment and, furthermore, I'll wager that Billy Harold wasn't a professional gambler," Mrs. Jeffries explained. "Kimball is."

"Luck be my lady, luck be my friend, give me good winnings again and again," Luty chanted. "That's a gamblers' sayin', and Mrs. Jeffries is right, the pros are always worried about gettin' on the wrong side of Lady Luck."

"Or the goddess Fortune," Hatchet added. "Alright, we can see how you eliminated those two from your list of suspects. But what about the Merry Gentlemen? Why did you focus on Ralston and not one of the other two?"

"Because once I thought about it logically, Ralston was the only one with a motive. Furthermore, he was the only one who could have done it."

"Why was he the only one who could have done it?" Ruth asked. "The other two didn't have decent alibis—they could have easily come back that evening and murdered Edison."

"But only Ralston knew two important things," Mrs. Jeffries said. "First, he knew the house was going to be empty. He was with Edison when Mr. Dempsey came with the theater tickets so he knew he could get in and out without getting caught by the servants. Second, he was the only one of the three that knew Edison was leaving for New York right after he testified in the bankruptcy hearing, and the murderer wanted Edison dead and not on a ship for America."

"How did he know Edison was goin'?" Luty asked. "Seems like the only people he told were his cousin, Mrs. Flurry, and Henry Lofton, his lawyer."

"He found out because he read Edison's letter to Mrs. Flurry," Mrs. Jeffries explained. "At least, that's what I think must have happened—we'll know for certain if Laura Hemmings had the letter with her when she went to see Ralston tonight and it's now in the possession of the police."

"'Ow many letters are there?" Wiggins smiled sheepishly. "I think I know but I'm a bit confused."

"There was only one," Mrs. Jeffries said. "The one Edison wrote to Madeleine Flurry. My theory is that Ralston read the letter when he was alone in Edison's study and the letter not only said that Edison was leaving the country, but it also contained something else that Ralston didn't want made public and that was why he decided Edison had to die. Ralston offered to post the letter for Edison, but instead of posting it, he stole it and put it in his overcoat pocket, where Laura Hemmings found it."

"Right, I understand that bit, but why did you want me to find out 'ow long Ralston was alone in the downstairs 'all?" Wiggins persisted.

"Because that's when Ralston unlocked the tradesmen's door." Phyllis glanced at Mrs. Jeffries. "Sorry, but am I right?"

"Clever girl, yes, you are. I suspect he told Edison that he needed to use the water closet as an excuse to get out of the room. Then he went downstairs and used the excuse of needing a headache powder to get the servants out of his way so he could unlock the door. But that was the key to his plan: He needed that door unlocked because he knew it was the only way back into the house. He also knew that Edison used the miner's shovel as a doorstop, so he had a weapon." She grimaced slightly. "Bashing someone on the head isn't a very efficient way to commit murder and Ralston knew this—that's why he spent time in his study that afternoon practicing his aim."

Phyllis looked doubtful. "How do you know that?"

"Enid Carter; remember she told you that on the afternoon of the murder, Ralston was in a particularly bad mood. She said, 'He came home that afternoon, shut himself in his study, and thumped his fist against the sofa pillows for half an hour.'"

"Oh, my goodness, you're right, he was practicing and he had his own miner's shovel. All the directors had one."

"Ralston came back that evening and waited for his moment to strike," Mrs. Jeffries continued. "He had a bit of luck when the carolers arrived at Edison's door at the time the servants were leaving—that provided both a distraction and a cover for any noise he might have made going up the stairs. As soon as the carolers left, he committed the murder and then left, went home, and quite calmly ate his dinner. What he didn't count on was Laura Hemmings going through his coat pockets and finding the letter."

"But if he planned the murder, why use the shovel?" Ruth asked. "Why not a knife or a gun?"

Mrs. Jeffries thought for a moment before she answered. "I don't know for certain, but I think his original plan was to have the police think the murder had been done by an intruder, a burglar or robber who picked up the shovel when they were unexpectedly discovered by Edison."

"Which means he wouldn't have brought another weapon with him," Ruth said.

"Right, but when the carolers arrived just as the household was leaving, I think he made a spur-of-the-moment decision so instead of waiting till all was quiet, he used the music of the carolers to cover any noise he might make getting into the house, grabbed the shovel, and murdered Orlando Edison."

"Is that why he left Edison's body lying in the doorway?" Hatchet asked. "To make it appear as if the assailant slipped in right behind the carolers?"

"Something like that." Mrs. Jeffries shrugged. "But it could also be that, like most people, he didn't realize a corpse is heavy. Hence the expression 'dead weight.' He might have left him there because he didn't have the strength to move the body."

"And a corpse lying in an open doorway could be a way of making the police think that it was indeed a robber who had forced his way in and that Edison had made a fight of it," Hatchet added.

"So Laura Hemmings found the letter in Ralston's pocket, read it, and thought that Ralston had written it to one of his fancy ladies and decided to blackmail him." Mrs. Goodge was fairly sure she understood everything, but some of the details were a bit hazy.

"That's what I think must have happened," Mrs. Jeffries said. "She probably thought she could threaten to give the letter to Ralston's fiancée."

"But didn't the Hemmings girl notice that it was signed by Edison, not Paul Ralston?" the cook pointed out.

"He might have signed the letter with an endearment," Ruth suggested with a self-conscious smile. "That's what my late husband did—he never used his name when he wrote me a letter. Neither of us did. We used, uh, other names."

"That makes perfect sense," Mrs. Jeffries hastened to say.

She could tell that Ruth was uncomfortable and didn't want to admit that she and the late Lord Cannonberry might have signed their letters to one another with silly pet names.

"But why did Ralston want Edison dead?" Luty muttered. "I can see *how* he managed it but the *why* don't make sense to me. The other Merry Gentlemen were in the same fix as Ralston—they lost their investment, too."

"That's right, but as your source confirmed, Bagshot's wife is wealthy so he'll not starve, and even with the investment loss, Downing still has plenty of money. Paul Ralston was the only one of them that had a real motive to murder Edison but it wasn't because he'd lost his money in a bad investment."

"What was it, then?" Betsy demanded.

Mrs. Jeffries took a deep breath. "Ralston murdered Orlando Edison to keep him from testifying in the bankruptcy trial. If you'll remember, the inspector told us that both Bagshot and Downing had tried to influence what Edison would say in court, but he would have none of it and told them he'd answer all questions asked with the full truth. Ralston came to see him that afternoon in a last attempt to ask him to be discreet. I think when he read Edison's letter to Mrs. Flurry he realized that his task was hopeless and that's when he decided Edison had to die."

"But everyone already knew the company had gone bankrupt," Betsy said. "So why did it matter what Edison might testify about?"

"Oh, but it did. I suspect that Edison was going to tell the court that he'd paid the Merry Gentlemen to sit on the board of directors. Luty's source hinted there were rumors to that effect and, as several other sources have pointed out, once the Merry Gentlemen were part of the company, investors flocked to buy the shares."

"That ain't exactly ethical, but it ain't illegal," Luty pointed out.

"But if it became public knowledge, Ralston would lose the one thing he was determined to have: his marriage to Anne Waterson," Mrs. Jeffries announced.

"Oh, my gracious, you're right." Ruth sighed in disgust. "Sir Thomas Waterson would never have allowed his daughter to marry Ralston if it was known that he'd taken a bribe to sit on the board and attract investors."

"And he had to marry the girl to get the big fat marriage settlement and the leg up to the upper classes," Hatchet said.

"So poor Orlando Edison was murdered because he was goin' to tell the truth." Mrs. Goodge sighed heavily. "That's disgustin'."

"That's my assumption," Mrs. Jeffries admitted. "But I'll not know for sure unless we find out what's in the letter."

"Poor Laura, she was almost killed." Phyllis took a sip of tea.

"She was tryin' to blackmail Ralston." Wiggins helped himself to another sandwich. "Mind you, I hope she's not dead, but she's not as pure as fresh snow, either."

Fred, who'd been lying by the cooker, suddenly leapt up and raced down the hall, and a second later they heard the back door open.

"Hello, old fellow, you've come to meet me," Witherspoon said.

Everyone went still. There was no time for Luty, Hatchet, and Ruth to make their escape, so they'd have to brazen it out. Mrs. Jeffries put a welcoming smile on her face as the inspector and Fred came into the kitchen.

He stopped in the doorway, his expression puzzled, but not annoyed. "Gracious, this is a surprise. Is there a party?"

"It's more like an impromptu gatherin'." Luty stood up and put her hands on her hips. "You know good and well why me and Hatchet are here. We're pestering your poor housekeeper about this case of yours. Come on, Inspector, you know how much we love hearin' about your work, but this woman"—she jerked her chin at Mrs. Jeffries—"has her mouth closed tighter than a bank vault. She won't tell us nothin'."

"I came by to see if you're still coming to my Christmas Eve dinner," Ruth said quickly.

"And we brought the little one to see you," Betsy said. "But you're home so late she's fallen asleep."

He laughed and came to the table. Mrs. Jeffries started to get up, but he waved her back into her seat and sat down next to Ruth. "That explains it, then. I'll not be needing dinner tonight, Mrs. Goodge. I've got to go back to the station and I don't want you staying up until the wee hours, but I will have one of those sandwiches. They look wonderful."

"Help yourself, sir." Mrs. Jeffries shoved the food close to him as Phyllis got up to get another plate and cup.

"I was going to make you a steak for your dinner, sir," Mrs. Goodge said. "And I don't mind waiting up."

"No, no, these sandwiches will do nicely. I'm going back to the station in a few minutes to meet with Chief Inspector Barrows."

"Inspector Barrows?" Mrs. Jeffries repeated. "Is something wrong, sir?"

"Not at all, but it's a bit complicated. We've charged the suspect with attempted murder but, based on the evidence we now have, we're going to charge him with murder as well. Barrows wants to do that himself."

"You've made an arrest," Ruth said. "That's wonderful. Can you tell us what happened?"

"We've arrested Paul Ralston for the attempted murder of Laura Hemmings." He nodded his thanks as Phyllis handed him a cup of tea. "And when Barrows gets to the station, he'll be charged with Orlando Edison's murder as well." He shoved a huge bite of sandwich in his mouth, glanced at the clock, and chewed furiously.

"What has this person, this Laura Hemmings, got to do with the case?" Mrs. Jeffries asked. They had to be careful here as she couldn't recall if the inspector had specifically mentioned Laura's name to her in any of their previous conversations. "Why did Paul Ralston assault her? Is he a madman?"

"She tried to blackmail him and he bashed her over the head and knocked her unconscious. Luckily, Constable Barnes and I had gone to question Ralston this evening and we heard her moaning for help." He told them about Laura stealing Edison's letter, then he took another bite of his sandwich. They waited patiently for him to chew and swallow. "But the doctor said she'll be alright," he continued. "Ralston made a run for it and Constable Barnes gave chase. He almost made a clean break, but he tripped and the constable was able to subdue him until help arrived."

"Now you see why we were here tonight pesterin' poor Mrs. Jeffries," Luty exclaimed theatrically. "Your cases are more excitin' than a penny novel."

"Or a play," Phyllis added.

"Gerald, thank God you were there. You saved that poor girl's life." Ruth patted his arm. "You're so brave."

He sat up straighter and smiled in pleasure. "I did nothing more than any other officer, though I will admit we'd only gone to interview him this evening because I'd put together a sequence of events involving him that needed to be explained. When we got to his house, he was decidedly uncooperative and both the constable and I sensed something was terribly wrong. Then we heard Miss Hemmings moaning and we searched the house. We found her on the floor of the morning room."

"How dreadful." Mrs. Jeffries clucked her tongue. "Thank goodness you and the constable were there."

"Divine Providence was looking out for the girl. Luckily, she regained consciousness. She gave us the letter she'd stolen from Ralston's pocket and his motive for trying to kill her became obvious." He looked at the clock again.

"What was the motive, sir?" Mrs. Jeffries blurted out. She could see he wanted to get back to the station.

"The letter was a love letter to Madeleine Flurry. But Edison hadn't signed the letter with his name. He'd written 'Your beloved' instead. When Laura Hemmings read it, she thought Ralston was the one who'd written it and that he and Mrs. Flurry were lovers. She threatened to show the letter to Ralston's fiancée."

"But how does that have anything to do with Edison's murder?" Hatchet asked.

Witherspoon got up. "Because Ralston foolishly boasted to Laura Hemmings that he wasn't afraid to commit murder, he'd already killed Orlando Edison. I must be off. It would be very bad form if the chief inspector had to wait for me."

It wasn't until the next morning that Mrs. Jeffries had her theory about the real motive for Edison's murder confirmed by Constable Barnes.

"It was right there in the letter," he said. "Edison promised to turn over a new leaf, to be an upright family man once they were together in New York. He insisted he wasn't abandoning her and their child, but wanted her to have a safe delivery of the baby before traveling to meet him. He wrote that he knew she had some doubts about his character, but that he'd prove he was worthy of her love. He asked her to come to the court when he testified; he was going to be completely honest and was even going to volunteer the information that he'd paid the Merry Gentlemen five thousand pounds each to be on the board of directors."

"I knew it." Mrs. Jeffries' spirits soared. "I knew I was right."

"The letter explains why Mrs. Flurry and he hadn't married," Mrs. Goodge said. "She worried about his character. What's going to happen to the letter? Will you give it to her?"

"The inspector has already instructed a constable at the station to make her a copy and we'll take it to her today," he explained. "She'll get the original when the trial is over."

"It's sad, isn't it." Mrs. Jeffries shook her head. "Ralston murdered so he could marry a woman he didn't love and poor Orlando Edison lost his life because he wanted to prove he was worthy to a woman he did love."

"There's lots of sadness in this old world, Mrs. Jeffries." Barnes put his teacup down and got up. "But let's not forget it's not all doom and misery. There's also lots of good people like yourselves who take the trouble to help serve the cause of justice."

"And that's the best Christmas present there is," Wiggins announced as he came into the kitchen. "Exceptin' for a good football match."